KINGS
OF THE
BOYNE

Reviews for Nicola Pierce

Behind the Walls

'This is not glorified history; it is history as it really happened with
its gritty and realistic depiction of the terror-struck city of Derry
in 1689 where Protestants are threatened by the Catholic army. It's
a vivid evocation of life in a city under siege – boredom contrasted
with times of real fear. Memorable characters help us share in the
feelings of the people trapped and give us an insight into those
feelings, both in historical times and today. Heart-breaking in
places, the story is testament to the resilience of people;
a moving read'
parentsintouch.co.uk

'An excellent novel'
Robert Dunbar, *The Irish Times*

Spirit of the Titanic

'Gripping, exciting and unimaginably shattering'

Guardian Children's Books

'Captivating'
Sunday Business Post

'Intriguing'
Belfast Telegraph

'I absolutely adored this book. It makes you feel like
you were there'
Finty, reader review

City of Fate

'This fantastically written book will hook you from the start ...
this is historical fiction at its best'
The Guardian

'A compelling novel, combining rich characterisation with a
powerfully evoked sense of time and place'
Robert Dunbar, *The Irish Times*

'Excellent ... vivid and moving'
BooksforKeeps.co.uk

Nicola Pierce published her first book for children, *Spirit of the Titanic*, to rave reviews and five printings within its first twelve months. *City of Fate*, her second book for children, transported the reader deep into the Russian city of Stalingrad during World War II. The novel was shortlisted for the Warwickshire School Library Service Award, 2014. *Behind the Walls*, a rich emotional novel set in the besieged city of Derry in 1689, followed in 2015. To read more about Nicola, go to her web page, www.nicolapierce.com.

KINGS
OF THE
BOYNE

1690:
THE BATTLE DRAWS EVER CLOSER ...

NICOLA PIERCE

THE O'BRIEN PRESS
DUBLIN

First published 2016 by The O'Brien Press Ltd,
12 Terenure Road East, Rathgar, Dublin 6, D06 HD27, Ireland.
Tel: +353 1 4923333; Fax: +353 1 4922777
E-mail: books@obrien.ie
Website: www.obrien.ie
The O'Brien Press is a member of Publishing Ireland.

ISBN: 978-1-84717-627-1

Cover image: Shutterstock

Printed and bound by Nørhaven, Denmark
The paper in this book is produced using pulp from managed forests.

For Susan Houlden

ACKNOWLEDGEMENTS

If you have even just a little interest in the Battle of the Boyne, please visit the fantastic battle site and museum at Oldbridge House, the Battle of the Boyne Visitor Centre in Drogheda. I also recommend visiting Drogheda's Millmount museum and fort, the site of that bloody massacre committed by Oliver Cromwell's army. An unexpected thrill for me was when my mother brought me to Christ Church Cathedral, in Dublin, and I found myself standing right in front of a chair that had once cushioned the rear of King William III.

The title of the book came from a former student of St Peter's School in Rathgar. I met his class in Rathgar Books and mentioned my difficulty in choosing a title. I had barely finished my sentence before Dylan Harold blurted out 'Kings of the Boyne'. Cheers, Dylan!

I am grateful to history buffs Aisling Heffernan of the Battle of the Boyne Visitor Centre, Eamon Thornton of the Old Drogheda Society, historian and musician Aideen Morrissey and former MLA for East Belfast Michael Copeland for their wonderful anecdotes both about the Battle of the Boyne and 1690s Drogheda.

Thanks to my brother-in-law, Doctor Ciaran Simms, for lending me his grandfather's books on Irish history.

Thanks also to David Doyle for telling me all about meadows.

I first read Saint Teresa's poem on the Facebook page of poet and writer Nessa O'Mahony.

A big thanks to the readers of that difficult first draft: my other brother-in-law Donagh McCarthy, Rachel Pierce, Damian Keenan, Marian Broderick, Niall Carney and Conor Geoghegan. It's a long story, almost as long as the book itself, but they had their work cut out for them, and I appreciated all of their responses and suggestions.

Once again designer and artist Emma Byrne blew me away with her work. And thanks so much to my ever-patient editor Susan Houlden who propped up my confidence following *that* first draft and prodded me to move in a different direction.

Finally, thank *you* for reading this book!

CHAPTER ONE

Ardee, 1 October 1689

For a second or two Gerald O'Connor wanted to be back home in Offaly, in his tiny bedroom that was too small for him now. Even before he had left, he had already begun to dream of a bigger bed and grander window.

Instead, that room continued to shrink as he grew taller, longer and wider. There were nights when he felt the whitewashed walls inching their way towards him; he could stretch out a toe from beneath his blanket and prod the coolness of the stone, challenging it to push back.

His bedroom window was the size of his sister's sewing basket so he could not see the ruin of his grand-father's castle. For that, he had to step outside and there it was: broken stubby walls covered in weeds, long spidery cracks and ancient matted webs dotted with the dusty, dried-up corpses of a multitude of flies and beetles. The roof was long gone and only one window, minus the glass, remained. This had been his own private empire when he was a child. It was where he had hidden himself after he threw a stone at his sister, dropped the cat down the well (it was an accident!) and fell into the biggest puddle around while wearing his best cloak. His family had always known where to find him, marvelling that he didn't realise this himself.

On summer days he sat in its shadow and dreamed of a time when the castle had stood tall and pristine – the bustling home of a busy, important family, his family, the O'Connors. He had begged his sister Cait to draw the castle as it would have been. Following a brief discussion with their father, Cait sketched the shape of what Mr O'Connor described from memory. He had been a little boy when it was destroyed by the English army of Oliver Cromwell. Cait did her best, and the little sketch, after spending years nailed to Gerald's bedroom wall, was now sitting in the pocket of his tunic. It was faded and worn, but Gerald would not leave it behind, though he rarely so much as glanced at it since he could see it perfectly in his mind's eye.

That castle represented his family's once-glorious past, and Gerald was determined to retrieve that glory once more. It was the reason that he was standing here, in the middle of a crowd of fellow soldiers belonging to King

James, in some place called Ardee, staring at a tree and the forlorn couple standing in front of it

The chosen tree had weathered its fair share of storms. It was tall and grand, its bark a variety of reddish hues that reminded Gerald of numerous scabs he had gleefully picked from his knees as a child. There were still a few leaves clinging on, doing their best to ignore the wintry temperatures, but they would be gone soon enough, to join their companions who curled up and rotted on the ground. Death was all around the Jacobite army on this gloomy day.

Having done his duty, Gerald fell back into line. Jacques, his friend, nudged him, a comradely shove that Gerald could not bring himself to acknowledge. He was too anxious; his breath was short and slight while he felt every strand on his head twitch in nervous anticipation.

The young couple in the centre of the circle of soldiers kept their eyes on the ground in front of them. The damning evidence was in a grey sack that was slumped by their feet, its open neck displaying the fine, white powder that was deadly lime.

Gerald stared at it in awe. How innocent and harmless it looked now, reminding him of snow that had been trampled into the mud.

Next, he glanced at the girl. It had been his job to bind her wrists together. He had had to hide his gentleness from his commander as he stood behind her and brought her hands slowly to meet at the small of her back.

She showed no fear, no emotion at all, but he saw the tremor in her fingers that were topped with cracked nails, as he folded them together and wound the rope around her wrists. He saw the bluish marks on the inside of her arms where her captors had grabbed her. He saw the rip in her dress; the sleeve had been torn away at the shoulder seam.

Something about the girl reminded Gerald of his only sister Cait. Cait only ever wore long, white woollen tunics. Not that he thought that this was particularly remarkable, only that no matter what she did or wherever she went she rarely stained her dress – unlike the Protestant girl standing before him, whose dress was a rainbow of stains and grubby patches.

Gerald moved closer to his friend Jacques so he could ask quietly, 'Is it really necessary to tie them up like that?'

Jacques shrugged. 'You are forgetting, my friend, that they were hoping to murder all of us!'

It was true, not that the boy and girl had admitted as much, but they had been discovered by Jacobite soldiers in the very act of lifting that hefty sack between them to pour its deadly contents into the only well for miles around.

Once it hit the water the lime would disappear from sight but would sicken and kill any mortal that consumed the merest sip. Such a simple plan, but then the best ones usually are.

To the casual onlooker, the atmosphere might have seemed relaxed and even good-humoured, though every now and then a single word was murmured, 'Murderers!'

Yet no murder had actually been committed. Gerald thought that this was important, but Jacques shook his head. 'If we had arrived any later than we did, we might be drinking their poison, and then, a few minutes from now, the agony would begin.'

Gerald tried to scrape some rage together for the girl, but he was distracted by her vulnerability.

Jacques found it necessary to add, 'Remember, Gerald, you are a soldier of the king's army. In wartime the lives of your fellow soldiers should be your only concern.'

The young criminals were refusing to acknowledge the Jacobite commander's questions. Therefore, it remained a mystery who they were, where they were from, who had directed them to poison the well and who had supplied the lime. Ah ... at last there was a response. The girl remained mute, but her partner betrayed his true feelings by blurting out, 'We needed nobody to tell us to do this!'

Seeming satisfied with this, the commander nodded and

scribbled a line or two on the sheet of paper in his hand. He made one more attempt to push for final confirmation of their guilt. 'So, you do not deny it? You both intended to poison the well?'

The youth scowled. As far as his audience were concerned, this was as good as an admission of guilt.

Then there was a moment full of promise when anything might have happened, when someone might have called out, 'Stop! Let them go!' or when God might have struck that tree with a bolt of ferocious lightning. Alas, the moment passed, as all moments do, and the commander, folding up his report, issued his verdict: 'I hereby pronounce you both guilty and sentence you, in the name of King James, to hang from the neck until you are dead.'

Desperately, Gerald tried to think of some kind of argument he could make to change the commander's mind, or at least to, in some way, delay his reckoning, but he was just a lowly soldier, with absolutely no right to an opinion in matters like this. This was army life.

To shatter the tension, someone somewhere behind Gerald said something that caused a ripple of barely suppressed laughter. Gerald did not hear the exact words, but he recognised the tone and knew it was crude, tainting the very air around them. Doing his best to ignore the ugly atmosphere, he wished the commander would silence the fools in their midst.

Perhaps this was the biggest challenge of soldier life, having to get along with the rough as well as the smooth. Some of his companions were the sort of fellows that Gerald would ordinarily have nothing to do with. Just like him, they were poor Catholics, but Gerald had little in common with the rabble who spoke coarsely and preferred to use their fists to debate a point, which explained the broken noses, torn earlobes and blackened holes for teeth. Few of them could read or write.

Gerald, on the other hand, was an O'Connor. His father was a respected soldier in King Louis' army; his grandfather had been a chief in Offaly, while his great-grandfather had been a prince back in those glorious days when Ireland had her own royalty. And if all that wasn't enough, his mother's ancestor, and his own namesake, 'Gerald the Great', the eighth Earl of Kildare, had ruled Ireland for thirty years. Furthermore, Mrs O'Connor's mother wore a diamond cross that had been given to her father by that splendid hero Hugh O'Neill.

Throughout Offaly they even had a special saying about the O'Connors: 'Fortune had taken their honours but had left them kings.'

Before he took his first steps, it was made clear to Gerald

that he was the product of greatness and had a duty to uphold that greatness. Sometimes he worried that he might prove unworthy of his family's past, but he kept that to himself.

The sniggering continued behind him, and Gerald fancied that the girl's head dipped a little lower.

Meanwhile, two horses had been summoned to do their duty. Gerald was much relieved that his and Jacques' horses, Troy and Paris, had not been chosen for the gruesome task.

'Don't bother saddling them,' said the commander. 'They won't be sitting on them for long.'

Nobody laughed; nobody was meant to.

Feeling like he might still intervene, Gerald shot a questioning look at the commander that went unnoticed. Two soldiers held the horses steady. The animals were restless, not liking the intensity of the crowd. They shucked their heads as if to say 'Yes! Yes!'

Gerald fretted that the chestnut mare might tread on the girl's bare feet. Instead, the horse lifted its tail to release a gush of greenish, brown sludge that splashed the girl's right foot. She never flinched, refusing to move away from the stinking mess. After all, why should she care about that now?

Now Gerald longed for it all to be over.

The priest stepped forward, his Bible already open at

the verse he intended to read. Nobody had asked him to do this, and Gerald wondered if this was the priest's way to inflict a final cruelty on the Protestant pair as they had no way to escape the Papist ritual, right down to being sprinkled generously with Holy Water.

Jacques muttered something in French, and Gerald was confident that his friend was agreeing with him.

Up went the ropes into the tree where two soldiers waited to feed the tail ends back to those on the ground. When they were satisfied that the ropes hung straight, they signalled all was ready, not wanting to call attention to themselves by shouting down to the soldiers below. The boy and girl were shoved up onto the bare backs of the horses. Perhaps there had been some earlier discussion about whether to blindfold them or not. Their faces were left uncovered.

Having carried out the last rites, the priest addressed the pair for the final time, 'Pray, my children, will you beg God for His forgiveness?'

For the first time in his life Gerald found himself questioning a priest. He thought: *for goodness sake, what use are prayers to them now?*

The confusion persisted in his head: *But she – they – didn't do anything. We stopped them in time.*

Why didn't he say something to try and save them, just open his mouth and make a sound?

However, it was the joker behind him who spoke once more. Oh, it didn't matter what he said, only that Gerald was now ready to prove himself. He swung around, startling Jacques, to defend the girl's honour, his sword clenched in his hand as he asked, 'What did you say?'

He hardly knew who he was speaking to and, besides, it did not matter since he could not be heard above the sound of the horses' backsides being slapped and the soldiers' shouts. The animals wasted no time in jumping forward and running a few paces before realising that they were riderless.

It was Jacques alone that witnessed the torment on Gerald's face, as the young soldier turned back to see the boy and girl's last dreadful moments.

Out of the corner of his eye Gerald saw a few men bless themselves. So, not all of them were ignorant savages bent on bloodshed.

Finally, it was over.

It was only then that Gerald realised that the commander was gone. The priest stood by, his expression heavy with sorrow, waiting for the bodies to be cut down. Gerald stepped forward to help but Jacques held him back, saying, 'We are to move on, to set up camp before nightfall.'

'But ...' began Gerald until he saw the determination in his friend's face. It was time to go. The priest licked his thumb to flick through the pages of his Bible. Jacques rolled his eyes. 'He will try to convert the dead, no?'

Gerald sighed.

Falling into step behind their comrades, Jacques allowed a few minutes to pass before asking quietly, 'Did you not know that even women die in wartime?'

Instead of answering Jacques' question, Gerald said, 'An old woman was killed in our camp last year, outside Derry.'

Swiping at a persistent fly that threatened to land on his nose, Jacques guessed, 'She was a Protestant, yes?'

Gerald looked at his friend impatiently. 'No! I mean, yes, I suppose she was. I don't know. Is that really the point?'

He kicked the ground, understanding that Jacques would not answer such a silly question, because the woman's religion was the entirely the point. Of course it was.

Gerald tried to explain his feelings. 'She was desperate for food. Some of the men saw her picking seeds out of horse manure and decided that she must be a witch. I did nothing when they surrounded her. I said nothing when they taunted her, stabbed her and shot her dead. I just stood and watched, exactly as I did just now.'

He walked ahead of Jacques, not wanting the Frenchman to defend their fellow soldiers.

Jacques let him go. He understood the boy's struggle. This year marked his tenth as a soldier in King Louis' army, the busiest army in the world. He reckoned that the life of a soldier was a simple one as long as you followed orders. Let someone else struggle with their conscience about trouble-some matters like this. The death of that pretty brunette and her friend was the commander's doing, not his.

The Frenchman made sure to keep Gerald in sight. He understood the boy's confusion. Perhaps he even welcomed it. Wasn't it good for an old hand like himself to be reminded that war was a horrible business?

CHAPTER TWO

King James in Dundalk, 1690

The flames of the candles flickered against the canvas walls of the tent, continually throwing shadows and shapes into light and then into darkness again. King James watched them without interest. Every now and then the tent dented and belched, or so it appeared, as the wind pummelled it from outside.

The king had had an early supper, some chicken that was a little tough, cold potato, followed by fruit and a glass of sweet wine. Since then he had not moved from his chair, only moodily staring into space. His servants had no choice but to ignore the gloomy expression on his face. Certainly they were not allowed to ask what was wrong. The only thing they could do was clear the table, spirit away the dirty dishes and see that his bed pan was placed between the sheets of his bed to heat it up.

The Comte de Lauzun, His Majesty's advisor, waited impatiently for the servants to leave. Eventually they were left in peace, allowing Lauzun to ask, 'Is something troubling you, sire?'

The king clicked his tongue against his mouth, saying moodily, 'That is rather a stupid question, even for you.'

Lauzun, who had already written in confidence to his own king, Louis, in France, to complain about James's temper, sought to keep the atmosphere peaceful. 'My apologies, Your Majesty. But of course!'

The Frenchman felt as gloomy as the king, but he had to keep his real feelings hidden. His job was to keep James happy and focused on getting the English throne back. Catholic France simply could not have William, that Dutch upstart, as a Protestant king of England, Ireland and Scotland.

If King Louis XIV was going to rule all of Europe – and that seemed to be an ambition of his – he needed Britain as an ally, a Catholic ally to help him to crush the Dutch vermin. Therefore, Lauzun surmised, the upcoming battle in Ireland was not James's alone. It was France's, too.

James had been slow to understand what was motivating the hordes of Irish soldiers who rushed to join his army. In

Dublin Lauzun saw how the crowds cheered James, throwing up their arms in welcome. Flowers were strewn on the ground before the king's horse while, here and there, bewildered babies were held up and cajoled into waving their pudgy fists.

Lauzun understood the reason for the ecstatic welcome in Dublin. The Irish were not really celebrating James as their king. No, indeed. They were celebrating James as a Catholic on the throne of England, who had the power to return their riches and privileges to them. The comte smiled as he remembered the blush on James's cheeks. The king had sweetly flicked his wrist at the people, in acceptance of their goodwill ... even love. Those crowds had turned his head. *Mais oui, the Irish are clever, yes?*

God knows it was their fault that James insisted on going north to the besieged city of Derry. What folly it had been, to imagine that those mulish Protestants would change their minds about him, on seeing him arrive in person at their gates. As long as he lived, Lauzun would never forget that awful day. Because, instead of opening their gates and their hearts to him, the king was actually fired upon; one solitary gunshot that killed the boy beside him and shook the king's stubborn confidence that he would be embraced by all.

'So, is there any change in our situation?'

It sounded as if it had taken the king a supreme effort to ask his question which was followed by a deep, shuddering sigh.

Lauzun shook his head sadly, saying, 'No, sire.'

Although there was the fact ... 'Only that, Your Majesty, the Williamite army is definitely in trouble. The dead are being carried off every day in dozens, maybe even more than that.'

King James was unimpressed, only allowing himself to surmise, 'I suppose that is one good thing about this dreadful climate and landscape. It is fighting our battle for us.'

Lauzun shrugged, unwilling to state his true opinion one way or another. They had been stuck here for weeks overlooking the Williamite camp. Naturally, every single Jacobite had assumed there would be a clash of arms, to send William's most experienced commander, the elderly Duke of Schomberg, and his army scurrying back to Hell, or wherever they had come from. Lauzun waited to be told to prepare for a fight, but that order never came. It was downright peculiar.

Lauzun sent a letter back to Louis, in which he was free to rant:

My Lord, if you could see how we are being used – that is to say, not used. The men polish their guns, sharpen their swords and pikes, and

I can only assume that they are mimicking the actions of the enemy who are camped in a sort of ditch.

As you can imagine, the weather is as bad as it can be, and the only battle taking place is between the men and clouds of flying midges that bite into any exposed flesh. At least we are camped in superior grounds, somewhat higher than the enemy. I fancy their proximity to the ditch is making them the perfect meal for the biting insects.

Schomberg is just sitting there while his army loses men day after day. Our physicians tell me that the Williamites are also being carried off by disease, owing to the wet climate and muddy ground. There is scarcely a decent tent amongst them. And we just sit here watching their misfortune unfold.

Meanwhile, King James sulked, or that is how it seemed to his companions. Inwardly, he comforted himself with the thought that just because he had lost one battle in Derry did not mean he would lose the war.

This is what James believed he was waiting for – an almighty confrontation with William of Orange, the Dutch king who had stolen away James's English crown, an adversary who was both his nephew and his daughter Mary's husband. James could see no other way to resolve and bring about his rightful return to the throne.

James was on a mission; his Catholicism was like a torch with which he intended to banish the darkness from his nation. God knew what he had suffered so far and the difficult sacrifices he had made. How many friends had his change of faith cost him, not to mention his family, his own precious blood, his daughters, Mary and Anne.

Never would he have guessed that at this late time in his life he would be living in a tent in the middle of an Irish nowhere. But if this was what God needed him to do then what choice had he? *There is nobody in this world who can truly understand what a wronged king has to put up with. Yet, wasn't Jesus also forsaken by all he knew? I should be proud to bear his cross of isolation.*

James did acknowledge that he was blessed with a loving wife in Mary Beatrice, who prayed every day for his safe return.

Young and beautiful, she had fulfilled all the king's requirements when he went looking for a second wife after poor Anne, mother to Mary and Anne, passed away. Oh, he knew how he was spoken about in court – how they whispered that he began his search for a new wife before poor Anne's body was cold in her grave.

He chose to ignore the gossip. A future king did not have time to dwell on the past. Anne was dead, and he urgently needed a son, a Catholic son that would inherit the throne after he was gone. Otherwise, the throne would pass to his eldest daughter, Mary, a staunch Protestant. This is what separates royalty from the masses: one must always think of the future. And plan for it.

In no time at all, he was peering at painted portraits until he came upon the likeness of the fifteen-year-old Catholic Mary Beatrice of Spain.

Despite their differences, regarding Church and faith, James's new bride and his Protestant daughters, Mary and Anne, became friends, in the beginning. There was lots of giggling and girlish parties with dressing up in funny costumes to put on plays for family and friends.

Who could have foretold just how much things would change?

After disappointing her husband with a daughter, Mary Beatrice had a second opportunity to provide the next heir to the throne. James assumed that she spent those long months praying as hard as he did because, in the end, their wish was granted. But was it really worth it?

There are some folk who would advocate taking care in what you wish for just in case you get it.

James would never forget that day as long as he lived. That tiny boy – James Edward Francis – was the best news his father had had in a long time. Because of his new son, King James now had a Catholic heir; and because of his new son, King James was no longer on his throne.

His enemies' reactions to the newborn were a little more dramatic than James had expected. His Protestant Dutch son-in-law was invited ... *invited* ... to invade England, making it necessary for James to flee, first sending his wife and baby to France and following on himself later.

It was Lauzun who escorted Mary Beatrice and the child to the safety of King Louis' castle, and that's why the comte was here now in his most official capacity. James looked at the Frenchman in front of him. True, he owed Lauzun a lot, but he did not particularly like him, suspecting that the young comte would rather be back in sunny France drinking fine wine and gorging on chocolate.

As James listened to the rain outside and rubbed his hands together to keep them warm, he had to admit that perhaps to be back in France would be no bad thing at all.

He sighed. 'If I only had five or six more French battalions, then we should drive the Duke of Schomberg out of Ireland.'

Since there were no Irishmen nearby, Lauzun was free to shrug his agreement: '*Mais oui*, Your Majesty. *Mais oui*.'

CHAPTER THREE

Waiting Around in Dundalk

'This is Hell!' declared Jacques as he wiped his nose on his sleeve. A greasy lock of dark hair fell over his eyes and he testily pushed it to the side.

'No,' grinned Gerald. 'This is still Dundalk, I think!'

Jacques refused to laugh. 'What in God's name are we doing here, growing older by the day?'

Gerald tried to cheer his friend up with a compliment: 'Your English is much improved.'

'Pah!' was the sour response.

The truth of the matter was that they were good and stuck, all of them, in the middle of nowhere.

Gerald and Jacques were sitting around their small camp-fire that spat angrily thanks to its wet ingredients. All its energy was put into the spitting so that there was little actual heat coming from it. The miserable fire was just one of hundreds in the Jacobite camp.

Gerald did his best to ignore the dampness from sitting on the wet ground. There was an unpleasant chill around his backside any time he moved so he tried to keep still.

They had been joined by a handful of colleagues, all troopers ready to fight for King James or, at least, they had been when they arrived weeks earlier.

Jacques' mood was dipping into frustration and impatience, and boredom: 'What are we waiting for? Why do we not fight, is that not why we are camped out here in the rain?'

Everyone agreed that it was a fair question, but no one had an answer to it. King James was somewhere out there in his tent and he must have his reason for not attacking the Williamites, mustn't he?

Michael O'Dwyer, an older, red-faced man from Tallaght, near the city of Dublin, began to peel a potato with his dagger. He ventured his theory: 'Maybe James does not like to take advantage of Schomberg's men that are dying away like May flies. His conscience might forbid him from launching an attack.'

Jacques yelped, 'But he is at war. You cannot feel sorry for the enemy. It is nonsense.'

Michael eyed Jacques to see if he was being insulted. If the Frenchman really wanted a fight, he would be happy to oblige him … if he was being insulted.

Sensing trouble, Gerald spoke up, 'Well, perhaps he is waiting for help, you know, more reinforcements. Maybe Louis is sending more men and horses?'

Some of his listeners shifted on their wet patches of grass; there were not enough rugs to go around and they preferred to keep their jackets on than spread them beneath their buttocks. The worry was that they were all being insulted as a group of proud Irishmen. Jacques wisely made no comment on this practical explanation. He sniffed instead.

Michael O'Dwyer, however, was able to appreciate the truth behind Gerald's words. 'Maybe the lad has something. I mean, how many of us have fought in a proper battle before?'

Gerald piped up immediately, 'I was at Derry!'

Michael shook his head at this. 'But that was not what you could call a *real* battle. That was more about skirmishing and ambushes. You know, like fighting fellow ruffians on the street when you were a youngster.'

Gerald was unsure as to whether he should admit, in front of these tough men, that he had never fought on a street when he was younger. He had never found it necessary to defend himself since no other boy would have dared to hurt him or they would have suffered at the hands of their mortified parents. Gerald was an O'Connor and even if the castles were in ruins, the memories were not. His family still commanded a huge amount of respect amongst their fellow neighbours.

Also, he had had no time to play rough and tumble what with never-ending chores and daily lessons, courtesy of plump Father Nicholas.

No, he would not share this story with these fellows here. At the same time, he could not agree with Michael O'Dwyer's assessment of his military experience in Derry.

'What about the trench where the Williamites attacked us in the dead of night?'

Jacques leapt in before anyone could sneer at Gerald's question. 'Ah *oui*, yes, that was quite a battle. We were set upon as we slept and then struggled to arm ourselves in the dark while being shot at from above. We were fish trapped in a puddle.'

Michael O'Dwyer listened patiently. He had not taken part in the siege of Derry and had been convinced that he had not missed much. However, young Joseph O' Leary, a skinny red-head from Trim in County Meath, was much engrossed in the story. He asked Gerald and Jacques the obvious question, 'And how many Williamites did you kill?'

Ah.

Now it was time for Gerald to squirm, while Jacques shrugged and answered plainly, 'Kill? No, my friend, there was no time for us to kill anyone.'

Gerald explained, 'We were ordered to get out of the trench and run as fast as we could. I suppose the important thing was that we should survive the attack.'

'And not fight back at all?' queried Michael, looking a little shocked.

Jacques cursed. 'I lost a good musket that night. They told us to forget about our belongings. Fortunately I was wearing my boots.'

His companions nodded, sending his smart French boots, with their shiny brass buckles, envious looks. Yes, to lose those to a Williamite would have been a great shame indeed.

Fixing Michael with a certain look, Jacques added, 'A good soldier knows when to abandon a fight that is doomed from the outset. What use is dying over a badly dug trench? We run away, we come back and fight again in the daytime. Makes more sense, no?'

Michael took a large bite of his potato and made a face that might have meant that he agreed, or maybe not.

Gerald sighed. 'Being stuck here reminds me of being back in Derry. All of this waiting around for the enemy to make the first move.'

Jacques sniffed again and despite the fact that no one stirred themselves to query his health, he announced: 'I have a cold.'

Only Gerald's smile contained any sympathy.

'*Mon Dieu!*' Jacques said. 'When this is all over I am going to return to my village and spend the summer teaching a pretty blonde how to throw a stone across the lake so that it skips and jumps before sinking to the bottom.'

'What?' asked Gerald. 'You would really spend a whole summer doing just that?'

The Frenchman stretched and yawned: 'Her name is Marie Thérèse. She is a slow learner.'

Only the laughter of the others made Gerald realise that his friend was joking.

CHAPTER FOUR

Outside Belfast, June 1690

The people stared in silence. King William cracked his mouth into a smile of sorts. It was important not to overdo it or look false. His horse twitched her ears forwards and backwards and he patted her on her neck, encouraging her to keep trotting.

So, this was Belfast, and this silent watchful audience that lined both sides of the dusty street were her citizens and, presumably, his loyal servants.

Of course, it's their first time to see a king.

He could appreciate their shyness and curiosity. Some of his men, however, did not share his understanding. He heard someone from the Derry regiment, which marched behind him, mutter, 'This is a pretty poor welcome for their king. Maybe they prefer to see the Papist James and his army.'

'Hush, Henry Campsie! It's not your place to say such things!'

William almost smiled at this and silently blessed the bold Henry, whoever he was, for being defensive of his king's feelings.

At least the sun was shining. Indeed, the people of Belfast seemed somewhat dazzled at the spectacle of King William and his massive army, some thirty-five-thousand strong, on horse and foot. And who would not be awed at such a sight?

William rivalled the sun in his blood-red cloak which clashed dramatically with the plainness of his white tunic. Large buttons of gold glinted from his cuffs and various collars, all the way down to the purple sash around his waist. Everything about him, from the glamorous curls of his dark wig to the folds in his knee-high shiny boots, suggested money and power.

A dog suddenly appeared out of nowhere. It darted forward, barking and snarling at William's horse. The mare shucked her head in annoyance, checking that she was not going to tread on him. The manic barking snapped the spectators out of their reverie, and there was a collective gasp of horror from the crowd as one young lad was roughly pushed out to fetch the rude animal, which he did, grabbing it by the scruff of its neck, all the while keeping his eyes to the ground.

A pathway began to open up behind him as his neighbours shuffled aside, assuming he would drag the dog and himself backwards to disappear amongst them. And that was exactly what the boy wanted to do and was trying to do.

However, King William had other plans for him. Raising his arm in the air, he cried out an imperious 'Halt!' to be obeyed by his cavalry and infantry, and the boy whose crimson cheeks matched the fiery red of William's cloak.

Making sure that all eyes were on him, William addressed the trembling youth, 'What is the name?'

Swallowing hard, the boy just about managed to utter 'Scruffy'.

A hiss from somewhere in the crowd reminded him to tack on the necessary 'Your Majesty' to the end of his reply.

'Scruffy, Your Majesty.'

Looking perplexed, His Majesty raised himself in his saddle to peer down and ask: 'Really? That is the name your parents gave you? How peculiar!'

Feeling trapped, the lad looked around for help while the dog turned to nip at his ankles. William saw a few smug smiles break out here and there, but it was left to the poor boy to try again: 'It's ... it's the dog's name, Majesty.'

'Ah!' nodded William. 'That makes more sense. He is rather a scruffy creature, isn't he?'

The boy looked even more miserable than before: 'Er ...

it's a girl, Majesty. Sorry.'

William pursed his lips and said, 'Oh, there's no need to apologise.'

One woman called out, 'Tell the king your name. That's what he meant, you fool!'

She followed this up with a wide smile of apology, feeling obliged to explain her intrusion. 'Beggin' your pardon, sir. He's my grandson, sire. Your Majesty. Sir.'

Then she curtsied rather awkwardly, which is not surprising considering it was the first time she had ever curtsied to an actual king before. To keep things simple, William chose to ignore her, preferring to concentrate on the boy; however, the grandson did not have the luxury of being able to ignore his grandmother.

'My … my name is Archie McKenzie, Your Majesty.'

'Well, Archie, now I know your name, but do you know mine?'

Young Archie was at a loss to know why the king persisted in dragging out a conversation with him, of all people. The only adults that ever bothered speaking to him were his parents and grandparents and they usually just shouted at him about his chores or clipped him around the ears if he made a mess of things, which was usually the case. In truth, he felt exhausted from holding the dog and having to participate in this nerve-wracking interview. What he really wanted to do was plop himself down right there on the road and let someone else take over.

More than a few people, including his mortified grandmother, felt it necessary to prompt him: 'It's William!'

Again, the king pretended not to hear the extra voices. Instead, he called out, as loud as he could without actually shouting, 'Allow me to introduce myself.'

Archie, it must be said, looked rather dejected, sunken by that familiar feeling of having failed in every way possible. Thanks to years of practice, he recognised that, once again, the moment had passed when he could have proved himself worthy in some way, though he knew not how.

Meanwhile the king was now addressing the crowd at large: 'I am King William. I was asked to chase the Papist James from the throne and now I will undertake to chase him off this very island.'

His army raised a cheer to this and were watched politely by those on the sidelines.

Indicating one of the newer battalions, whom he had asked to march closely behind him as thanks for their devotion, William continued, 'The city of Derry showed her loyalty to me and her church.'

The boys and men cheered once more, while those holding banners waved them with pride. Amongst their unit were some of the boys who had shut their gates against the redcoats; each one of them had gone without food, preferring to starve than surrender to that pretender king James.

William beseeched his listeners: 'Can I be so bold as to hope for similar support from the people of Belfast? I would welcome new recruits to join the ranks of this army that will – once and for all – end the ambition of James and his Catholic French cohorts.'

At this, he removed his sword from its sheath and held it above his head, looking every inch the mighty warrior. Finally, he was rewarded with a roar of excitement from the audience. Who knows who shouted out first, but within seconds the shopkeepers, fishermen, farmers, politicians, clergymen, servants, housewives and their children took up a resounding chorus of 'Three cheers for King William: Huzzar! Huzzar! Huzzar!'

CHAPTER FIVE

Killaughey, County Down, June 1690

Reverend George Walker was both a man of the cloth and a man of the battlefield. As governor of Derry, he had seen the good city through months of siege and starvation at the hands of the Papist James's Jacobite army. Of course Derry survived – God bless her! Moreover, Reverend Walker felt that this was largely due to the passionate, morale-boosting sermons that he shouted from the altar in the city's cathedral.

Now, a year later, he was leading her soldiers south to support their saviour, King William of Orange, in the long-awaited battle against James. But first he had an important task to carry out.

Summoning a handful of his most trusted young soldiers

to him, he informed them: 'Right, lads, we have been told that King William needs more horses and as soon as possible. As it would take too long to bring them over from England, it has been decided that we will make use of what is available to us.'

Private Daniel Sherrard grew concerned. Neither he nor his brother owned a horse or else they would hand them over to His Majesty. However, this was not what the clergyman meant.

'The quickest way to make up the numbers is to borrow horses from the local population – that is, our local brethren. And you, my boys, have been especially chosen to round them up. So, off you go. And, mind, we need every single horse you can find.'

'Borrow, sir?' asked Daniel, wanting to be clear about his orders.

Reverend Walker shrugged impatiently. 'Well, yes. I suppose. Isn't that what I said?'

Daniel did not look convinced, while Robert, his older brother, who had recently been promoted to corporal and had no interest in the finer details, snapped at him, 'Come on, Dan!'

Robert saluted the reverend and gave him a confident, 'Yes, sir. Right away!'

As usual Robert's best friend, Henry Campsie, whose

father had twice been elected Mayor of Derry, walked with them and tutted loudly. Daniel ignored him. However, he could not pretend to be deaf to his brother's exasperated lecture: 'Why, oh, why must you always ask questions? A soldier's lot is to carry out orders, not study them. You're worse than Father!'

If Robert had meant to insult Daniel, he failed. Instead, Daniel was flattered to be compared with their father, whom, he fervently believed, was the most intelligent man that ever walked the earth.

Henry smirked. 'Perhaps you should have stayed at home, Daniel. I always thought you would become a physician like your father.'

What could Daniel say to this? To take offence would mean sounding critical of his father's profession, which was, to be honest, something he *had* thought about for himself. However, he was not going to admit this to Henry, who seemed to think he alone knew all there was to know about anything at all.

Robert might have distracted his friend, but he was still embarrassed and, therefore, annoyed over Daniel questioning the Reverend Walker, of all people. Surely this sort of behaviour reflected badly on him too. His little brother had a lot to learn.

'It is funny how ...' mused Henry.

Daniel was absolutely sure that whichever way that sentence ended he would not find it the least bit funny.

'I still have trouble imagining you on a proper battlefield even though you're wearing the uniform and carrying a musket. Yet I have no problem at all imagining you looking after sick people ... yes, and sick animals too. Sure, why not, you'd be great at it.'

'Oh, shut up your mouth, Henry!' Daniel sniffed, pretending not to care.

'Hey, that's Corporal Henry to you, Private!'

Daniel uttered some words that would have displeased his parents had they been there to hear them. Henry laughed and slapped Daniel on the shoulder, saying, 'Righto, I'm off to steal some horses for the king. See you two later!'

'He makes me so mad!' declared Daniel unnecessarily.

Robert rolled his eyes; it was not the first time his brother had said that and nor, he suspected, would it be the last.

'Just ignore him. You know he just likes to annoy you. Anyway, right now, we've more important things to think about.'

'Where are we going?' asked Daniel.

'Let's just walk for a couple of miles. There are some farms dotted around the place and there's bound to be a few horses about.'

Daniel had a thought. 'Why don't we split up? We'll

cover more ground that way. Or do you not trust me?'

In truth, Robert did not trust Daniel, not really, although it was not something he'd had to consider before his promotion. But he was a corporal now and hoped to make sergeant one day. As far as he was concerned, it was best to be safe. Where possible, he would supervise his little brother until he felt Daniel has earned his trust. However, he could not confess this aloud. Therefore he fibbed, telling Daniel, 'We're to travel in pairs in case there are any Jacobites hanging around.'

They walked along in companionable silence. For now, the rain had stopped and the clouds seemed impatient to shed their wintry shades of wearisome grey. Daniel could hear plenty of rustling in the undergrowth and wondered whose day they were intruding upon: a stoat, a hedgehog or maybe just a plain old rat.

The winding road was dimpled with puddles, varying in size and depth while the trees were budding with the promise of new life. Robert breathed in deeply. The reverend had told them they were in County Down, in other words a long way from Derry.

'This time last year ...' said Robert.

He didn't have to say anything else. Daniel understood his brother was comparing their present surroundings with being cooped up for three miserable months behind the walls of Derry, simultaneously feeling safe and imprisoned while the Jacobites pounded the city with bombs and bullets. Their every waking moment was dominated by a fierce hunger that would not leave them. It was that hunger that drove the people of Derry to eat candlesticks, mice, grass ... having first devoured their beloved pets. Daniel did not like to dwell on it.

Instead he focused on the good things. Surviving the siege meant that they might always appreciate afternoons like this, following a road to God knows where and never forgetting to be grateful for the freedom to do so.

'Aha!' said Robert suddenly. 'Do you see what I see?'

Daniel followed his brother's gaze and saw, in the distance, a farmer ploughing his field with not one but two horses.

'Well done, Corporal Sherrard!'

'Why thank you, Private Sherrard. Shall we?'

Robert led the way; they left the road behind and strode through the wet grass that squeaked beneath their feet.

'Do you think he'll mind?' asked Daniel.

Robert shook his head. 'The people here are loyal to William. They'll probably consider it an honour to assist him.'

To the right of the field, they saw a thatched cottage, guessing it to be the farmer's home. It was modest in size;

a thin line of smoke drifted from the chimney. Just out-side the open door, they could see children playing. An older-looking girl was bent over a tub of clothes, prodding them with a stick. She was the first to see the two soldiers approaching.

Instinctively, Daniel raised his arm in acknowledgement but then changed his mind and brought it down again.

'Whatever are you doing?' asked his brother.

Daniel replied, 'Well, we're too far away to greet them, and they should know that we mean them no harm.'

Robert laughed. 'They'll know soon enough. Besides, the only one we need to talk to is him.'

At last, the farmer had spotted them and stood, waiting for their approach. He fished out a large, red handkerchief and proceeded to mop his face and the back of his neck. The horses flicked their tails and stared off into space or maybe they were concentrating on the green grass in the next field and wishing it was nearer.

'Now, leave this to me!' Robert was taking his position of corporal seriously.

Daniel was going to protest but knew there was no point. He had long ago learned that if Robert wanted to be in charge of something, it was best to let him be.

'Good day to you, sir!' Robert's voice was hale and hearty. 'We bring you greetings from King William himself.'

Daniel rubbed the ear that his brother had virtually bellowed into and looked ahead of him.

And looked again.

No. It couldn't be.

Oblivious to Daniel's confusion, Robert continued shouting in a cheerful manner. He had a job to do and, unlike Henry Campsie, he also had a younger brother to tutor in the ways of the world. As such, he was too busy to notice Daniel's twitchy attempts to attract his attention.

And so it was that they were only a few feet away from the farmer when Robert finally understood that he was not actually addressing a farmer. No, he was addressing the farmer's wife.

'Oh!' he exclaimed, for that was all that came to mind, and then he glanced at Daniel as if to say, 'Behold, this is a woman!'

However, Daniel only muttered, 'I did try to tell you!'

CHAPTER SIX

Drogheda, June 1690

Having seen that their horses, Paris and Troy, were fed and watered, Gerald and Jacques were wandering around the small walled town of Drogheda. Their walk was hindered by overcrowding. People were nervous. Catholics streamed in from miles around, trusting the safety of their families to the bricks of the garrison town — exactly like the Protestants who made their way into Derry in 1688 to take shelter from the coming storm of a Catholic army. Accordingly, the population of Drogheda had exploded.

The noise was incredible thanks to screaming children, lowing cattle, barking dogs and the hawkers selling their wares. Because of Drogheda's proximity to the sea, fish was a popular product. Here and there, the fishmongers, with their ruddy hands and sleeves pushed up past their elbows, delighted in the flamboyant gutting and beheading of their goods, spurts of blood splattering their already filthy aprons as they worked.

The traffic was thick and fast on the streets: weary horses pulled carts that held all manner of things and then there were the horses of the well-to-do that pulled the grander carriages; young boys herded bleating goats and sheep to the butchers'; women scurried along doing errands; while bands of children got in everyone's way as they played their games of chasing one another or daring one another to grab the tail of a passing horse, thereby risking being whipped by the rider or being kicked in the head by the irate owner of the tail.

At one stage, Gerald thought he might have to go to the rescue of a young child who had become separated from its mother and stood lost in the midst of a bustling crowd, bawling at the top of its voice – 'Mama! Mama!' – until he was too overcome to pronounce the word and only bawled.

People rushed by, too absorbed in their own business to notice the toddler in distress. Gerald had been about to snap into action when the mother suddenly emerged out of the throng of strangers and did nothing more than grab the child by the hand and drag him off, ignoring his moist smile of relief and happiness.

Gerald would not have thought to admit it to himself but

since he had been forced to watch that girl hang, he was determined that he would not just stand by again.

Jacques made a face. 'Phew, this town smells worse than Paris!'

Gerald grinned. 'Do you mean your horse or the city?'

Jacques laughed. 'Both!'

On their way into the town, they had passed what they assumed was a dumping ground, sitting just outside the walls. It was a towering mass of rotten fruit, fish guts, ancient potato skins and perhaps other types of skins too, broken crockery or what was once crockery, and, yes, the rotting remains of at least two animals, possibly dogs, or goats – really, it was impossible to tell. The dump seemed to throb with life thanks to the rats and the large birds scavenging for meals. The gulls and the crows screamed in protest at the thieving rats that were too big to confront.

Jacques had pointed out to Gerald that it was far too near the River Boyne, and even as they stood there and watched, they saw yellowish thickened globules and muggy, shapeless forms of God knows what slide free from the stinking mountain into the water.

Not surprisingly, the entire area was besieged by clouds of flies which made standing around almost impossible.

'Do not,' warned Jacques, 'touch the water here unless you have seen it come out of a well with your own eyes.

Believe me, after twenty years of being a soldier, I know all about bad water.'

Gerald did not need to be convinced. It was an unusually warm summer's afternoon which probably explained the heightened smell that plugged the back of his throat and hastened the pair on their way through the city gate.

Drogheda, like Derry, was a garrison town. For years now the army had taken up residence within its walls. Three thousand Jacobite soldiers were the current occupants, holding the town for King James, who was making frequent visits from his base in Dublin.

Thanks to his tutor, Father Nicholas, Gerald was already well-schooled on the town's experience of bloodshed. Pointing to an impressive mound topped by a watch-tower, he said, 'You see there, that is where Oliver Cromwell's men slaughtered the garrison soldiers and the bodies were stacked on top of one another for days on end because the people were too afraid to go near them.'

Jacques nodded. 'That is understandable.'

Gerald continued, 'The officer in charge of Drogheda at the time was Sir Arthur Ashton and he had a wooden leg. I heard that the enemy soldiers ripped the leg off him and bashed out his brains with it.'

Having infused the story with as much drama as he could, Gerald, quite naturally, expected a passionate response from his listener – be it a show of disgust or some abominable language. Instead, Jacques scratched his chin and glanced around them, muttering, 'Terrible. Yes.'

'Terrible?'

Gerald echoed the word in such a way as to suggest that it was not enough.

Jacques was looking for something or so it appeared. He kept turning this way and that, checking who was around them. It was unsettling.

Gerald asked, 'What is the matter? Have you lost something?'

'No. Not really.'

Gerald was confused: 'Not really?'

Jacques sighed. 'Are you going to repeat every word I say?

Then the Frenchman tried a different tact. 'Wasn't there something you particularly wanted to do here? After all, we don't know how long we have left until we are called to arms. Didn't you mention a bookseller's? You wanted the grand tour ... no?'

Gerald nodded. 'Yes, I wanted to see about getting a new Bible. I lost mine somewhere between here and Ardee, I think. And I was hoping to have a proper look around Drogheda. My tutor talked about it often and now I am here with time on my hands.'

Looking relieved, Jacques said, 'Well, then, you go look-ing for your Bible and I'll meet you later.'

Gerald almost said 'later?' but then he definitely would be repeating a lot of Jacques words. Instead, he said, 'Oh, but I thought we could go together.'

Jacques sighed and said, 'Look, I will meet you at the gate we came through and …'

But he was interrupted by a young woman who rushed up behind them to exclaim loudly, 'There you are! At last!'

Jacques grabbed the girl's hand and kissed the back of it. 'Ah, forgive me!'

Gerald wondered if he should make a quick exit. How-ever, Jacques made this impossible by turning to Gerald, to say, 'Allow me, my young friend, to introduce you to a wonderful girl … indeed the most wonderful girl I have ever met …' he paused to add effect to his joke. 'What was her name again … ah, I remember, Nancy!'

'Oh, you!'

Gerald found himself somewhat awestruck when Nancy then focused all her attention on him, curtseying playfully while saying: 'You must be the Master Gerald from County Offaly. Jacques has told me all about you.'

It would have been rude, Gerald thought, to have asked exactly when this conversation about him might have taken place. Likewise, he did not like to mention that he had never heard of her before so he only smiled politely and said, 'A pleasure to meet you, Madam!'

'Goodness, what manners!' said Nancy.

To Gerald's surprise, she linked an arm through each of theirs and asked, 'Well, what are we going to do? I have to be back in an hour so I can't stand around here dawdling.'

Gerald glanced over at Jacques, fully expecting to be dismissed, but it seemed that his friend had undergone a slight transformation. His dark eyes sparkled in a way that Gerald had never seen before, while his expression, so bright and full, was free of its usual sulkiness. In fact, Jacques looked years younger and gazed at Nancy as if she were the sun making an unexpected appearance on a drab winter's day.

'But what would you like to do, Mademoiselle?'

Nancy scrunched up her face, and Gerald thought he might venture an idea: 'I would be grateful if you would direct me to the bookseller?'

She squeezed his arm and proceeded to walk the two friends forward. 'Of course. This way, mind how you go. There's cow dung everywhere.'

Unfortunately Gerald was so busy feeling shy that he skidded on a stinking pile, ending up with it clinging to his feet. The other two teased while watching him do his best to scrape the mess off against a nearby rock.

The bookseller's shop was a large, dark, misshapen room

that held an impressive amount of books and scrolls. A couple of dusty windows let in little light so the owner had provided two dusty oil lamps. Altogether, there was just enough light to see the names of the books that sat either pressed together on wooden shelves or piled in tottering towers that Gerald warily tip-toed by, not wanting to be the clumsy clod that knocked one over.

In the centre, on a table, a large book of maps lay open, inviting customers to have a look. Jacques turned the pages carefully, to find a detailed map of France, showing Nancy the town where he came from, and so on. Gerald peered over his shoulders to admire the intricate gilded lines of a country laid bare for all to see. He and Jacques had already decided that when all this trouble was over he would accompany his friend back to France.

There were no booksellers where Gerald came from, in Offaly, while there had been one or two in Dublin, but that city, with its universities and students, intimidated Gerald so much that he had found himself quite unable to walk into them.

It turned out that Nancy knew the bookseller; he was a friend of her father's, and she proudly introduced her friends to him.

Mr Patrick Mahon was, as one might have expected, completely absorbed in a book as the trio made their entrance. With his bushy grey hair and tiny spectacles that barely stretched across his face, his slightly bulky figure and smooth hands that had never farmed nor built a wall, the bookseller reminded Gerald of his tutor Father Nicholas.

'Ah, welcome my boys. Soldiers, I see.'

Gerald smiled. Since he and Jacques were in uniform one would have had to have been blind not to know that they were soldiers. Naturally they had received a lot of attention on the streets outside, mostly positive – depending who was looking at them. The children gawked and pointed, some even calling out to them: 'Can we come with you when you go fighting? We could hold the flags and polish the guns. Go on, let us! Can we watch you kill the Williamites? Can we?'

By way of reply, they received nothing more than a dark scowl from Jacques, while Gerald ignored them completely.

Of course the people of Drogheda knew there was a battle coming. There were soldiers everywhere, though Gerald and Jacques remarked that there wasn't much to the new recruits – hardly any of them owned a musket, while none they had spoken to had had any previous battle experience.

Furthermore, some of their uniforms were decidedly shabby and ill-fitting. A young corporal from Dublin, whose too-small jacket barely allowed him to put his two arms down by his side, explained to Jacques, 'They told me this was all they had and that there was no money to buy any more.'

Jacques had pressed his lips together. Gerald knew this sort of thing troubled him, filling the more experienced soldier with a sense of foreboding. As far they both knew, there was no shortage of money for the rival army under William, and money represented power, especially when it came to outfitting an army.

Mr Mahon asked, 'How can I help you? Are you looking for anything in particular?'

Now that he was here, Gerald wasn't so sure of himself. He was struck by the leather covers, some of which seemed to be inscribed in gold lettering. Everything looked so expensive, and he fretted that he might waste this learned man's time.

'Well, I thought I might look at your Bibles, that is, if you have any?'

Mr Mahon smiled. 'But of course I do. They are my biggest sellers. Step right this way.'

As Gerald stepped forward there was a cry of protest from a dark bundle near his feet – a dark bundle with claws.

'Ow!' cried Gerald in fright, quickly following this up with an embarrassed apology. 'I'm so sorry, sir. I didn't see him.'

'Do not blame yourself, my boy!'

Mr Mahon stood over his cat and waggled his finger at it. 'Odysseus, what do you mean by hiding yourself there? Can you blame this young chap for walking on you? Have some sense, sir!'

The cat meowed in a tone that could only be described as rude.

'Please accept my apologies, Master Gerald. I am afraid that I have spoiled him.'

Gerald could hear Jacques and Nancy tittering behind him as he fell in behind the bookseller who led him to a small shelf of Bibles.

'Here you are, some of the finest Bibles available. Of course, I imagine that the big ones are too bulky to carry around but, see here, these little ones can easily be carried in a pocket.'

The bookseller was right; there were at least three squat, thick Bibles that would fit into the palm of his hand. Gently, Gerald pulled one free from its companions and instinctively raised it to his nose to sniff the almost transparent pages. Father Nicholas had taught him how to appreciate books, telling his pupil, 'I'd rather the smell of a new book over any flower – may God forgive me!'

Next, Gerald let the book fall open. The print was tiny, to be sure, but its cover was mottled in reddish hues and, well, it just felt right. He was not in a rush to query the price of the Bible and allowed his eyes to travel over the other books on the shelf. Right at the end, he spied a much thinner book squashed up between a large, imposing book about the Gospels and the wooden slat that signified the break in the shelving.

Gerald reached for it, almost crushing his fingers as he worked the book free until, finally, out it came, toppling into his hand, no doubt glad to have escaped its ample neighbour. It was only then that Gerald realised there was no way he could put it back as the Gospels book seemed to have somehow expanded leaving absolutely no room.

It was a prayer book and much more decorative than the Bible which Gerald placed gingerly on the table behind him. The cover felt almost soft, like a cushion, and was tinged with gold, glistening in the drab light of the nearest oil lamp. The back of his neck tingled when he read the name on the opening page: Saint Teresa of Avila – his sister's favourite saint.

Cait collected saints like Gerald used to collect rocks. Father Nicholas usually helped with this, returning from his trips abroad with pamphlets and books that he thought she might appreciate. She once said that Saint Teresa was an inspiration to women everywhere because she wrote several important books and helped to found convents all over

Spain. Cait also admired her because: 'She did not allow herself to be pushed into marriage, preferring to keep herself free to pursue her own work.'

Gerald could not imagine either of his parents attempting to push their daughter into doing anything she didn't want to.

The Spanish saint was a mystic and was jeered for her visions of Mary and Jesus. Cait was not blind to the looks that some of the locals gave her while she claimed strange occurrences for herself. Hadn't she heard the banshee wail her terrifying lament not three days before their grandfather died? Afterwards, man to man, Gerald's father had wondered to Gerald if she had not just heard the screeching of an owl.

Cait spent her days looking after the sick and the poor. Nobody had asked her to do this; it just sort of happened, as Gerald remembered it. Naturally her favourite saint was also a healer, bringing a child, her nephew, back from the brink of death just by laying her hands upon him. In truth, Gerald found himself more interested than he expected, and he was definitely impressed by the coincidence of finding one of her books here in Drogheda.

The pages were edged in more gold, and, with an obstinate puff, the book fell open on a page where Gerald felt obliged to read the following:

Let nothing disturb you
Let nothing frighten you
All things are passing;
God only is changeless.
Patience gains all things.
Who has God wants nothing.
God alone suffices.

It was as if he could hear the saint herself, her breath cool against his ear, the slightest hint of blossoms in the air, the gold colouring suddenly suggesting the gold of evening sunlight as it stretches across the fields in front of his home.

Completely absorbed in his thoughts, Gerald almost screamed when Jacques crept up behind and tapped him on the shoulder, asking, 'Did you not hear me calling you?'

Ignoring his friend, Gerald called over to Mr Mahon, his timidity gone, 'May I ask the price of this book?'

Of course it cost more than he had in his pocket. In fact, it cost more than he had ever had in his pocket. Well, it was beautiful, it would be an insult to attach a mean price to it. Yet, Gerald lingered, turning the book this way and that, wondering what he could do.

However, Patrick Mahon was not a bookseller for nothing. He recognised and appreciated when a customer had fallen in love. And this young soldier looked truly smitten.

'If you like, I can hold it here for you. Just pay me a deposit and the rest as you go. I promise that no one else shall get their hands on it.'

Gerald hesitated. As of yet, there was no firm information available regarding the payment of wages for the Jacobite army. The deposit was the easy part; simply hand over the contents of his pockets and hope for the best. He looked down at the book again as if waiting for guidance. It was the perfect gift for Cait and, yes, for him too. How odd it was, that those few words moved him to remember that he was never truly alone but also served to remind him that he was about to take part in what promised to be a momentous, not to mention dangerous battle. After all these months, it was easy to forget why he was wearing this uniform and what all these days were tumbling him towards. How small he suddenly felt. No, he *needed* to have this book because he needed to believe that he would survive what was coming if only to press this precious book into his sister's hands.

He nodded to himself, thinking, *If worst comes to worst and I can't pay for it, I'll just tell him to put it back on the shelf, but he can keep my deposit.*

Still, he heard the tremor in his voice as he told Mr Mahon, 'Thank you. I would be most grateful if you held it for me, although I am not exactly sure when you will see me again. I mean if ... or ...'

The bookseller hushed him. 'Do not trouble yourself, lad. See, I will keep it right here with your name on it. Just give me half of those coins in your hand. There's no need to clear yourself out completely. A man should always have a bit of money in his pocket, just in case.'

Stuck for words at Mr Mahon's kindness, Gerald could only obey him, dutifully counting out the larger coins into his hand before mumbling his thanks.

He turned and walked out the door, fighting the tears that threatened. Outside, he had time to collect himself. What on earth had come over him? Perhaps it was just as well he didn't brave the bookshops of Dublin.

The other two were taking their time saying goodbye to the bookseller. *How wonderful it was that Nancy knew him.* A passerby glanced at Gerald, and the boy hoped that his face wasn't red. *Well, as long as I don't look like I'm about to cry … that would be embarrassing.*

Unfortunately for Gerald, he was destined to be embarrassed when Jacques and a grinning Nancy joined him.

Doing his best to look normal, Gerald smiled in all innocence. 'What?'

Nancy nudged Jacques. 'Best give it to him now. I have to get going in a few minutes.'

Gerald turned his head from one to the other as Jacques handed him a hastily wrapped package. Again he asked,

'What?'

Then he opened the package and found that gorgeous book, and Nancy, who couldn't wait any longer to explain, exclaimed, 'We bought it for you.'

In fairness to him, Gerald managed to open the book and also managed to read aloud the new inscription: *To Gerald, a good friend and the best of companions. From Jacques and Nancy.*

The next words that Gerald remembered hearing were from Jacques: 'I think we need a bigger handkerchief!'

CHAPTER SEVEN

County Down, June 1690

There was a confused silence and the woman glanced from one Sherrard to the other as if trying to guess who would speak first.

'You are so tall!'

The words were out before Daniel could stop them. Immediately he felt foolish and ashamed, saying, 'Forgive me, I did not mean to be rude.'

The woman blinked and replied, 'Well, I am tall. There is nothing I can do about it.'

She was Scottish then or, at least, that was what her accent suggested. Her voice was softer than they expected.

Robert speedily pieced together the various reasons why he had mistaken her for a man. For starters, Daniel was right, she was the tallest woman he had ever seen, plus her shoulders were broader than his own. The wide-brimmed hat nicely camouflaged her long, thin nose; high cheek-bones and the odd wispy strands of blonde hair hinted at the rest of her crown. Furthermore, she had misled him with her attire. Unlike every other woman and girl he knew she was not wearing a dress. Robert wondered at the farmer allowing his wife to appear in his jacket, trousers and even his old boots. Corporal Sherrard could not even begin to imagine his mother wearing anything else except her skirts and apron.

She sighed and asked them, 'Are you lost?'

Robert was instantly huffy. 'Lost? No, we are not lost. We are soldiers from King William's army, as I have already said.'

To counter the sting in his brother's tone, Daniel offered her a small smile and decided to make a formal introduction, saying, 'My name is Daniel and this is my brother Corporal Robert Sherrard.'

The woman did not look impressed and only asked a second question, 'Where are you from?'

Robert answered first, 'Derry. It's fifty miles from here.'

The woman shrugged. 'I've never been to Derry but I would imagine that it's a lot more than fifty miles away.'

'Well, we live there and have walked from there. So ... I think we ought to know!'

Robert could not bear to be criticised and the slightest whiff of being faulted in any way made him choppy in manner.

It seemed to Daniel that the woman suppressed a fleeting smile.

'Mama! Mama!'

And just like that, they were surrounded. Six children in all, including the girl they had seen washing clothes. She was younger than Daniel had supposed, no more than thirteen or fourteen years old. She carried a chubby baby who reminded Daniel of his sister Alice. The baby sat upright against his sister's hip and fearlessly met Daniel's gaze while sucking on its thumb.

'What's wrong, Mother? Who are they?'

Robert would not deign to introduce himself to children, and Daniel followed suit, leaving the woman to say, 'Hush, Marian. Nothing is wrong. They are just soldiers, that's all.'

This was all getting a bit much for Robert's patience. If he owned a pocket watch, he would surely have checked it by now to see how much time had already been wasted. Clearing his throat, he asked, 'Can I speak with your husband?'

Daniel wished his brother did not sound quite so imperious. However, neither Sherrard was prepared for the woman's solid reply: 'No.'

In particular, Robert was taken aback and repeated her answer, 'No? But I ... I ... we need to speak to him at once.

Can't one of the children fetch him?'

The woman caught a strand of her hair and pushed it beneath her hat before answering again, 'No, they cannot.'

Of course Robert took the reply personally and believed that he specifically was being thwarted in every way possible. He gulped in air and then spoke slowly as if he were addressing someone with little intelligence: 'I must order you to summon your husband to us and I do so in the name of King William ... and Queen Mary. Therefore any refusal to fetch him is treason.'

He added the queen's name, instinctively feeling that this misguided woman might be more considerate of Her Majesty over the king himself.

Daniel flinched inwardly at the mention of treason. Traitors were hanged or shot. Surely Robert was not threatening to hurt this woman because she didn't call her husband. What was his brother thinking?

But there was something wrong. Daniel detected a flicker of something in the woman's expression and noticed the mortification on her daughter's face which propelled him to ask the obvious. 'Excuse me but why can't we talk to him?'

It was the boy who answered. He had dark hair, a slimy nose and big brown eyes that looked older than his years, which were maybe eight or so. With a solemn look, he explained, 'Because he's dead.'

Ah.

As embarrassed as he felt, Daniel was somewhat relieved for his brother's sake. The woman was not disobeying him nor was she trying him for a fool. Indeed, he was not the least bit surprised at hearing the relief in Robert's exclamation, 'Well now. I see.'

It all made sense. The husband was dead and so his widow was wearing his clothes and ploughing the field.

'What did you want him for?' The daughter Marian asked her question at the exact same time that Robert asked, 'When did he die?'

There was a pause and the two questions hung between them. Robert and Marian looked at the woman for guidance, and she naturally chose to repeat her daughter's question, asking, 'Well, what did you want with my husband?'

Up to now both Sherrards had steadily avoided looking at the two large items they had come for. Daniel, for one, would have preferred to have found the horses idly grazing and of no use to anyone.

The baby reached for the nearest horse and his sister obliged it by stepping forward so that the child could knock at the animal's neck with its pudgy fist.

The eight-year-old boy lodged an immediate complaint. 'Georgie! That's not a door! Mama, tell him!'

But his mother only said, 'Hush, Samuel!'

Next, Georgie launched himself forward and planted a moist, sloppy kiss that left an oval-shaped blot on the horse's coat. Daniel smiled along with the family, leaving Robert all alone to make his declaration.

'Madam ...' he began.

'Jean Watson,' she replied.

'Uh ... I beg your pardon?' said Robert.

The woman took a breath, possibly to hide her impatience, before saying once more, 'Jean Watson. My name is Mrs Jean Watson.'

'Oh, right. Thank you!' said Robert, obviously feeling that he was starting to get somewhere at last. 'Well, Mrs Watson, as you might have heard, King William plans to confront James Stuart and his Jacobite army. In fact, that is where my brother and I are headed. However, the king has recently discovered that he needs more horses.'

Daniel watched Mrs Watson's lips almost disappear as her gaze became a glare.

Robert kept talking because he simply had to. Gesturing at the horses, he continued, 'And he hopes to depend on the generosity of the Protestant population ... that is ...'

Marian was incredulous. 'He wants our horses?'

She hoisted Georgie onto her other hip as she faced her mother. 'He wants our Bess and Star?'

How Robert wished the widow would send the children back to the house. They were complicating matters needlessly.

Daniel reckoned that he had better help his brother and added, 'Just for a while.' He hoped he was telling the truth as he rushed on to explain: 'You see we have a lot of equipment and thousands of men and, well, it's faster on horseback.'

The only listener who looked convinced was Robert who nodded and said, 'I'm sure you understand. When you think about it, you would be a part of King William's campaign, without having to fight.'

Even as he spoke, Mrs Watson was already shaking her head. 'Absolutely not. I need these horses. I wish the king well on his campaign, but these animals are my only farm hands.'

Robert opened his mouth to argue, but she interrupted him, asking him sharply, 'How many children do you see?'

He stopped short and counted them. 'Er ... six?'

'Yes, six!' she snapped. 'Six hungry mouths to feed. And how many parents do they have?'

Samuel wanted to help the conversation along and did so by answering, 'Just you, mama.'

'But ... ' protested Robert.

'No!' said Mrs Watson. 'I don't care about your "buts"; I

don't have time for them. If I cannot work this farm, my children will starve.'

As if to emphasise her point, she prepared to return to her ploughing and called the horses to attention. She also told Marian to bring her siblings back to the house. 'Everyone now back to your chores.'

Robert kept quiet while the children reluctantly walked away in line behind their leader Marian. Samuel stuck his tongue out at Daniel, filling the young soldier with shame. When they were finally alone, Robert tried to sound as civil as he could. 'I'm sorry, Mrs Watson. I understand your predicament but orders are orders. His Majesty needs more horses. Right now your neighbours are being told the same thing by our colleagues. You don't have a choice.'

Daniel longed to distract himself by scuffing at the upturned earth with his foot, but he knew he had to show complete support for Robert and for King William.

The widow spoke through gritted teeth. 'If you take my animals I have no way of feeding my children or paying the rent. We'll lose our home.'

Robert shrugged helplessly. 'I understand ...'

'But you don't care, is that it?' She looked as if she might spit at him, at the both of them. She tried another approach: 'Does His Majesty wish more children to die in his name? Surely enough children starved to death in Derry.'

Daniel felt winded by her words because they were absolutely true. She was right; hundreds of children had died during the siege. A whole generation of youngsters had been wiped out and now slept underground within the cathedral grounds. An idea came to him then and he said to his brother, 'Robert ... I mean, Corporal, couldn't we just take one of the horses? Wouldn't that do?'

Daniel was desperate to appease the woman and save her children; he pleaded with her, 'You could plough with one horse. Couldn't you?'

It was a most practical solution, really the only one available to suit everyone as far as Daniel could see.

Alas he had made a mistake which worsened when the widow tilted her head to consider his suggestion and seemed to agree with it, asking Daniel, 'And when will you return my horse to me?'

It was an impossible question to answer, right then and there, in the middle of the half-ploughed field as the rain began to spill once more.

Daniel saw fury on his brother's face and realised his dreadful error. He bowed his head in shame, noting how the raindrops sprinkled the earth; it reminded him of his mother sprinkling flour on the old kitchen table where she made the bread.

Why hadn't he just kept his mouth shut?

He heard Robert say to the widow, 'We are taking both horses.'

Robert didn't shout, he didn't even sound angry, but there was something about his voice that made the woman drop her arms to her side. Daniel could not bring himself to look at her.

'Unhook the horses, Private.' With that, Robert turned and strode away, making it abundantly clear that there would be no further discussion.

Mrs Watson didn't help, of course she didn't. She just stood there and watched Daniel fumble with the reins. How many moments dragged by until he managed to free the horses from the plough? Raindrops sank into the horses' coats and disappeared without a trace. Daniel wished he could do the same.

It required all of his strength not to apologise, either for his brother or himself. Yet, he had to say something and what better than those two words his mother had drilled into him as soon as he could talk: 'Thank you.'

The farmer's widow didn't soften her gaze, though she must have guessed at the young soldier's inner turmoil. He took a step and pulled at the animals, who surely wondered who he was and where he was taking them.

'Just a moment, Private.'

His heart sank but he turned to face her.

'They are used to being fed twice a day. Watch that Bess doesn't gorge herself on sweet apples, and the shoe on Star's right foreleg will need replacing soon.'

Daniel nodded. He had already thanked her and it seemed a little pathetic to say it again.

'Where is King William now?'

The question surprised him.

'He's ... he's a few days ahead of us, going south. Two or three days, I think.'

'Good!' was all she said to that.

Now that he had removed the horses from her side she seemed taller than ever.

He asked, 'Why do you want to know?'

She gave him a bitter smile. 'Because he has left me no option. I'm going to ask him to return my horses to me.'

Now it was her turn to march away, calling over her shoulders to him as he stared after her, 'You see, Daniel Sherrard, sometimes men need to be reminded that there are more important things than war.'

CHAPTER EIGHT

Drogheda, June 1690

Gerald and Jacques had spent the entire afternoon on horseback, Jacques pushing Gerald hard on performing manoeuvres that might well save his life in battle. They both agreed that Troy knew exactly what was required of him; it was just his rider who needed to practise.

Years of training had gone into Troy, Paris and the rest of the horses in the French cavalry. Gerald could not help but be impressed. He only needed to lightly pull the reins this way and that to signal to Troy to walk forward or backwards or to the side.

Jacques repeated what he said in every training session: 'You must trust yourself as much as your horse trusts you. That is what it is all about, trust.'

'I know. I know. You've said that before!' Gerald flexed

his fingers to prevent them from cramping after holding them in the same position for so long. It struck him that his life was one long list of instructions, from his parents to Father Nicholas, and now his friend who enjoyed torturing him with endless repetition of directions and exercises.

Ignoring his pupil's cheekiness, Jacques continued on with the lesson: 'A horse is a brave and noble creature. Just think how he allows a man to mount him. As far as the horse is concerned, every rider imitates an attack by a predator. The big lion jumps onto the horse's back to bite down on his spine while hugging the horse's neck in order to tear it open with its claws.'

Gerald rolled his eyes. He had long ceased reminding Jacques that there were no lions in Ireland.

'Remember to keep your musket straight. Your arms must get used to holding it straight in battle while guiding Troy this way and that.'

'I guide him just as well by pressing my knees against him. Really, Jacques, we have done this so many times. I'm not a beginner anymore!'

Jacques grinned at him. 'It is true you have made excellent progress, but I think this is thanks to your most excellent horse and most excellent teacher.'

Troy snorted his agreement.

As they trotted past the town, they could see their fellow

soldiers sweating in the sun, digging trenches and fortifying Drogheda's walls. Gerald remarked, 'Isn't it peculiar that this is exactly what went on in Derry only we were on the outside of the walls, we were the threat?'

'No, my friend, I do not find it strange at all. In life, everything is repeated, with the same things, and they happen again and again only to different people.'

Jacques was in a philosophical mood.

'You mean like, the next time we're here in Drogheda, I'll be the one to fall in love?'

Jacques grunted. 'Maybe so. If you're lucky and only if we ever return to Drogheda again.'

Gerald smirked. 'So, you still plan to leave then, after this is all over?'

Jacques answered with a shrug, 'But of course. I am a soldier. I go where King Louis wants for me to go.'

'Really?' asked Gerald. 'But what if you don't want to go anywhere else? What if you want to make a home for yourself and have a family?'

The Frenchman reminded his friend, 'Your father has a home and a family and he fights for Louis. He has everything, yes?'

Gerald thought about this. 'I suppose so. I mean, for all I know he misses Ireland and Mother terribly, but they both believe in doing their duty. They told us that Father would be better placed to help Ireland if he joined up with your king.'

Jacques waved his hand. 'Well, there you go. We are all doing our duty. Isn't that why you are here?'

Gerald said nothing to this. They brought the horses back to their pen, dismounted and removed the heavy saddles. Then they spent the next hour rubbing the animals down and making sure they had plenty of water.

When they were finished, Jacques slapped both horses on the flank. 'See you later, my friends. Enjoy your evening!'

He had already decided how he and Gerald would spend the following hour. 'Come, I need some of your horrible Irish beer to cool me down. Let's go to the tavern and continue this interesting talk.'

Gerald knew that his mother would hardly approve of his entering such an unworthy establishment. The ale-house was nothing more than a dark basement, found at the bottom of a few rickety wooden steps that did their best to trip up the customer who had indulged himself with too much alcohol. It was far from clean, the atmosphere thick with the smell of sweat and urine. The battered furniture had certainly seen better years, better decades, but the customers did not make their way down those treacherous steps to take in the interior decoration. The dank basement was for drinking and conversation.

Besides, his father was no stranger to the tavern in Offaly and, according to Jacques, a variety of taverns in Paris. Jacques had known Gerald's father in Paris. Indeed, it was Mr O'Connor who had asked that Jacques look out for Gerald, ensuring that the two met up as soon as possible by asking the Frenchman to deliver Troy to him. It had taken Mr O'Connor some time to be able to afford the horse because of the animal's specialised training Horses represented extra soldiers on the field but required months of tough conditioning to prepare them for the noise and chaos of battle. Finally, the day had arrived and Mr O'Connor was delighted to be able to send his son this tremendous gift that meant that Gerald was immediately promoted from the lowest echelon of any army, the infantry, to the highest, the cavalry. Although he and Jacques were rather low down in terms of the cavalry, where the wealthier members owned two or even three horses and had their own groomsmen. However, this did not bother Gerald in the slightest. He was perfectly satisfied with having just Troy and looking after him himself. This was the first time he had ever owned a horse, a fact that would have shocked his wealthy ancestors.

The room was crowded, the summer temperature creating a thirst that could only be satisfied by a mug of brown ale. Gerald insisted on paying for their two drinks, still determined to repay, in some way, the price of the book.

They found two worm-ridden stools and sat down close to one another.

Gerald had been thinking about the word 'duty' and even before Jacques could enjoy that all-important first sip, he asked, 'Can I make an observation and, pray, do not be offended?'

Jacques swallowed a mouthful of warm beer as he nodded his permission.

'Well, it's just that you said we are all doing our duty ... but, you see, your country is not really under threat, is it? I mean, you have a Catholic king, one of the most powerful rulers in the world. He has plenty of money and a huge army.'

'*Oui*, this is so,' conceded Jacques, concentrating mostly on his beer, making sure none of the house flies ended up swimming in it.

'But, well, it's just that ... you are only here because Louis told you to be.'

Gerald had rushed out his last few words and seemed to expect an explosion of some sorts.

Slightly baffled, Jacques simply agreed, 'Yes. I know that. You know that. What of it?'

Gerald paused, feeling slightly lost himself. What was the point he had wanted to make?

'Look,' said Jacques, 'you told me why you are here, about your grandfather's castle that was burned to the ground, about your mother that longs to be a great lady again, like her mother before her. You fight to win back the riches of your family, and I fight for Louis to hold onto his riches. Don't pretend, my friend, there is a nobler reason for us to be here. Really, war is usually about the power and the money.'

He rewarded himself for his speech by draining his drink and then looking pointedly at that of Gerald, who was not as keen on the taste and, without thinking, swapped cups with his friend.

'*Merci bien!*' muttered Jacques happily. 'This is the life, no?'

The first beer had settled him in nicely and, with a contented sigh, Jacques took in their fellow drinkers. 'Ah, see, there is Michael and Joseph.'

He waved at the other soldiers, saying: 'Now, I do not much care for either of them but tonight let us all be merry. Yes?'

At long last, Jacques glanced at Gerald's face and was perplexed at not seeing the usual friendly expression. However, just before he could investigate matters further, he was obliged to deal with Michael and Joseph, the two soldiers from Tallaght and Trim who had found a stool each and were pushing in beside them.

Michael glanced at Gerald and asked, 'What's wrong?'

When Gerald made no answer to this, Michael smirked as he said rather too loudly to Jacques, 'Oh dear, I hope we're not interrupting anything.'

The younger soldier, Joseph, had not noticed anything and had no idea what his friend was talking about and certainly was not prepared for Gerald's furious bark.

'How dare you!'

Jacques was mystified, looking from Gerald to the new arrivals and back again. 'What? Who are you talking to?'

Gerald spat out his answer. 'You, Jacques, you! You think it's so easy, don't you? You have met a girl you like so now you are perfectly happy. It doesn't matter where you are, only that you can drink beer and chase girls. That's all you care about!'

Michael was understandably thrilled with this. He had hardly expected a performance to go with his beer and certainly not one that involved the pompous *Frenchie* being made to look as sorry as he did.

Doing his best to ignore the eager audience, Jacques sought to calm his young friend. 'I do not understand. What have I said?'

However, Gerald refused to dignify the question with a reply, forcing Jacques to work it out for himself.

'Wait!' said Jacques, before declaring, 'This is about me

saying there are no noble reasons to fight. I am right, no?'

He paused, not wanting to upset Gerald anymore than he had already done. Nevertheless, he had finished the second beer and, therefore, was not going to indulge any silly whims. He was nobody's nursemaid.

But, first things first.

He stood up quickly, startling them all, announcing quietly, 'I need more beer!'

Gerald rolled his eyes to the grimy ceiling while Jacques called out his order to the plump barmaid, who sloppily filled a jug and brought it over to share out between the four beakers. Joseph and Michael were mightily appreciative of Jacques' generosity and drank up quickly, to make room for more. Only Gerald did not offer up his empty cup.

Jacques pretended not to notice and focused on the late-comers, asking them, 'So, tell me, you two, why are you soldiers in King James's army? Why will you fight his battle for him?'

Gerald scowled while the others seemed surprised at such a strange question.

However, Joseph wanted to be helpful and offered, 'My father told me I had to go because we needed the money.'

Jacques seemed surprised at this and stared at Joseph, who suddenly looked far too naive for his red coat. Joseph's face was covered by a dizzy blend of orange and brown freckles, and Jacques pitied the boy for his giant front teeth that refused to stay hidden.

Feeling that he should elaborate, Joseph added, 'I'm the eldest of seven.'

Michael nodded. 'I have a family to feed back in Trim and this uniform is an improvement on scrabbling in other men's fields, planting their vegetables.'

Gerald now stirred himself to ask, 'So, you believe in King James and in returning to the old Ireland, where we can be free to better ourselves?'

Michael smirked. 'Do you mean Tir na nÓg, the Fianna, Oisín, Niamh, Cuchulainn and his hound, and all that lot? Do not forget, my lad, that we are lining up to fight for an Englishman. I doubt that the Fianna would be so proud of us.'

'But James can give us back our religion, our rights.' Gerald was adamant that at least one of them would see sense.

Michael slurped his beer noisily and swallowed quickly. 'As far as I'm concerned, James is the one who pays my wages.'

It was Jacques' turn to become tetchy. If they were going to drink his beer they had to get their facts straight: 'Correction! King Louis is the man who pays your wages. Without him, none of this would be happening. Your children would starve and you, Joseph, would be still sitting at your poor parents' table.'

'You know what,' said Michael rather loudly, 'I don't like your tone. And I don't care who pays me as long as I get paid!'

Joseph seemed lost. He sent Gerald a worried look, which was promptly ignored.

'There!' Jacques nudged Gerald lightly. 'Is Michael any better than me? He might have an Irish accent but at least I know who I'm fighting for.'

Wanting to keep his two hands free to hit someone, Michael shoved his mug at Joseph. Joseph, however, scraped enough courage together to refuse it. He stared at his feet and pretended he was elsewhere.

'You don't know anything about me, Frenchie.' Michael spoke slowly and precisely. 'Remember you're not in France now. You have no idea what we've been through.'

Jacques was confused. 'Huh?'

Michael twisted around suddenly, making Joseph flinch, as he pulled up his tunic and shirt to show them his back which was crisscrossed with shiny welts that they could just about make out in the candlelight.

'You know who gave me them?' he asked. Without waiting for an answer, he told them, 'the English lord that caught me looking for potatoes on his estate. I was twelve years old and my parents were dead. I was hungry, dressed in rags, and he had his gardener whip me as if I was a rabid dog.'

The others stared at Michael's red face. Feeling a little

embarrassed, the older soldier slid his clothes back into place. Lowering his voice, he said, 'That Englishman told me that I had no business being alive! Has any foreigner said that to you in your own country?'

His question was for Jacques who was struggling to understand the turn in conversation.

Adamant that Jacques concentrated on what was being said, Gerald added, 'You hear that, Jacques and that's only one story. There are plenty more! I spent my childhood being walked for miles by Father Nicholas so that he could show me burnt-out churches and graves that had been dug up just because the corpses were Catholics.'

Michael nodded at this, as Gerald continued, 'People are starving, *our* people. We're not allowed to farm our own land because it belongs to England. And when we can't afford to pay the rent for our homes the English landlord evicts us without a second thought. Babies, old people, sick people, left sitting on the side of the road, hungry and with nowhere to go.'

Jacques shifted on his stool. 'But we have our poor in France too. Is it not worse that rich French people do not care about their own poor?'

'Oh!' cried Michael. 'So, now we see your true colours.'

'Colours?' Jacques scrunched up his features. 'I do not understand.'

Still stuck on an earlier point, Gerald snapped, 'And your King Louis is only involved because he hates William of Orange, and for no grander reason than that.'

'You lot, keep it down!' yelled the barmaid. 'No fighting in here or I'll put you out.'

'Sure. Why not?' shrugged Jacques. 'Louis wants to rule Europe so he uses James to beat William, and James uses Ireland to beat William, while William fights to remain king of all England. So what?'

Gerald's face was white with rage. Why had he come into this awful tavern? He hadn't wanted to. He knew his mother and Father Nicholas would be disappointed, not to mention his sister who would despise each and every one of these drunkards.

When he bade his family and tutor goodbye, he thought he knew exactly who he was, where he was coming from and what he was going to do. All he had ever heard from them all was how marvellous Ireland had been in the past.

For Father Nicholas the matter was simply explained: 'The English have infested our landscape and heritage and the only way to deal with them is to flush them out. Do you understand what I am saying, child?'

And, of course, Gerald did understand because he had been brought up to view the world through the eyes of his family and the priest.

To be sure, things got complicated in his mind when he saw Derry's skeletal citizens and soldiers guarding her walls, and he could not help wondering if they should not just leave the city to herself.

And hanging that girl and her friend ... well, he still doubted the necessity of killing them.

But, here in Drogheda, it was easier to re-arm himself with Father Nicholas's and his mother's rage. Hadn't he just walked along Scarlett Street, so called because it was soaked with the blood of those whom Oliver Cromwell had slaughtered in *his* God's name?

Ireland was under attack once more, but this time he was here to fight for her.

Taking a deep breath, Gerard said, 'James may well be using Ireland to get what he wants, but we, the Irish, are using him.'

His three companions considered this for a moment.

'I accept that we are all here for different reasons and that some of those reasons might not be as ... admirable ... as others. But I know why I'm here. I want Ireland and her Catholics, which – yes – includes my family and me, to be free from tyranny.'

Jacques fidgeted at the word 'admirable' but did not contradict Gerald. However, he was not going to let the moment pass without attempting some sort of apology. 'My friends, perhaps the richest man is not the one sitting in a castle, counting his coins. Rather, it is the man who is free to choose his lot in life. Yes?'

Michael studied Gerald. Up to now the boy had not interested him. It was obvious that his own childhood had been vastly different from Gerald's and presumably they had little in common. Yet he noted the fire in the boy's eyes and wanted to believe – yes, Michael did – that there could be a better life for him and maybe for all of them sitting here. He said, 'I don't know much about riches or freedom but I can agree to fight for a better future.'

Joseph surprised everyone by asking, 'Have any of you heard of Ireland's "Sleeping Army"?'

They shook their heads, and Joseph explained, 'There is a cave somewhere between Drogheda and Ardee containing an ancient army of Irish warriors that were put to sleep long ago by some sort of spell. In order to wake the soldiers, who neither belong to our world or the next, one must enter the cave and fire the loaded gun that sits in the middle of them. My father met a man who swore he found the cave. He saw the soldiers lying on the ground, their eyes closed, looking as near to death as any dead man. Then he saw the gun and, without thinking, picked it up and half-cocked it. Immediately, every single soldier sat up but their eyes remained closed. The man got such a fright that he dropped the musket and left, leaving the gun half-cocked and the soldiers sitting halfway up.'

Joseph's listeners waited for him to continue but he was finished. It was the longest speech he had ever made and it had exhausted him.

To make up for his rudeness earlier, Gerald smiled at Joseph and said, 'Of course! The sleeping army could be like us and the man could be King James. All he has to do to waken our army is to fire a single shot and leave the rest to us.'

CHAPTER NINE

Around the Campfire

The campfire spat and spluttered as Daniel prodded the potatoes in the pot. Henry Campsie sat nearby, cleaning his musket. Against Daniel's wishes, Robert had just told his friend all about the widow. His response was typical. 'Are you sure that she was a woman?'

Daniel refused to acknowledge such a stupid question but Robert was immediately intrigued. 'What do you mean?'

'You said she was huge, was wearing trousers and had a bit of a Scottish accent,' said Henry.

When Robert nodded, Henry produced his own theory. 'Maybe she was actually a Jacobite soldier ... you know, one of those Scottish giants, the Redshanks.'

Back in 1688, the Redshanks were the first Catholic soldiers to arrive at Derry's walls and demand to be allowed into the city. They hailed from Scotland, wore red coats and were handpicked for their height – a man had to be at least six foot tall to join them.

'Oh, my God!' exclaimed Robert. 'Did you hear that, Daniel? Why didn't we think of that?'

Daniel was astounded. Ignoring the usual smirk on Henry Camspie's face, he asked his brother, 'Are you serious?'

Robert was determined that Daniel's dislike for Henry should not cloud the issue. 'Come on, Dan. He has a point. How can it be that the tallest woman we have ever met also happens to be wearing trousers and a pair of man's boots?'

'We both heard her speak, and she didn't sound like any man I know.'

'True,' agreed Robert. 'But she only spoke quietly, remember? She kept her voice low so she could have been disguising her true self.'

'Or *his* true self,' added Henry with a wink.

Robert was furious at himself. What a mistake to make. Noticing his brother's eyes on him, he asked him, 'What were we thinking? Why didn't we check?'

'Because ...' said Daniel in an exasperated tone, 'we both knew she was a woman. Because we were there, while Henry was not.'

'But we should have checked at least,' said Robert, already thinking how this might look to the likes of Reverend Walker and King William himself.

'Checked how?' asked Daniel. His grip so tightened around the wooden spoon that he felt his fingers cramp. He stirred the hot water in a poor attempt to release the tension from his hand.

'You're the doctor,' said Henry, laughing. 'How do you think?'

Even Robert flinched at this, but he would not hush his friend. Instead, he looked at his brother in the hope that he might have something useful to say.

Realising that his big brother was in a real fix, Daniel followed his usual urge to help him out. 'Robert, she had six children and the ones that spoke called her "Mama".'

'Yes!' Robert slapped his thigh. 'Exactly! Six children. That's right. We met them all, so we did.'

He looked at Henry waiting to receive his blessing, or something like that. However, his friend just slowly shook his head from side to side as if he could scarcely believe his ears. 'Oh, I see. Well, of course. I mean, children never ever lie to save their father's life.'

'You fool!' snapped Daniel.

Henry put his musket on the ground and gave Daniel a peculiar look, asking him, 'Just who do you think you're talking to?'

Daniel flung the spoon into the boiling water, causing

it to splash a little, the water burning his hand. 'What kind of man – and a soldier at that – would pretend to be a woman?'

'Steady on, Daniel,' said Robert. Not for the first time he wondered where his little brother had gone. Where was the boy who only wanted to be liked and would not have picked a fight with anybody?

'You always take his side, Robert! How can you be persuaded she was a man by someone who wasn't even there?'

Henry stood up; he had something to say and it felt appropriate to get to his feet. His father had been mayor of Derry and someday Henry hoped to be mayor himself. With that in mind, he practised his oratory skills whenever the opportunity arose. His father had always warned him against losing an argument through bad temper so he smoothed himself down and put his thoughts in order.

And then he began. 'Look, you two, we are in the middle of a war or soon will be. Nothing is as it seems in times of war. Daniel, you ask what type of man would pretend to be a woman and the answer is a desperate one.'

Robert nodded absentmindedly, while Daniel just stared, successfully hiding the fact that in the farthest corner of his mind he was starting to question Mrs Watson himself.

Henry continued, 'James and his army are desperate men; they have to be. They lost in Derry, and now King William has arrived with a bigger army than their own. Imagine it, Jacobite soldiers hiding out so that they don't have to fight to the death ... doing whatever is necessary to save their skins.'

He paused here, to allow his words to sink in. It was a trick he had learned from watching his father presenting unpopular proposals to fellow councillors.

'Look, as Daniel has pointed out, I wasn't there, but maybe that makes it easier for me to query her story. You two were after the horses and had enough to do to make sure you got them. So, you come back and describe her to me and I can jump to conclusions because I wasn't there and therefore can't be distracted by the children or her voice, or whatever else. Do you see what I mean?

Robert nodded yes while Daniel stabbed a potato with a knife.

'All right,' said Robert. 'So, what do we do now?

Daniel looked at him warily. 'What do you mean what do we do? We got the horses, didn't we?'

Robert ignored him and waited for Henry to answer his question.

Henry scrunched up his features as if deep in thought, but Daniel felt that the would-be politician had known all along what he was going to propose. 'Well, if you ask me, the only thing we can do is get proof of her identity.'

Robert understood him immediately. 'You mean we should return to the house to check if she is truly a woman or a Jacobite soldier in disguise?'

'Well, yes,' said Henry. 'There's no other way, is there? You have to get inside the house and look for a red coat or something like that.'

'That's settled then,' said Robert, as he dusted himself down and prepared to take his leave. 'It's all right, Daniel, you stay here. I'll do it.'

'Wait,' said Daniel.

He wasn't sure how he felt or what he believed but he wished to spare the Watson children any unnecessary upset. He felt he owed Marian and her siblings that much. He sighed heavily and said, 'You lost your temper with her. She'll let me into the house quicker than she'd let you. I'll go.'

Henry blocked his way. 'Take your gun with you. If she's a Jacobite you need to arrest him ... or kill him if he resists.'

Robert was suddenly unsure. 'I should come with you, Daniel.'

Thinking fast, Daniel told his brother, 'No, we need to hide this from Reverend Walker and everyone else in case it's nothing. If it is as Henry believes, then I'll come straight back for you and Henry.'

CHAPTER TEN

Returning to the Watsons'

Sometimes when Daniel was alone he imagined that his dog, Horace, was with him.

Indeed, there were times when he found himself on a street in Derry looking around to confirm that his pet had not come back from the dead, because he thought that he'd heard the familiar pattering of four scruffy paws against the cobbled stones.

How Horace would have loved this, thought Daniel as he retraced his steps down the long country road, hoping he could remember where the widow's cottage was. It was not difficult to picture Horace scampering in and out of the puddles, barking loudly in great excitement.

Maybe he would tell the widow about Horace to show her that she wasn't the only one to lose an animal in the name of King William. Or he could ask her advice on cooking potatoes. Different scenarios were conjured up as he prepared for his mission. He needed to come up with something special in order to be invited into her home.

A part of him wanted to curse Henry, but what if he was right? She *was* strange to look at, what with her immense tallness and the fact she was wearing men's clothing along with those mucky boots. Plus what Robert said was true; she did keep her voice low even when she was angry about losing her horses. Any other woman would have cried and made a terrific scene.

He found the field and the cottage and made his way to it, wondering if he should have let Robert come with him. What if she was a Jacobite who felt she had been rumbled and was waiting for him to come back to arrest her? She could be hiding at the window, a loaded musket in her hand, watching his lonely approach. *Well*, he thought, *I'm hardly going to turn back now.* There was nothing for it but to keep up a steady pace until he reached the front door.

As he approached the cottage, he heard sobbing inside and had no time to consider how this might affect his visit. He knocked and placed his musket in the crook of his arm ... just in case. Suddenly nervous, Daniel asked God to protect him as the door was slowly opened just enough to allow Marian to use one eye to identify him.

She had to raise her voice above the noise of the crying

and wailing to ask him what he wanted. She looked scared and upset.

'I'm looking for your mother. Can I talk to her?'

'No. She's not here!'

Inside he could hear little voices crying, 'Mama!' and 'Where's Mama?'

Daniel imagined Henry whispering to him that this was all part of an elaborate act to make him leave.

Marian wiped the tears from her eyes and blurted out, 'It's all your fault!'

'What do you mean? Where is she?'

Wait a minute, thought Daniel. *No, she couldn't be.*

Samuel appeared beside Marian and, on seeing Daniel, bawled at him, 'You took our horses. I hate you!'

Daniel ignored him and asked once more, 'Marian, please tell me where your mother is.'

For an answer, the girl stepped away from the door, bringing her brother with her. Daniel pushed the door open. Inside was smoky from the small fire that barely thrived in the grate. Apart from the baby, who was stretched out on his belly on the grubby floor, the rest of the children were seated at a small, square table, seemingly competing with one another to see who could cry the loudest. Samuel took his place beside them and scowled at the young soldier.

Marian sounded weary as she told him what he wanted

to know. 'She's gone to get our horses back.'

Daniel had not really believed the widow when she'd said as much to him. What on earth was she thinking? Foolishly he asked the girl, 'Are you sure that's where she went? Absolutely sure?'

Marian nodded her head. 'I tried to stop her. We all did.'

Georgie, the baby, seemed to recognise Daniel from earlier and babbled some form of greeting before launching himself in his direction. Daniel tried to think. The whole thing was ridiculous. Suddenly, it occurred to him that when his brother and Henry heard about the woman's disappearance they might well be convinced that this was the proof they were looking for, that Mrs Watson was actually a murderous Jacobite spy who was now, thanks to the Sherrards, in hot pursuit of their king. He imagined Robert's embarrassment at having allowed her to escape.

'We begged her not to go. Even our neighbours told her it was too dangerous.'

Daniel felt something tugging at his leg and looked down. Georgie was staring up at him expectantly. Without thinking he bent down and lifted the baby into his arms.

Samuel shouted, 'NO! You can't take our Georgie. Tell him, Marian.'

Fortunately his sister realised that little Georgie was not about to be whisked off to help King William on his campaign. 'Oh be quiet, Samuel Watson. He's not taking Georgie anywhere.'

Daniel felt obliged to add his own assurances. 'It's just that I miss my own sister, Alice, she's about Georgie's age. But I can put him back down on the floor, if you prefer?'

Samuel shrugged and announced, 'I'm hungry!'

There was a chorus of 'Me too! Me too!'

Daniel felt sorry for the harassed girl who muttered, 'I'm doing my best!'

'Of course you are. Do you have food for them? I can go and shoot a rabbit; there are plenty of them around.'

'No,' said Marian. 'Mother left us plenty. I have some rabbit left over from yesterday with potatoes boiling in the big pot. I was about to check them.'

Marian was rather shocked when the soldier suggested that he'd take a look at them to see if they were ready. He explained, 'I do most of the cooking for our group in the camp.'

The meat was soft enough, while the overcooked potatoes were starting to break apart. Marian placed six bowls on the table and took Georgie from Daniel so that he could carry the pot over and begin ladling up the steaming food.

'Will Georgie eat the meat?' asked Daniel.

Marian shook her head. 'No, he hasn't the teeth to chew but I'll mash up some potato with milk for him; he likes that.'

Georgie began pointing at his bowl and bellowing something that might have meant, 'Please hurry up, I'm simply starving!'

'Let me do his potato,' said Daniel. 'You just eat your dinner.'

Grateful to have someone else be in charge, Marian handed the baby back to Daniel and sat down to eat.

Daniel mashed up the already mushy potato for Georgie and, taking the last stool, he folded the baby into his lap and began to spoon-feed him, being careful to blow hard on the potato first to cool it down.

The children ignored him and he was glad that all the crying had stopped. Briefly he worried that their mother might have a change of heart and suddenly appear in the doorway. What would she make of him sitting at her table as if he was one of her family?

'So,' said Daniel, 'you said your neighbours told your mother not to go. How did they know?'

Marian replied, 'She went to all of them whose horses had been taken and tried to get them to come with her.'

Daniel guessed what happened. 'But nobody would go with her?'

'No,' said Marian. 'They told her to forget about it, that the horses were gone and that was that.'

Marian couldn't help looking proud as she continued,

'Mama told them she wasn't scared and that she'd go to the king herself. Some of them laughed at her but they aren't nice people.'

Samuel nodded. 'They never helped Mama when she was tired.'

'I see,' said Daniel, feeling somewhat triumphant that Samuel was talking to him in a civil fashion.

'Anyway,' said Marian, 'Mama told us that she had to go to King William and make him listen to her.'

Samuel butted in, 'I wanted to go with her but she wouldn't let me!'

The boy sounded upset which propelled Daniel to say, 'Well, that's because you're the man of house. You're the oldest boy, aren't you? So, you have to look after everyone here.'

Samuel took a moment to see the truth in Daniel's words and rewarded him with a smile, albeit one that was covered in bits of potato, as he declared, 'Yes. I am! I'm in charge!'

Typically, big sister Marian attempted to burst his bubble. 'Samuel clung onto Mama to stop her from leaving. I did my best to hold them back but I had Georgie and they ran after her, crying all the way.'

One of the others, a girl of about four, quietly stated, 'Mama kicked the wood away.'

Daniel looked to Marian for an explanation. She told

him, 'There is a stream behind us and the only way to cross it is to walk along the plank of wood. When Mother saw Samuel and the others coming after her she kicked the plank away.'

'She didn't want us,' said Samuel.

'Oh, but she does want you!' said Daniel. He was surprised at how upset he felt on behalf of the children. 'She didn't want to leave you but she needs to keep you safe and make sure that you have enough food. She'll be back before you know it.'

'When is she coming home?' It was the little girl again.

'What's your name?' asked Daniel.

'Isabel Watson. I am four!'

'What a lovely name!' gushed Daniel, stalling for time. 'And who is that beside you?'

Isabel checked who was sitting next to her before making any introductions. 'That's just Anna. She's three.'

There was just one more child to go. Daniel nodded at the littlest version of Marian who was too absorbed in her food to realise the attention she was receiving. Her potato was sliding around the bowl and it was proving quite a challenge to catch it with the spoon.

Isabel obliged. 'That's Sarah but she can't talk. She's too small.'

Daniel held up his fist to count out the names: 'So, there's

Marian, Samuel, Isabel, Anna, Sarah and baby Georgie. Did I get it right?

The thing about four-year-olds is once they want to know the answer to a question they are almost impossible to distract.

Isabel proved this superbly by repeating her question, 'When is Mama coming home?'

Daniel looked at Marian to see if she knew the answer; however Marian was gazing at him waiting anxiously for his.

Well, he was not going to lie to them. He made some quick calculations in his head. If William was, let's say, three days ahead of them and the widow had only just started out, it might take her about five days to catch up with him. Although she might be faster since a massive army on the move could be slow and cumbersome. Then, she finds William – here, Daniel struggled to imagine her actually meeting the king but that had nothing to do with the question — so, she meets William and gets the horses and makes her way home. Of course, by now, she's on horseback which would speed up her return. Yet, that still meant ...

'I think that she'll be gone two weeks. It shouldn't be much more than that.'

He did his best to sound confident but poor Marian looked utterly distraught. The others, Daniel sensed, knew as much about the length of 'weeks' as they did about the stars in the sky. Marian bit her lip and did her best not to cry.

It was a desperate situation for the widow who was caught between leaving her young family alone but having to do so if she wanted to keep a roof over their heads and food on the table. Daniel was filled with sympathy. *What a horrible decision to have to make.*

A loud explosion broke the silence in the room. Daniel then felt a fierce rumble in his lap followed by the sensation that someone was pouring something warm down his leg. A moment or two passed before the smell was suffocating. Daniel stared at the placid baby who was busying gnawing on his spoon and looking the picture of innocence.

'Phew!' gasped Daniel. 'Perhaps King William should have taken Georgie instead of the horses. He'd send any army running for cover!'

Marian smiled through her tears.

CHAPTER ELEVEN

Location! Location!
June 1690

James heaved a heavy sigh, ignoring his French and Irish commanders who waited to discuss locations for the battle.

The last few weeks had dragged by, and it had recently occurred to him that he was far from happy. Apart from everything else that was going on and the fact that he hadn't seen his wife and baby son for the best part of a year, he was homesick. The city of London had just about framed every major event in his life, from the death of his father, King Charles I, at the hands of a Cromwellian mob, to the reign of his brother, King Charles II.

His brother had shared his love for the grimy, dirty city. Perhaps one of the most exhilarating experiences of James's life was accompanying his brother out into the middle of the street during the great fire of 1666. He and Charles had rolled up their silk sleeves and carried umpteen buckets of water, directing the line of helpers back and forth, the smoke blinding them and giving them a hacking cough that produced phlegm as black as tar.

Of course he still loved England as much as he ever did. It was not England he had declared war on, only William, his nephew and son-in-law and, therefore, most unnatural enemy.

In his last letter to France he had shared a little of his predicament with his wife, Queen Mary Beatrice:

I sense I am losing my popularity amongst the Irish. However, my dear, you know me well enough to appreciate that I will not do something just because others think I should. For example, a printer that I hired to print the pamphlets about the new rules for Protestants says he has lost the original copy and cannot do the job. Of course he has lost nothing. He is merely looking out for his fellow parishioners and I rather admire the plucky fellow. The Irish wanted me to imprison him but I refuse to. They only want him punished because he is a Protestant.

Oh, how I wish we were all together again and back home in London where we should be!

His mood of the last few days was so different from the night before he left France.

King Louis had embraced him and said, 'I hope, sir, never to see you again. Nevertheless, if Fortune decides that we are to meet, you will always have my support.'

James had bowed his head graciously, feeling most honoured, if still somewhat dubious, about what lay ahead. A tiny part of him felt he was being wrapped in a spider's silk web and that he was not moving entirely of his own free will.

For the onlookers, however, it was a touching scene. The French king gave an eloquent speech, describing how he had placed five hundred thousand francs and ten thousand muskets at James's disposal.

Playing the part, James replied for all to hear: 'My thanks indeed to you, sir, but you have forgotten one thing and that is to arm me!'

With a grave flourish, Louis unbuckled the sword and belt from his own waist and leant across to fasten it around James. It must be said that Queen Mary Beatrice was not the only person in the handpicked audience to succumb to tears.

Up to the last few weeks that distant memory kept James warm at night, but now, today, it only served to remind him that had it not been for Louis he would be with his wife and son back in France. At times like this, it felt like he had been cast adrift on a bare plank of wood on which he was expected to sail the seven seas.

Thus while James was temporarily lost in his worry that he was merely being used by the French king, his French and Irish commanders could only wait politely for their king to return to the task in hand.

The portly Richard Talbot, Lord Lieutenant of Ireland, sat patiently, or at least pretended to. He had known James for thirty years or so, and James realised that this proud man had a lot in common with the king of France. Both seemed to expect so much from him.

'Do you mean to stay in Dublin, Your Majesty?' The Lord Lieutenant tried to make his question as casual as possible.

It was young Colonel Patrick Sarsfield who piped up with an answer: 'Surely not, sire. Why would we want to bring William's army to Dublin? I'd rather burn the city myself than leave her vulnerable to an enemy army.'

Born and bred in Lucan, eight miles from the city of Dublin, the colonel was understandably passionate about his birthplace and the city. James had recognised the young man's loyalty by promoting him to the position of colonel but secretly considered the Earl of Lucan too much of a hothead to be taken seriously. However, the man did his have followers and his regiment had recently proved successful in taking

Sligo town, beating a Williamite battalion into submission. James could not ignore victories made on his behalf and thus congratulated Colonel Sarsfield while confiding to Talbot that 'The colonel is undoubtedly a brave man, but I fear that his abundance of courage makes up for lack of … well, intelligence.'

Richard Talbot was thrilled by this confession. He detested how the men cheered the dashing Sarsfield. As Lord Lieutenant of Ireland he believed that he should be the cherished leader since he was the actual leader of Ireland when James was not around.

For his part, Patrick Sarsfield disliked the Lord Lieutenant and was one of many who called him 'Tricky Dicky' behind his broad back. It was widely felt that the Lord Lieutenant played up to James, befriending the King's friends and giving them presents in order to insert himself into their intimate circle.

By now, James realised that the longer he put off the inevitable battle, the longer he would have to stay in Ireland. He knew he could not, would not, return to Louis without a fight. Privately, he determined: *I have no choice but to get this over with, come what may.*

A map of Ireland was stretched out on the table. William, they knew, had recently left Belfast and was marching south. The area between Dublin and Belfast had never seemed so small. An ornate clock was ticking on the mantelpiece; time was also marching on.

'I was thinking,' James said aloud, 'of heading towards William. I assume that he is planning to approach us, thereby stopping us in our tracks.'

'You mean,' said Talbot, 'travelling north to meet him?'

James allowed a brief nod of his royal head.

His French commanders shared a worried glance, and it was left to Lauzun to ask: 'But, Your Majesty, is it wise to stray so far from Dublin? What if you need to … that is … leave Ireland in a hurry?'

Lauzun congratulated himself on his own bravery: *somebody has to point out the practicalities*. Also, the French prime minister had warned him severely against risking the lives of the French soldiers, while Louis, it could be safely assumed, wanted no harm to come to James. Lauzun's shoulders drooped beneath all this responsibility as he followed up with a sincere: 'Your safety is my first priority, Majesty!'

James raised an eyebrow to this and did not altogether dismiss it.

Neither Talbot nor Sarsfield were pleased by this blatant hint of possible failure. Perhaps the only thing they had in common was their belief in a successful outcome. They had to win this battle because so much was riding on it.

Patrick Sarsfield rushed to say, 'My Lord, may I assure you

that your Irish soldiers have no intention of losing. Every man has sworn to do his very best for you and, surely, after our victory in Sligo we should be confident in ourselves.'

Richard Talbot discreetly rolled his eyes but had to respect the colonel for grabbing the opportunity once again to mention his success. Self-promotion was an important aspect of any military career.

'And,' said James, 'when I am returned to the throne of England, will every Irishman continue to swear allegiance to me and bow his head to me as his monarch?'

An awkward silence followed.

James leant forward as if afraid he might not be heard. 'Make no mistake, gentlemen, I know why my Irish supporters are so eager for war. Now, let me be clear: I do not believe in a divided empire and have no intention of releasing Ireland from her relationship with England. I believe in the union of our nations and I shall always believe in the union of our nations.'

Richard Talbot was obliged to close his eyes, as if trying to stave off a headache. What could he say to this? Ever since James became king and made him Lord Lieutenant, he had dreamed of an Ireland being ruled alone by an Irishman and a Catholic. However, first things first – until they got James back on the throne they were well and truly stuck.

Talbot opened his eyes and said, 'Yes, Your Majesty', as

he thought to himself, *that blond upstart had better copy me or else ...*

He need not have worried. Patrick Sarsfield did the exact same thing, bowed his head and echoed his chief. 'Yes, Your Majesty!'

James went back to studying the map. 'What about returning to Dundalk and meeting him there?'

Lauzun tried to stifle his panic. Should he risk James's infamous hot temper by repeating what he had only just said? Yes, he should! He'd rather have James shouting at him than King Louis.

'Sire, don't you think it would be better to stay in reach of Dublin?'

'Oh, for God's sake, Lauzun!' It was Richard Talbot that glared at the French advisor, thinking to himself, *that little weasel doesn't care whether we win or not.*

Ignoring Talbot's grouchiness, James suddenly pointed at the thin blue line that weaved its way in and around Drogheda and asked, 'What about that river?'

The men moved in closer to look, with reluctance, upon the line for themselves. It was Patrick Sarsfield who politely argued, 'Your Majesty, if we choose to make a stand before a river, we'd have to divide up our army to prevent the enemy from crossing it and that, sire, is a long line. We'd have to stretch ourselves the length of its banks.'

James seemed not to hear the colonel, while Lauzun felt torn all over again. Sarsfield was the youngest man in a room that was otherwise occupied by aging warriors who had not proved themselves in battle for many years now. Surely they should be listening to anything he had to say. Accordingly, Lauzun decided to ask: 'What do you mean, Colonel?'

Talbot gazed earnestly at the map, allowing Sarsfield to make the valid point: 'What I mean is that a successful army does not weaken itself by breaking up into smaller groups. No, it sticks together at all times because this is where its strength lies. With all respect, Your Majesty, I suggest that we choose a stretch of land that does not contain such a tricky obstacle as a river.'

James looked annoyed, but Talbot felt obliged to support the colonel, 'Your Majesty, I must agree with Sarsfield in this matter. A river will present God knows how many possibilities to the Williamites, who will scour the area looking for places to cross. We'd never be sure of having covered every conceivable danger, while what we do know for sure is that there are more of them than there are of us.'

The Frenchmen looked from the Irish to the English, feeling they had nothing to add to this particular discussion. At least the river was not too far from Dublin. That was something.

James thought for a moment, before leaning over to fold the map in two and say, 'If the river forces us to split into groups it will do the same for the Williamites. And since they have more men it is best to avoid meeting their entire army head on.

'Gentlemen, I have made my decision. We shall meet them at the River Boyne.'

CHAPTER TWELVE

Heading South, June 1690

It was almost seven o'clock on a beautiful bright morning and King William's Derry regiment was on the march once more.

Daniel was doing his best to hide his anxiety about the Watson children and also his guilt.

The night before, he had found an agitated Robert and Henry waiting for him on his return from the cottage.

'Well?' asked Robert. 'What happened? What took you so long?'

Daniel was hungry and made for his bag, where he had hidden some bread for himself. He bit into it and only then replied, 'I had to wait until it was dark. I mean, I could have tried to get in the house but they would've just hidden any evidence like a red coat or a rifle.'

Henry did not look convinced.

'So I thought,' continued Daniel, 'that it would be better to spy on them through the window.'

To his relief, his brother nodded and said, 'Hey, that's good thinking, Daniel!'

'All right,' said Henry in a gruff tone, unwilling to compliment the young soldier on his clever plan, 'and what did you see?'

'She's definitely a woman!'

Robert waited for Daniel to justify the declaration, but his brother merely took another bite of his bread.

'How do you know?' Robert wanted to shout the all-too-obvious question aloud.

'Because ...' said Daniel, chewing again, enjoying keeping his listeners in suspense, 'I watched her nurse the baby.'

Henry sniffed. 'Really?'

Daniel kept his tone light. 'Now, Henry, you cannot believe that a soldier would pretend to feed a baby if there was nobody around to catch him out. Even you couldn't pretend to believe that.'

'You swear that's what you saw?' Henry asked.

Robert answered his friend, 'If that's what Daniel says he saw, then that's what he saw. He's no liar!'

Henry shrugged. 'Yes, I know. Sorry, Daniel. I just wanted to be sure.'

This was a surprise indeed. When had Henry ever

apologised to him before?

Daniel experienced a twinge of gratitude and shame. It wasn't often that Robert defended him to Henry and for him to accidentally choose an occasion when Daniel was telling an out-and-out lie did not made the younger Sherrard feel proud or one bit clever.

'Left, right! Left, right!'

How many hours were passed thus, moving one foot in front of the other in a definite rhythm that lulled a young soldier into believing he was part of something huge and momentous?

Mrs Sherrard had urged her son to take in the sights so that, on his eventual return, he could tell her all about the different places that she would never get to see for herself. Like most women, his mother had no need, or ambition, to step out of the city she was born into; her entire life would be lived behind the walls of Derry.

Daniel wondered what his mother would make of Mrs Watson. Would she be appalled at the widow's single mindedness or might she applaud it?

How would he describe the landscape now? Was it so different from where he had come from? It was the one island after all; a person would be forgiven for thinking it was an island of fields. Since leaving Belfast they had seen little else. Daniel hoped to visit Dublin city; now that would be worth describing around the Sherrard dinner table. He had heard it was almost as big as London and contained colleges and students and libraries and the Lord knows what else.

The day passed steadily, as expected, in hundreds of thousands of footsteps until the sun began to slide towards its bed and word went round to break for camp. The scouts would have suggested this location because it provided access to fresh water and trees. Soldiers busied themselves erecting their tents while others were summoned to carry out necessary tasks.

As usual Robert had orders for his little brother, confident in Daniel's trustworthiness when it came to gathering firewood.

Daniel didn't mind. Having spent the entire day walking in the middle of a tightly packed crowd, the boy yearned to be released into the nearby forest to search for fallen branches or whatever else he could find. He wasn't the only one sent out for wood, but he quickly dislodged himself from the pack and tried not to fret about wild animals.

In any case, he could hear his wood-gathering colleagues complaining about their aching feet and their empty bellies and that made him feel safe enough.

He moved farther away from them but could still hear their voices in the distance. Robert nagged him about not being friendly enough but Daniel felt no great urge to get along with his fellow soldiers. Wasn't he surrounded by them night and day? The only time he didn't see them was when he closed his eyes. Certainly it was no surprise to him that he should want to linger in the forest, even if it was a little creepy in the strained light of the setting sun.

He grudgingly began to look around for twigs, feeling he should at least do this much before it got too dark to find any. Of course there wouldn't be a lot on offer as the forest was in the whole of its summertime health. He walked on, following meandering threads of pathways, wondering if anyone had stepped here before him. Finally he found some old, dried-up twigs dangling from bushes and foliage, never having made it all the way down to the ground. However, he knew that they would burn too quickly without providing any warmth and continued looking for newer branches to add to his bundle.

He could still hear the others calling out to one another as he spied a tree in front of him from which a long, solid branch hung low. *That's more like it*, he thought, and put down the twigs. He leapt and fastened both hands around the branch which barely creaked in protest. Then he swung himself back and forth, back and forth. When he realised this wasn't working he began to jostle the branch up and down, feeling that it should give at any moment. It didn't. The tree had no interest in delivering up one of its own, though Daniel was doing his utmost. He decided to raise both legs until his feet wrapped round the branch. Next, he hauled himself into a precarious sitting position that he managed to hold for one glorious moment until he lost his balance and smashed heavily to the ground.

He lay there stunned and embarrassed, grateful that there were no witnesses. Or so he thought.

The ground was cool, but it was pleasant to lie there awhile and breathe in the smell of the undergrowth. He closed his eyes, just for a moment, and imagined that he could start a new life here and set up home beneath this very tree. *Well, why not? No more army, no more war talk and no more of Henry's taunting. Oh, wouldn't it be wonderful to hear only birdsong and the quarrelling of animals … and nothing more serious than that.*

As he lay there, Daniel found himself thinking of Horace. He imagined he heard his dog by his side and could feel his eyes upon him, waiting for his young master to stir himself. And then Daniel fancied he could smell his pet, his meaty breath and … and then … Daniel heard him … a low, guttural growl.

Only Daniel knew that it couldn't be Horace because

Horace was dead. Slowly, very slowly, he opened his eyes and pushed himself up to lean on his elbows and looked around … meeting the hungry gaze of an enormous wolf.

The beast's black coat and dark eyes lent it a dreadful majesty while it displayed its fangs in a fleeting sinister grin. Both wolf and boy acknowledged their roles in the scene. The wolf was in charge. It stared at its prey calmly as if they had signed some sort of contract in which Daniel had promised not to run, not even to move. All Daniel could think was that he hoped death would be immediate.

The wolf sniffed half-heartedly at the ground, nosing through the twigs that Daniel had dropped, all the while building itself up to the moment when it would finally act. Daniel watched it because he couldn't do anything else. Briefly he wondered about reaching for his knife. But he knew the second he moved the wolf would pounce, as it was going to anyway. In fact, he fancied that the wolf was simply waiting for him to make the first move and start the proceedings.

'Stay where you are.'

For a moment, Daniel thought he had dreamt the voice, or stranger still that it was the wolf itself offering advice. In his terror, he could only whisper, 'I can't move.'

'Good,' said a familiar voice. 'Keep staring at him, exactly like you're doing.'

Already shocked to his core, Daniel made no reaction as he recognised the voice of Mrs Watson. He merely did exactly what she told him to; he maintained eye contact with the wolf, who showed some confusion at the sudden arrival of this tall woman in her floppy hat. She was somewhere to Daniel's right and he resisted the urge to look at her which meant that he received as nasty a shock as the wolf when an axe suddenly soared between them and thudded into the tree behind them.

Daniel croaked in panic, 'You missed!'

Mrs Watson ignored him while the wolf was startled by the large flying object that had just about bumped his nose. Briefly he considered holding his ground until the woman quickly followed up with a large rock that bounced clumsily off his forehead. He yelped in fright and, with a speedy twist, darted off into the bushes, tearing them as he ran. Mrs Watson listened to his fading footsteps but Daniel could only hear the blood pumping inside his head. He shivered violently while his body seemed encased in a freezing sweat.

'I didn't want to kill him. There's no need for murder when he could be so easily frightened off.'

Daniel didn't know what to say to this. He was still distracted by his thumping heart and clung to the grass beneath him as if afraid he might fall a second time.

Mrs Watson strode over to the tree and tugged her axe

from it, giving the blade a quick wipe of her sleeve.

'You ... you saved my life!'

His rescuer shook her head. 'All you had to do was stand up and show him how tall you were, make some noise, hold his gaze. Wolves are opportunists; he saw you lying on the ground and assumed you were wounded and would not put up a fight.'

She was standing over Daniel, reminding him that he had yet to move an inch. Suddenly mortified, he got to his feet, feeling more than a little unsteady.

'What were you doing anyway, taking a nap in the middle of a forest?'

Daniel blushed as he confessed, 'Um, I fell out of the tree. I'm gathering firewood for camp; at least that's what I'm meant to be doing.'

He pointed to the small scattering of twigs. She did not look impressed.

'It's getting late,' said Daniel. 'I'd better get back in case they come looking for me.'

He could have explained about Robert and Henry believing she was a murderous Jacobite but he was embarrassed enough as it was.

'Stand back!' Her manner was brisk.

'Pardon?' asked Daniel politely while glancing around to see if the wolf had returned.

'I said, stand back!'

He obliged and had to move sharply again as she swung her axe and hacked at the branch that has caused him all the trouble in the first place. She made a present of it to him. He took it from her in awkward silence, though he very much wanted to tell her that he had seen her children and also he wanted to ask what on earth she was doing here in the forest. Furthermore, he wanted to warn her to stay out of sight of the camp. But there was no time for any of that.

They heard his name being called from afar.

'It's my brother!' Daniel explained.

He was ashamed of the anxiety he knew she could see in his eyes and tried to hide his feelings. 'He ... Robert looks after me, you see, because he's older than me.'

She nodded and said, 'You'd better get going.'

He offered a fragile smile of apology and turned to go.

She could have told him not to worry, that she understood enough to hang back in the shadows. Instead, she said, 'Just remember never to turn your back on a wolf.'

Daniel was in a rush now and only said, 'Goodnight, Mrs Watson, and thanks again ... for everything.'

CHAPTER THIRTEEN

The Day before the Battle, July 1690

On a sunny Monday morning, William sat in his carriage and watched the lush, green fields of Ireland slowly roll by his window. Curious about this little island that sat next door to his adopted country, he had asked his wife and James's daughter, Mary, about it. 'There must be something special about the place since your ancestors sought to colonise it as soon as they could?'

She was of little help, only saying that she thought it was to do with the fertile land. 'One hears that anything can be grown in it.'

Well, William was pleasantly struck by the place. It was rather quaint compared to London and The Hague, but when he looked upon such scenes of mottled greenery, with its jagged coastline and miles upon miles of forest, he felt awed. *Perhaps I will return after this is all over.* He had been told that the forests were full of deer and the most gigantic of stags. There had once been a dangerous population of snakes too, but a saint, who had herded goats, had managed to rid the island of them, which was, William thought, quite an achievement for any man.

The travelling was taking its toll on the king, though he did his best to hide it from his men. Long hours on horse-back had him struggling to breathe properly – his lungs ever his weakness. He had promised Mary not to be foolish, but he knew well that his popularity depended on his being the fearless leader that rode out in front. In any case, once the battle commenced, he would forego his promise to his wife and be damned.

Only the previous evening, he had decided to start a diary, imagining that it would make a keepsake for his as yet unborn son. It struck him that his diary would be a sort of instruction book on how to be a king.

Amongst the massive throng following his carriage were the artists who bore the responsibility of painting the battle scenes, thus capturing the events forever in paint and making all who took part immortal.

Amidst the jostling of the coach, William, being careful not to spill ink on his cloak, wrote:

As King and acclaimed saviour of the Protestant Church I have
to be seen fighting in every painting. How I perform in battle will
undoubtedly affect how I am viewed in London and throughout
England. As I see it, my bravery will win over my critics because who
does not like a hero?

William read over what he had written and smiled.
Something shifted within him and he truly believed that
he was embarking on something tremendous. Between the
covers of his diary he was free to explore his feelings and
explain himself properly in his own language.

He continued writing:

I go to make war with my uncle, James, who is your grandfather.
There are so many worries that I have scarcely time to explain them.
I will admit to my greatest fear, however, which is that I may actually
kill him. That is the point of war, is it not: to defeat the enemy and
take his life? Yet how can I take pleasure in robbing your mother of
her father and you of a grandfather, but why else am I here? James
has placed us all in an impossible position and I am only forced to
act in response to this.

Somewhere behind his carriage was the king's wooden
house in which he camped out in the midst of his men. As
far as he was concerned it was important to show his soldiers

that he would only ask of them what he was prepared to do himself. That, in his mind, was the mark of a good and fair leader. Loyalty and respect had to be earned.

His army was made up of a variety of nations. It was a joy to listen to the different voices and languages: Dutch, French, Finnish, Danish, Prussian, English and Irish. William was determined to treat every battalion fairly in order to install unity in the ranks; he felt this was his special responsibility because if these men were not prepared to risk their lives for him personally then what was the point of all of this?

According to his spies, his father-in-law was taking the opposite approach. William had remarked his surprise to the Duke of Schomberg. 'How foolish of him. No doubt this is his way of acting like a king.'

The duke had sighed. 'Indeed, My Lord. I hear that he keeps himself completely isolated from his own soldiers. In fact they complain to one another about never seeing him.'

William laughed. 'And how loyal will those soldiers feel when they have to choose between James and themselves? Does he not realise the importance of developing a good rapport with his own men? That is why I eat with my soldiers and pitch my cabin alongside their tents.'

William was not impressed by what he knew about the enemy. He had received colourful reports of drunkenness and quarrelling amongst the Irish soldiers who, when they weren't fighting each other over who drank whose brandy, were picking fights with their French colleagues; and with James ruling this most unruly army from a distance that he had himself created, well there could not be much to fear now, could there?

Then there was the appalling way the rival army treated the landscape. His soldiers had come across starving peasants, reduced to eating grass because the Jacobites had stripped their fields of barley and corn and burned any remains, before herding off their cows and goats – ensuring that the people had absolutely nothing to eat and so could not give any food to the Williamites. *Really, what was James thinking? This would only serve to turn the country against him while I play the king with the friendly face.*

After travelling through the night, the carriage finally came to a stop at nine o'clock in the morning. William's secretary, Constantijn Huygens, informed him that they had reached what was judged to be the best place for His Majesty to establish his headquarters.

Eager to stretch his legs after the long journey, William jumped down from the carriage and took a look around; he found himself standing in front of a group of rather impressive ruins.

Around him the orders were shouted along, to break

formation and set up camp. Firewood needed to be gathered in order for dinner to be cooked. The horses had to be unsaddled, watered and fed. Tents had to be quickly assembled, while the men's weapons and uniforms both had to pass inspection. This was an army of mostly professional soldiers and, as such, they needed to look the part before they fired a single bullet.

The scouts, who had reached the area earlier, had spied the enemy camp and informed William of the Jacobite position across the River Boyne. They had also learned a valuable piece of information in that the water level dropped, for a little while, at around ten o'clock in the morning.

'Good work!' said William. 'I should like to see it myself. Have my horse brought to me and we will go immediately.'

He was in a hurry to get started on his task of subduing his father-in-law's army.

Later on, he would write:

Always make a thorough inspection of your battlefield. You must know it as well as you can so that it cannot deliver any nasty surprises.

Assembling his staff around him, William informed them that they would be accompanying him on a reconnaissance exercise.

'I want to study the river for myself and make a note of exactly where it would be easiest to cross. We need to ascertain if it will prove to be our friend or foe.'

The group started out with William in the lead, showing off that he was not afraid to be seen by the enemy.

Accordingly, the Williamite convoy calmly ignored the sight of the Jacobite tents in the distance. William kept his horse at a stroll as he surveyed the landscape, commenting to his men, 'How beautiful it is.'

'Yes,' said the Duke of Schomberg by the king's side. 'It is certainly a land worth fighting for.'

'Worth fighting for, yes,' said William, 'but not worth dying for.'

It was necessary to keep swiping away the tiny flies that gathered along the riverside, while the horses swished their tails and flexed their ears this way and that. It was also necessary to keep a firm grip on the horses in case they got any idea about stopping to sample the lush vegetation, though William allowed his horse to sup from the river.

The noise was tremendous and distracting due to the sheer volume of soldiers, animals and the hangers-on that traipsed after both armies. Maybe all of Ireland was converging on the area around the River Boyne while the waters simply continued to flow as they always did, regardless of what would come on the morrow.

'Does it appear shallow enough to cross here?' William asked his companions.

Meinhard, son of the duke of Schomberg, shrugged. 'No doubt it depends on the time of day, sire, as the tide ebbs and flows. According to the scouts, this is the approximate time for an easy crossing.'

The men gazed at the water while Meinhard made an obvious suggestion. 'Would Your Majesty consider sending over a regiment now to see how they might fare?'

William shook his head. 'Mondays are unlucky for battles. We will just have to wait until tomorrow.'

The Duke of Schomberg cocked his head to the side and said, 'Well, Your Majesty, it seems that you have been spotted.'

Rude shouts and whistles poured out from the far side, but King William paid them no heed, only saying, 'They can consider this as my calling card to the Jacobite leader. Let them tell him that I am here.'

Pulling back from the riverside, the reconnaissance party moved in behind the trees and shrubs while keeping the water in sight. William needed to see how it curved and where it appeared shallow or, at least, shallow enough for his soldiers to cross on foot and on horseback.

Sniffing the air, he said, 'They are baking their bread, a not altogether unpleasant smell.'

Meinhard smiled. 'Indeed, Your Majesty. Perhaps you might like something to eat. It must be almost noon?'

William patted his horse's neck and replied, 'Yes, why not. I must admit that the smell from the Jacobite ovens is giving me an appetite.'

Taking in their immediate surroundings, the river with the sunlight flickering across it, he remarked, 'And this is rather a pleasant spot to stop awhile.'

Only the duke glanced a little uneasily at the opposite bank, but he felt it was beneath him to point out the obvious danger of sitting in full view of their enemy. He had to admit that it was mischievous to taunt the Jacobites like this and admired his king's arrogance.

Why not just dismount here and pass around their little cakes while their horses nibbled at the grass and weeds as if none of them had a single care in the world?

But then everything changed, and in an instant they were all brutally reminded that the scenic river was their ever-flowing battlefield.

The elderly duke had spied something ominous poking out on the far side, with flashes of red coats rustling through the bushes.

'My Lord, I would suggest that perhaps we move on from here as …'

BOOM!

The duke did not manage to finish his sentence before there was a dreadful explosion, causing birds to squawk and take flight, while a puff of grey smoke spat up from behind those bushes that barely hid the snout of the cannon.

It had all happened so fast, and suddenly there was a second echoing explosion. Two of the Williamite horses lay dead while the king ... the KING ... was bent forward, blood pooling from his shoulder, his cake fallen to the ground.

'Your Majesty!'

The duke heard his son's cries and quickly grabbed the reins of William's horse, who was preparing to turn and run. One of the dead horses had slammed back into her before crumpling to the ground. The frightened royal mount reared up and her eyes rolled back as the old man stubbornly held on, despite feeling that his arms were being wrenched from his body.

William was trying to talk but the duke was only interested in getting his king as far away from the river as quickly as possible. Meanwhile, the Jacobites had realised that they had hit their mark and were cheering and whooping in celebration.

'Blast this horse. Stand still, you brute!'

The duke got the horse to her master's side and William was roughly shoved up onto her back. His face was white and his breathing was forced but he was alive; his hand was clutching at the hole in his jacket from where the blood flowed. He tried to speak again but the duke shouted over him, ordering the group to 'MOVE!'

The remainder of the horses were pulled away in case there was a third cannonball. The bodies of the fallen horses were kicked in the ribs to make sure that they were dead, a last parting shot before the Williamites made for the cover offered by the trees and hedges.

Only when they were out of sight from the river did the duke and the others clamber up onto their horses while the two men whose mounts had been killed sprinted behind for a couple of minutes until they were judged to be out of range of the cannon and muskets that were probably being loaded frantically by ambitious Jacobites.

Now it was time to see to the ailing king.

Meinhard was furious and a bit shaken. *What were we thinking, presenting ourselves as irresistible targets like that?* He rounded on his father, needing to dissolve his rage. 'That was ridiculous! They could have killed him and maybe that's what we deserved for our stupidity.'

The duke bit his lip. It would not do any good to argue with his son when he was like this nor would he bother reminding him that it was his idea to have cake. He loved his son but even he had to admit that he was difficult to get along with. Ever since he was a little boy Meinhard seemed to thrive on making friends only to fall out with them. The duke had secretly blamed his wife for spoiling Meinhard when he was a child, encouraging him to believe that he was better than any of his peers.

Turning away from his son, the duke focused on William. 'Your Majesty, is the wound serious? Shall I call for the physician or can you make it back to camp?'

The king was trying to calm his breathing. His hand was practically glued to his coat by his own blood and he was not ready to lift it away. It took him a minute or two to realise that he did not feel too badly after all, if only his breathing would return to normal.

In the background they could hear the Jacobites boasting that they had killed him. William shrugged at the duke. It was a strange sensation to hear men celebrating his death.

'I don't think it is more than a scratch. The blood makes it appear worse.'

The duke wanted to be convinced by William's words but he still looked nervous. 'Well, perhaps we should visit with the physician.'

William shook his head at this, saying, 'I'll go later when I have more time. For now let us continue with the survey of the river.'

The duke opened his mouth to protest but he realised

that the king did indeed look better. William took a deep breath and did not struggle with it, and he sat up straighter in his saddle.

This was a test of his strength and courage and he was determined to pass it.

The group spent a further ninety minutes or so following the river and introducing themselves to the geography of the battlefield. Finally William felt their work was done and that a visit to the physician would be sensible. He was feeling light-headed and had ignored it for as long as he could, trying to convince himself that it was just the shock combined with the heat of the morning and the lack of a decent meal.

He led his men back to camp where he promptly slid from his horse to the ground. Meinhard and his father carried him between them to the physician's tent. The wound was cleaned and discovered to be superficial but sometimes it is the smallest cuts that cause the greater bloodshed. The king was ordered to rest, which did not suit him at all, but he had to admit he could do little when he felt so sluggish. In the end, he took to his bed for a couple of hours, during which the Jacobites continued to boast of having killed him. Rumours of William's death rampaged throughout the Boyne valley while he slept the sleep of the dead.

When he woke he found the Schombergs sitting at the

foot of his bed, both looking very much relieved.

'How are you feeling, Your Majesty?'

William checked before replying truthfully, 'Actually I feel very well! But I must eat before doing anything else. I rather think it was hunger that woke me up.'

After summoning food for the king, the duke made a tentative suggestion. 'Sire, when you have eaten I think it would be wise to take a ride around the camp, if you feel up to it. It seems that the men need to be convinced that you are still alive.'

'What?' exclaimed William. 'How could they think I am dead?'

'Well, sire, the enemy have been boasting of your murder to our boys. Also some soldiers saw you being carried into the physician's tent and they grow increasingly more worried that they have not seen you since.'

William shrugged. 'But of course. Let us go right now. I will eat afterwards. I cannot have my army doubting me.'

'Very good, sire. And I might also suggest that a letter be sent off to the queen. Just in case.'

William was immediately alarmed at the idea of Mary reading of his death. His secretary, Constantijn, was ordered to take down a brief letter explaining to her what had happened and to assure her that he was in good health. As he dictated the note his servant helped him to dress.

Meinhard appeared at the entrance to his cabin. The horses were outside, saddled, ready and waiting.

The king addressed the Duke of Schomberg. 'You will accompany me, old friend. I think they should see us both looking confident and happy.'

The duke was in complete agreement. 'Certainly, Your Majesty.'

The king exited the wooden cabin and already there were shouts of relief on sighting him which made William smile.

He and the duke mounted their horses and trotted on, intending to cover as much ground as possible. Their camp was sprawled across several miles and William meant for as many as possible to see him looking hale and hearty. Of course there were separate communities within the camp. The cavalry, those who could afford their own horses, had their own area, while the different infantries were spread around, only coming together to collect their rations of food and ale. The various nationalities were denoted by their flags proclaiming the battalion that would march behind it.

Within minutes of that first sighting, William learned exactly how popular he was amongst his English, Scottish, Dutch, Danish, Finnish and Prussian soldiers, and his French Huguenots. To his surprise, the men raced to stand either side of him, forming lines of welcome as he rode by, clapping their hands and cheering loudly: 'Long live King William!'

The Duke of Schomberg was amused at the expression of genuine emotion on the king's face. He said, 'You see how they cheer you, sire. Tomorrow they will seek revenge for that musket ball.'

They spent the best part of an hour meeting the men and then it was time to discuss the following day, with William enjoying a fresh boost in himself as a beloved leader and king.

CHAPTER FOURTEEN

The Williamite Council of War

After a good dinner William summoned his men for a council of war. They included the ever-faithful Duke of Schomberg, his son Meinhard Schomberg, Count Solms, the Dutch commander of the Dutch foot-guards, James Douglas, a Scottish commander, a couple of English colonels and the commander of the Danish regiment, the German Duke of Würtemburg-Neustadt. William also had Constantijn, his secretary, present, to take down an account of the meeting.

Just before his men arrived, William wrote in his diary:

Never underestimate the power of a good war council. This is where one's strategy is decided upon. My generals will be given a chance to present their own ideas, but ultimately the decision on how and when to fight lies with the king.

Across the river James was undoubtedly doing the same thing with his commanders.

'Well, my friends,' began William, 'you have all had a chance to scout our location. What do you make of it?'

Typically the Duke of Schomberg got to his feet before anyone else. He was the most experienced of them all and he also claimed a closer relationship to William over anyone else. When he spoke, William always listened, the younger man appreciating the duke's wisdom and expertise in military matters. The duke believed that over the years the king had come to regard him as a sort of a father figure, his actual father having died when William was a baby.

So, the duke stood and spoke as the second-in-command of the Williamites: 'Your Majesty, I suggest that we use the river to entrap the enemy. We stage a sizeable attack at the nearby village of Oldbridge, which is less than two miles from Drogheda, thus fooling James into sending his entire army to meet what will appear to be the bulk of ours. Then, as the Jacobites approach Oldbridge, we let loose the rest of our battalions, who will have secretly followed the Jacobite to attack them in the side and the rear. Those battalions should be moved into position tonight, about four or five miles upstream, when it is dark.'

There, he had given his presentation and it was a sound one. All the nodding heads around him testified to its merits. All but one. It took a moment for the duke to notice that one head was not nodding away like it usually did. In fact, the head seemed disinclined to move at all.

'Mmm,' said William.

This was peculiar. The duke quickly recounted to himself what he had said and could find no fault in it. Perhaps His Majesty had not heard him properly or maybe he was still suffering the effects from his narrow escape today. Yes, that would be it. Undaunted, the duke repeated his plan but in a simpler fashion.

'You see, we fool the enemy into meeting us at Oldbridge. They'll not expect to be attacked from behind and that way we catch them off guard. It means splitting our army in two, but we knew that was going to be the case as soon as we heard there was a river. We saw today, sire, how the river loops around the village so it seems logical to use that to trap the Jacobites within it, in one fell swoop ... as it were.'

Nobody nodded now, preferring to wait for William to give them the go-ahead, only he didn't. He merely rubbed his nose and avoided meeting anyone's eyes.

Meinhard Schomberg was stumped. He had never seen

his father treated like this and was confused, trying to decipher what was wrong with the plan. Wanting to support his father and take an active part in the proceedings, he stood up and offered: 'The plan is a risky one but if it is carried out just as my father says then we cannot lose. Our army is bigger and better equipped. I hear some of the Irish soldiers are still carrying scythes instead of muskets.'

He took his seat again, feeling pleased with himself, both as a dutiful son and contributing voice to the discussion. However, his words held no sway with the king.

Count Solms was pleased to see the old duke being sidelined like this. He was the oldest soldier there, and as a fellow Dutchman he felt he understood William better than anyone else. Surely it was time for William to listen to a new advisor and why shouldn't he step into the number one role? Feeling that William wanted him to say something, he rose to make his suggestion: 'My Lord, I commend the Duke of Schomberg on his grand plan but perhaps we should seek out a less complicated approach. What if something unforeseeable was to occur and we ourselves were caught in the loop while divided of our maximum strength?'

William gazed over their heads to think on this, while the duke blinked heavily at the pompous so-and-so referring to his plan as 'complicated'. He barely managed to sound civil as he addressed Count Solms, 'Well, sir, what would you suggest then?'

The Dutchman licked his lips and, without a hint of friendliness, replied, 'Why, sir, if you would hear me out, I was just about to tell you.'

'My apologies,' lied the duke.

William ignored the tension.

'I think, instead, we should keep the army together and make an all-out frontal attack at Oldbridge. I can't help feeling that it would be unwise to divide the army in two.'

None of his listeners looked impressed with his idea, leaving the count muttering somewhat huffily, 'That is my humble opinion, sire.'

William flicked some dust from his sleeve. He was biding his time, wanting to digest the two opposing ideas while searching for a way to put his own spin on them. Thanks to his ride through the camp his ego was stirred up, which was not a helpful factor when one is searching for the best battle plan. William was falling into a trap of his own, only this one was called 'vanity'.

Those English colonels are probably reporting my every move back to the parliament in London. How they gazed in awe at the Duke of Schomberg as he presented his plan. Well, I won't have it said that we won thanks to the duke. I am king and this victory must be mine alone.

William was caught in a bind of his own creation, not

wanting to outline a plan of his own in case it was flawed. *I must be careful. My kingship rests on not just beating my uncle but on how I beat him. It is essential that I impress those English colonels from the outset.*

Stuck for a better alternative, he brought the council to an end, saying, 'Very well, gentlemen. Let us retire for now. I will dictate your orders to my secretary and you will receive them within the hour. Good evening!'

The Duke of Schomberg was not the only one who looked momentarily stunned, but William's tone did not encourage any questions. They all stood up slowly, fixing their clothes and making sure they had not left anything behind, instinctively delaying leaving just in case William had a change of heart.

William left first, with his secretary at his heel. There was no need for the others to hang around any longer.

Willing the others to walk ahead of him, the Duke of Schomberg paused as if lost in thought. Meinhard stood beside him and felt uneasy about … well, everything. For the first time ever, his father looked properly old to him. He totted up the years in his head and thought, *My God, can he really be seventy-five years old?*

Meinhard was simultaneously shocked and proud. His father had been a soldier for all of his life and was a hero to both himself and his own young son, Charles, who idolised his grandfather and could be relied upon to make the great man smile no matter what. Tonight, however, the duke looked weary and not simply tired and in need of a good night's sleep but sort of … finished in a way. Right on cue, his father stumbled and Meinhard grabbed his arm to steady him. The duke gently shook his son away, explaining his confused state by saying, 'This has never happened before, to be dismissed along with everyone else until further notice.'

Father and son returned to their respective tents in silence, with Meinhard unable to find the right words, hardly knowing what he wanted to say, only thinking: *After tomorrow's battle, I will talk to him about giving up army life. If he won't for my sake, then perhaps he might for his grandson.*

CHAPTER FIFTEEN

The Jacobite Side of the Boyne

J acques was nowhere to be seen. *He must be with Nancy*, thought Gerald, not a little enviously. *It must be nice to have someone waiting for you to come back from battle.*

Gerald was surprised by the large volume of extra people that were gathering between their camp and Drogheda. Lord knows that if he had any more coins he could have had his pick of foodstuff, weapons, clothing and even animals. Dozens of hawkers had set up their stalls on the outskirts of the soldiers' tents. They kept the walls of Drogheda in sight just in case they needed to escape the Williamite guns and cannon. In the meantime, they appeared to be doing great business altogether.

A surprising amount of the new arrivals were women.

Gerald wondered if his mother or Cait might surprise him but the more he thought about it the more he realised that visiting him on the eve of battle would no more have occurred to his mother or sister than it would have occurred to him to invite them along. As far as they were concerned war was the business of the men but only because they were too busy to bother with it. He smiled as he considered the fact that the O'Connor women were tougher than any man he had ever met. That's what his father always said and Gerald was inclined to agree.

No doubt Cait was caring for the sick and the poor, while his mother ran the household and worked the family plot, in between helping Father Nicholas with his work in the village. They schooled the village children in the religion and history of their country. Would either mother or sister even stop long enough to worry about him? No, probably not. Of course they had no idea that tomorrow was the big day. Nevertheless, they were too practical and sensible to waste precious time on something like worrying, preferring to hand over their cares to God and get on with the things that they could control.

Their lives were continuing on in the same way as they always did when he was a boy in Offaly and would pre-sumably continue to do so whether or not he managed to return to them again. That was the wonder of it all – that no matter what happened to him tomorrow, the sun would continue to rise and fall, just the same as always.

His mother's favourite quote was 'This life is but a vale of tears', which was far from cheerful but it meant that she generally did not expect to be any happier than she was and, thus, could never be really disappointed. Not that Gerald could swear that she was happy, although he would admit that she never looked actually *unhappy*, which perhaps amounted to the same thing.

Briefly he wondered how his father was getting on in Flanders and if he knew that the battle was to be fought the next day. James would surely have had to let the French king know. According to Jacques, King James would not shake his right foot without first consulting with King Louis, though how Jacques knew this fascinating fact, Gerald had no idea.

It was hard to relax or settle down to anything. Unsure about what to do, Gerald had written a letter to his parents – in case, well, let's just say it was a letter of fond farewell – of which the wording had taken the best part of an hour but it did not look as if he had spent more than five minutes scribbling it down. It was hard to put his feelings about particulars on paper since he found it difficult to believe that he might actually die. Now, was that a good thing or bad thing? In any case, it seemed too incredible and unnatural to think of himself being dead.

Jacques was under orders to get his body back to Offaly if the worst should happen. That was a conversation that they had had months ago when there had been no battle in sight. Gerald had then asked his friend what he wanted him to do with his body if he died. Jacques' answer was typical – a disinterested shrug accompanied by the unhelpful words: 'Surprise me!'

Gerald had persisted. 'What about your family?'

'They are all dead.'

And that was that.

It was something that needed to be discussed since the usual practice when soldiers died in battle was to dig a deep trench for all the bodies to be piled into. If there were no friends or relatives present to alert families back home, parents and wives would simply have to assume that a death had occurred when they did not hear from their loved one again.

Worse than that was the knowledge that if a dead body was not claimed quickly enough by its fellow soldiers it was in danger of being stripped by the enemy. This explained why Gerald would not be carrying anything important on his person in the morning, aside from his sword and pistol. He would just have to trust that his belongings would be safe in his tent until they could be collected by himself or Jacques.

Gerald shook his head to rid himself of these depressing thoughts and dragged himself and his knapsack outside the tent to sit on the ground. In his hand was the book he had bought for Cait, already opened to his favourite page containing those lines about not being afraid of anything. All around him his fellow soldiers were trying to affect an air of relaxation or downright fearlessness. There was a lot of loud laugher at jokes that Gerald did not catch, but he could not fail to notice that the laughter sounded forced and hollow. Fellows talked too loudly and needlessly threw their arms about to make a point.

Fires were lit, though it was a warm evening. In fact, the fires had an important part to play in the preparations as it was up to the men to make their own bullets. Lead would be melted down by the heat of the campfires before being fashioned into round bullets while countless sheets of paper needed to be rolled up to hold the precious gunpowder. There was plenty to do, but Gerald made sure to appreciate that it was a most lovely evening too. The sun was beginning its descent to the other side of the world, its light sliding across the fields like butter melting on freshly baked bread. The men did their best to ignore the unmistakable fact that this last day of calm was slowly reaching its end.

The grass beneath Gerald's hand felt like velvet, and he found himself noticing little things of no importance, like strangely coloured beetles that were new to him and birds, miles above his head, journeying home. Their squawking, being carried unevenly in the summer breeze, had a ghostly quality to them. At such a height the birds must be able to see how the two armies were whiling away these last hours. Not for the first time Gerald wished he could fly.

Someone began to play a fiddle, the sorrowful tune barely competing against the raucous laughter and bad jokes. Gerald raised an eyebrow in surprise; normally the music did not begin until after sundown. Then again, there was nothing normal about this evening. Yes, the brandy rations would be supped, the ballads would be sung and those snooty French soldiers, who refused to mix with their Irish counterparts, would play their chess and their card games. However, no matter what pastime they indulged in, it was not for enjoyment's sake or even out of genuine choice, it was all about getting through the next few hours and avoiding any futile dwelling on possible consequences.

The one thing that each of these soldiers – Irish, French, rich, poor, infantry, cavalry – had in common was that they wanted to survive what was coming. The alternative was not to be borne. Gerald sniffed, thinking that exactly the same was true in the Williamite camp. They all had to fight but nobody wanted to die. Yet tomorrow was going to bring death – that much could be depended upon.

Just for a second, Gerald had a flash of foreboding and, in his mind's eye, saw the field in front of him as it might look tomorrow, covered in writhing and dead bodies, the green grass soaking up the pools of freshly spilled blood.

Enough!

He gazed around him and couldn't help but wonder who might already be marked out by God to die in his name. Would anyone be given a hint? Would anyone foresee their end in nightmares tonight?

Gerald O'Connor, this is silly! He chided himself, thinking that right now he obviously had too much time on his hands.

There was no more training or drilling to be done since they were trying to hide their numbers and questionable standards from the enemy spies who could be anywhere at all, although it was too late to worry about spies now since they could do no more damage. Unfortunately it was also too dangerous to go swimming in the Boyne.

He thought about checking on the horses but felt too lazy to make the trek to the pens. Instead, he preferred to enjoy the lingering warmth of the day and the last remnants of a peaceful existence. Later on he would go to see them. Later on he would make time to pray like he had never prayed before. For the moment he leant back and closed his eyes, pretending he was at home, sunning himself by the lake while waiting for his mother to call him for dinner.

'Jacques, stop. Wait!'

It was Nancy and she was shouting breathlessly and in between sobs.

As Gerald opened his eyes he heard stomping footsteps beside him and assumed it was Jacques that had kicked opened the flaps of their tent before flinging himself inside. He sat up quickly, blinded by the sun while trying to work out what was going on.

'Nancy, are you all right? What's wrong?'

It took his eyes a moment to adjust before he could see her standing in front of him, her hands to her face, wiping away the tears. She seemed in a daze, staring at the tent which had been slapped closed against her.

Gerald was horrified and studied his friend's shadow against the canvas wall as if it was a page of a book. He took a deep breath and asked, 'You … you have had an argument?'

In response, Nancy just cried and cried, wrapping her arms about her middle, not caring what she looked like, unaware that she was starting to attract attention from soldiers that were on the look-out for a distraction. Gerald roused himself to his feet, feeling immediately out of his depth. True, he had lived with women all his life, but he had never seen his mother cry, while his sister had only shed tears that one time when she had been unable to prevent a baby from dying. Even then all he had to do was step back and let his mother handle it.

He glanced around, wishing for the second time that evening that his mother or Cait might surprise him.

'Would you like to sit down for a bit?'

Nancy remained standing while a gruff voice from inside the tent called out, 'Tell her to go home!'

Gerald swallowed and tried again. 'I can escort you home, if you like? I'd be happy to.'

Nancy was miserable, saying in a low voice, in between hiccups, 'Am I that troublesome, that I would make two people happy if I just left?'

'Oh, God, no! No, not at all. That's not what I meant.'

Gerald felt the heat in his cheeks. How on earth did she reach that conclusion? He had only meant to be kind. Jacques had told him that women were complicated beings, but he thought that his friend was just being funny. Now, he wasn't so sure.

Nancy was too sad to reassure him. Her sobs had been reduced to weeping, using the cuff of her sleeve to wipe her face. 'I can't find my handkerchief,' she explained and looked on the verge of collapsing again.

Grateful to be able to do something, Gerald rummaged through his knapsack and pulled out his own handkerchief which was thankfully clean or clean enough. He has washed it out in the Boyne a few days earlier. Cait had embroidered his initials on it as her parting gift when he left home to join the army. Those carefully embroidered letters – G O C – were now wrapped around Nancy's damp nose. Gerald pretended to fixate on something in the distance while she did what she had to do, mumbling, 'Thank you, Gerald. I'll bring it home and clean it for you.'

'Oh, that's all right. You can keep it.'

She forced herself to give him a watery smile. 'Was it your sweetheart who initialled it for you?'

Gerald shook his head with regret. 'My sister, Cait.'

'You are lucky to have a sister who cares about you.'

Without thinking, Gerald said, in a tone that suggested he needed convincing, 'Am I?'

Nancy nodded. 'Better to have a sister who cares about you than fall in love with someone who wishes you would just disappear.'

Oh, dear. They were treading in dangerous waters again.

Gerald stared at her in the full knowledge that he had absolutely no idea what he could possibly say to this. So he said nothing. She shrugged, understanding he was in an impossible position, torn between loyalty to his friend and wanting to show sympathy for her sadness.

She changed the subject, noting the book lying on the

ground beside his feet. 'It's the book that … we bought you. Watch out it doesn't get grass stains. Maybe you should put it in your bag in case you forget to later on?'

Eager to display cooperation where he could, he immediately bent down to pick up Cait's present and dutifully shoved it to the bottom of his bag.

Needlessly, she added, 'That's better, isn't it? It would only have been ruined otherwise.'

Gerald nodded in agreement. He recognised that she was putting off leaving, in the hope that Jacques might reappear. There was no movement inside the tent and Gerald reckoned that his friend was lying on his blanket and staring moodily at the canvas ceiling while listening to every single word.

Stubborn mule! Why doesn't he come out? He must know that she doesn't want to leave until he does.

A moment of stricken silence passed while Gerald struggled to think of something appropriate to say. Nancy looked around her helplessly, trying not to look at the tent that seemed to grow in size the longer she stayed.

'Gerald!'

They both jumped guiltily, and Gerald dived towards the flaps and pushed his head inside.

'What?'

Jacques scowled at his naïve question. 'What do you

mean "What"?' Gerald widened his eyes to signify his utter innocence and ignorance, thoroughly conscious that Nancy would hear their every word.

'Bring her home. It's getting late.'

'But,' began Gerald, 'maybe you could ...'

Nancy called to both of them, 'I'm perfectly capable of getting myself home. I'm not a child.'

Gerald was glad that she could not see the thunder in Jacques' eyes. He defended her as quietly as he could. 'She's really upset. Can't you come out to her?'

'She wants to marry me.'

'Oh,' said Gerald, for the sake of saying something.

'Oh,' echoed Jacques and rubbed his nose. 'She refuses to understand that I am a soldier because I wish to be. I chose this life to see the world. I don't wish to be needed in this way. I don't want a house or children. It is not for me!'

It was a long speech and Gerald did his best to understand what his friend was telling him.

'She says she loves me. Pah! They all say that! But what does it mean for Jacques?'

Gerald shrugged. Nobody had ever said those words to him and he had been rather looking forward to the day that someone did. He did want to fall in love with a girl who made his stomach flip at the sound of her voice. Now, he wasn't so sure about having children but, certainly, he longed for love in the same way that he longed to be a great soldier and improve his family's lot back home. It was all part of a glorious but still vague future to be thought upon again after tomorrow's battle.

The fiddler in the camp was playing a sweet ballad about true love. Gerald pushed down his desire to smile as Jacques looked absolutely disgusted by the timely tune.

'You do like her. I know you do. You go all funny when you talk about her.' Gerald tried to think of a better description. 'Your eyes sort of light up, or something.'

Now, they both looked embarrassed.

'I have to be free!'

Gerald did his best to look impressed but ended up asking, 'For what? For some other girl? Jacques, you told me that she was the most wonderful girl that you have ever met. Can't you see how lucky you are?'

In truth, he had no idea where these lines were coming from, although it probably helped that he was just a little bit smitten with Nancy himself.

Nancy!

Gerald turned, expecting to see her still standing behind him, waiting for a peek inside the tent.

'Oh?' he said once more.

The change in his tone made Jacques sit up. 'What?'

'She's gone.'

Jacques half shouted at him, 'Gone? What you say, gone?'

Gerald was confused. 'But you wanted her gone. Jacques … really, I …'

Jacques cursed dreadfully in French and crawled towards Gerald, pushing him out of the way. Jumping to his feet, the French soldier looked up and down but there was no sign of Nancy.

Gerald slowly got to his feet, not knowing what to think.

What was left of the sun had been partially covered by cloud. Birdsong competed with the sound of the fiddle and the frequent bursts of laughter from the groups sitting around their fires.

'Where did she go?' Jacques' anger had been replaced by anxiety.

'How would I know? I had my head in the stupid tent talking to you,' Gerald snapped out of guilt at having done something wrong.

Jacques snapped back, 'But I wanted that you bring her home! Why did you not do that?'

'For God's sake, Jacques! She didn't want me to. She wanted you!'

Gerald instinctively balled up his fist and wanted to plant it in Jacques' sulky mouth. This was too much. 'You know, I could be dead tomorrow. Is this how I'm to spend my last night?'

Jacques' mouth actually fell open. 'Huh ...?'

He was still gazing around him, looking for a head of blonde hair while trying to digest the truth in Gerald's statement. '*Mon Dieu*! You are not going to die tomorrow. I will be right beside you the whole time.'

'You can't promise that, you know you can't.'

Grabbing his young friend by the shoulder, Jacques forced Gerald to look at him properly. 'Listen, I am not going to let anything happen to you. I promised your father and now I am promising you.'

Gerald nodded, wanting to believe him. This was such a strange night. Nothing felt normal.

'We can talk about this later, but now I must find Nancy. It is too dangerous for her to be out here alone.'

A loud burst of rude laughter interrupted them.

Jacques craned his neck to see what had caused it, adding, 'I don't trust soldiers on a night like this, when they are readying themselves for the action like wild animals in a pack who only live for the moment.'

They both began to look around them in earnest, Jacques instructing Gerald not to call her name. 'Do not draw attention or it will be more than us looking for her.'

Gerald followed Jacques' lead by reaching for his sword while his friend threatened the evening sky, 'I swear, if anything happens to her ...'

'You'll what!'

Nancy stepped out from behind their neighbour's tent, her hands on her hips, looking triumphant yet defiant.

'Nancy!' Gerald whispered in delight, mindful of keeping his voice down.

Jacques stared for just a second or two and then ran to her, pulling her into his chest so that Gerald could no longer see her.

Smiling at the entwined couple in the twilight, Gerald discreetly dropped to his knees and crawled back into the tent, dragging his sword behind him.

CHAPTER SIXTEEN

The Jacobite War Council

James found himself to be relieved when he was told that William was not actually dead.

I would not be the cause of my own daughter's widowhood.

He felt that he had lost Mary forever but that did not mean he wanted to cause her pain. He was still her father and, therefore, would always wish her well, her and her sister Anne, no matter what happened the following day.

His war council was rather subdued.

Richard Talbot looked uncomfortable, feeling guilty about a letter he had written to James's wife in Versailles with his own version of the situation in Ireland. He had actually told her that he felt there was no point in fighting a battle that one was bound to lose. Not surprisingly, his attitude to William's near-miss was the exact opposite to his king's. *Damn it! Why couldn't that cannonball have finished him off?*

What nobody could deny was that nothing appeared to be in their favour.

James had set up camp on the Hill of Donore, which overlooked the southern bank of the River Boyne. So far, his preparations had involved leaving Drogheda and the tiny village of Oldbridge well protected by a couple of battalions, which would force the Williamites to brave the water if they wished to penetrate the Jacobite territory. The Jacobite leaders had mistakenly believed that the Boyne could only be crossed using the bridge at Slane, so it had made sense to block off the bridge.

This was all very well until a few hours ago when it was discovered that the river was in fact passable beyond Oldbridge, where there was a ford – a passageway of shallow water – a few miles south-west of Rossnaree.

James was flabbergasted. 'What are you talking about? I was told the Boyne was too deep to cross. How can I only be hearing this at my council of war?'

The French commanders barely contained their own shock. Lauzun wanted to shout at the Irish leaders: how come not one of you knew this about a river in your own country? He could not wait to relay all this to Louis – if he managed, that was, to live long enough to write another letter.

Everyone began talking at once, with the French shaking

their heads in despair and accusing the Irishmen of wanting them all to be killed. One of them cried out, 'We should leave at once and head for the River Shannon. Let the Williamites exhaust themselves by giving chase. They are not familiar with the landscape, which can only work in our favour.'

This was loudly rejected by Patrick Sarsfield, who reared up. 'Oh, what a grand idea! We should just give up. Is that what you're saying?'

James was struggling to keep his temper under control. Recognising the warning signs, Richard Talbot called for calm, suggesting that they just accept this latest information and concentrate on finding a solution. 'Please, gentlemen! Why point fingers at this late stage? Let's just decide how to deal with it.'

James moved to take control again. 'I will send a small party of cavalry to keep watch over the ford at Rossnaree.'

One of the French commanders said as politely as he could, 'Your Majesty, might it not be better to send a large group instead, as many as we can spare? If this is the only ford then we must assume the Williamites will definitely use it *en masse*.'

Looking sceptical, James argued the point, 'But if the ford is narrow, it hardly matters how many Williamites there are. They will be slowed down and forced to cross in small groups. A few cavalry with enough ammunition should be able to hold them off.'

His listeners squirmed with disagreement, leaving the same commander to assume a begging tone. 'Please, sire, we know their guns are superior to ours. If there is too small a group of defenders, they will be easily picked off by the enemy rifles that are easier to use than our old matchlocks.'

The commander smiled nervously to show his respect. 'Sire, I really, *really* feel we need as many defending the ford as possible.'

The rest of the commanders agreed with the brave Frenchman but no one wanted to anger James into making a bad decision based purely on his ego. It was best not to crowd him.

There was no denying the superiority of the Williamite weapons. James wondered if Louis was aware of the poor condition of some of the guns he had supplied. The match-lock musket was out of fashion now, taking too long to reload, and it was useless in the rain. Its replacement, the flintlock, did not require a piece of rope to be set alight in order to burn the gunpowder. Hallelujah! James had also been made aware of the bayonet muskets that allowed the Williamite soldier both to fire his gun and use it as a stabbing sword. Once the matchlock fired its musket ball it was only a length of heavy, dull metal until it was reloaded again.

Therefore his soldiers needed to carry swords or daggers as well as their muskets. He deplored the fact that so many of his Irish soldiers carried only scythes and old knives. There were not enough guns to go around, and even if there were, they had run out of time to teach anyone how to fire one.

Knowing when he was beaten, James said, 'All right, all right. Send an entire regiment to guard the ford but have the bridge at Slane destroyed.'

The men hid their relief at this change of mind. A king should always know when to accept advice, especially in military matters when thousands of lives were at stake. It was decided that Sir Neil O'Neill and his Antrim dragoons would be given the responsibility of keeping anyone from crossing at Rossnaree.

And then they were dismissed, James suddenly desiring to be alone in order to think.

He was rattled by his own gloomy premonitions. In the middle of the arguing and shouting, James had found himself questioning once more what he was doing in Ireland.

Even if he won tomorrow, and he sensed that this would be a miraculous outcome, what would he actually achieve? Of course the Irish would be ecstatic because they would see it as their own personal victory over what they considered to be an English army, while the French Louis would be delighted to have his worst enemy ousted from England.

But what would it mean for James? As soon as he asked himself one question, another one quickly formed.

Did he really want a throne that might bring never-ending problems? Did he really want his baby son to rule a country that already hated him? What if his son ended up like his grandfather, murdered by an angry mob? What about his daughters? He may have lost them for the time being but who was to say that they could not be a family again, somewhere in the future.

A memory swooped upon him, dragging him backwards in time. He was in his sister's palace in The Hague, in Holland, playing with her toddler son who had made a run for him as he soon as he recognised his doting uncle.

'Ah, there you are, little man. Do you want to play "horsey horsey"?'

The child bared his toothless gums and flapped his hands in excitement as James picked him up and placed him on one knee, pretending his leg was a horse, bouncing it up and down to make the child scream with laughter.

His sister clapped and cooed to her son, 'There now, William, don't you have the best uncle in the world?'

James shook his head to return to his gloomy present.

His camp atop the Hill of Donore included the battered ruins of a small church and its graveyard.

Who were the dead? What kind of lives had they led? Was there anyone left who remembered them, or were they well and truly forgotten, along with their families and friends; an entire world long gone.

The overgrown graves and the worn, broken walls of the church were having an effect on James. Was it Talbot who told him about the jumping church in Ardee? An unclean soul had been buried in the church's graveyard causing the church wall to jump backwards, thereby excluding the interloper from the rest of its sleeping baptised community. The Irish loved their stories; there was no doubt about that. Sometimes James wondered if they were not obsessed with their history and their dead.

How does a nation move forward if it is continually trying to rake up its past? And what about France, what if I had to spend the rest of my days there?

France was all very well. Louis had treated him and his family like royalty but, still, it was not home. All of this thinking had only served to bring James back to the beginning again, full circle.

The only way I'd ever get to live at home again is by winning tomorrow. If a thing is worth doing, then it is worth doing well.

'I have to at least try, don't I?'

He shuddered at the sound of his own voice in the darkness.

Was it ghosts that moved just beyond the corner of his eye, or only bats flitting here and there in the twilight? The neighbouring trees seem to quiver with quarrelling crows that were certainly loud enough to waken the dead.

'What on earth is that?'

Of course the dead did not answer him. He stared at the dark blob in the sky that twisted and turned at great speed, like black coffee swirling around in a cup. It grew in size but then, suddenly, it was a flat line before exploding into the shape of a ball – no, a bell, and immediately after that into a flower, blooming instantly before shutting up once more. Ah, yes, he had seen this before. It was only a flock of starlings performing a frenetic, swinging dance across the sky. As he stood there, he felt blessed to be bearing witness to such a majestic sight that was created by the most ordinary of birds.

Surely it was a sign from the Heavens above. Feeling suddenly inspired James declared, 'I left London like an obedient servant following orders and now God has seen fit to give me yet another chance. Tomorrow I will avenge both His name and mine.'

CHAPTER SEVENTEEN

The Williamite Side of the Boyne

Afterwards, Daniel permitted himself a smile. How naive he had been to think that the night before the battle might drag too slowly for him or that he would not be able to think about anything else other than what might happen on the morrow.

They lit their campfires earlier than usual as it was generally agreed that they needed to eat earlier and then try to get a decent night's sleep. Daniel took out his musket for the umpteenth time to make sure it was in proper working order. He did his best not to think about the battle itself. If he were asked for his honest opinion he might have said that he *mostly* felt that his side would win. Everyone knew the Williamite army outnumbered the Jacobites by thou-

sands. In fact, Daniel was still getting used to the extraordinary sight of so many soldiers around him. Yet, still.

Oh, he was a little scared all right, but he was glad to
be. Only an arrogant man would profess to be completely
fearless on the eve of a battle. Henry Campsie, for instance,
had declared himself to be very much looking forward
to fighting as if it was some sort of chummy sport like a
boxing match or a horse race. Meanwhile, Robert tried to
mirror his best friend's confidence, but he could not fool his
brother, who suspected that if he asked Robert how he felt,
he would be smartly informed that Robert's only worry
was regarding Daniel's safety. So Daniel said nothing and,
instead, found himself missing his big brother though he
was not five feet away from him.

His weapon was in perfect condition or, at least, in the
exact same condition it had been in thirty minutes earlier
when he had last checked it. He sighed, realising that he
should – he really, really should – write a letter to his parents, just in case … just in case.

'Robert,' he called out. 'I'm going to write to Mother
and Father. Shouldn't you do the same? They'd want to hear
from the both of us.'

Robert shrugged. 'Leave me enough space to add a few
lines beneath yours. I'll be back later.'

Daniel was surprised. 'Where are you going?'

His brother sauntered over to him and made a quiet confession, 'I'm restless, I suppose. I'm going to take a walk.'

Daniel immediately suggested, 'I'll come with you!'

Robert looked embarrassed. 'No, no need. Henry said he wanted a walk too. I'll write to Mother when I get back. All right?'

Daniel nodded and pretended not to be hurt. He watched his brother and Henry fall into step together and gradually lose themselves amongst the crowds of various uniforms.

Dear Mother, Father and Alice,

I hope you are all well.

Well, that was the easy part. Now what? He decided not to tell them that he had almost been eaten by a wolf because it would only scare them. Besides, as he couldn't mention Mrs Watson, he'd have to concoct a lie about how he escaped the wolf's clutches. It was best to keep things simple.

Ah, of course, he knew what he would tell them:

We had a dreadful fright earlier as we believed that King William had been fatally wounded. He was out along the River Boyne, in full view of the enemy. A shot was fired and the next thing we heard the Jacobites cheering that William was dead.

Some men began to weep; I think they were His Majesty's Dutch guards, who seem to love him very much. We hardly knew what to do with ourselves until we saw the king's party return. William was carried from his horse by the Duke of Schomberg and his son. Their expressions were grave and we all expected the worst.

However, a few hours later he rode amongst us to show us he was fine. If you could have seen how the men gathered around him ... thousands and thousands shouting his name aloud. I would not be surprised if you heard us in Derry. I saw some Dutch guards crying again, but this time it was out of happiness.

Daniel stopped, aware that this was a most impersonal letter for his poor parents to read. But what else could he do? He didn't think it fair to admit his worries about the battle or about being so far from home and about ... well ... not being sure he wanted to be a soldier anymore.

There, he had finally admitted it to himself. He did not want to be a soldier; he had had a change of heart. He bit his lip and felt his cheeks flare, grateful that no one noticed his shame. He watched as some soldiers compared muscular arms, wanting to be wrestled to prove a point, whilst others played cards or just sat and chatted quietly as if it was any old Monday evening. Daniel took no pleasure from his surroundings and was swamped by a selfish desire to stand up and start walking away as fast as he could.

Mother, Father, I want to go home.

No, he did not write that. It would only break their hearts and Robert would be ashamed of having a coward for a brother.

So, what else could he write? As he continued to debate this exact question he heard shouting. Heads turned in the direction it was coming from, the more curious actually getting to their feet to see what was going on. It was no distraction to Daniel, who assumed that it was just an argument over something trivial. He considered describing exactly what he could see from where he was sitting but in doing so had to accept that all he could see were men staring off into the distance. The shouting was getting louder and louder. And then Daniel heard Henry's voice shouting across the camp, 'See what we've found, a spy in our midst!'

Daniel looked up slowly from his letter just in time to hear Henry's gleeful question, 'Is this not the tallest woman you have ever seen?'

Oh God, no!

Shoving the pen and paper into his pocket, Daniel jumped up and broke into a run. An audience had gathered around Henry and Robert, obliging Daniel to push his way through, already recognising the floppy hat and pale face at the centre of the staggered circle.

Horrified, Daniel looked to his brother. 'Robert, what are you doing?'

Robert shrugged as if to say this was nobody's fault. 'We found her on the outskirts of the camp. It looks like she's following us, spying on us.'

Someone rather unhelpfully suggested, 'That's no woman! Why, she's taller than any of us.'

'See,' called Henry to no one in particular, 'I told you so. She's a Jacobite spy!'

'Hang him!' It took just one individual to say this before it was instantly taken up as a maddened chorus.

'Kill him! Kill the spy! Hang 'im from the nearest tree!'

Perhaps the night before a battle is a most treacherous time in any army camp, when nerves are taut and men are building themselves up to commit bloodshed.

'No! No!' screamed Daniel. 'Leave her alone!'

'Daniel, for God's sake!' Robert was torn between the genuine terror on his brother's face and not wanting Daniel to make a fool of them in front of their fellow soldiers.

Mrs Watson never said a word. Just like Daniel giving himself up to the wolf, she felt trapped. The situation was reversed and now young Daniel was her only hope. She gazed at him, silently beckoning him to calm himself so that he would be listened to.

'Let her go, she's not a spy!' Daniel balled up his fists and took a step forward, hardly knowing what he was going to do.

Henry tried to reason with the boy. 'It's all right, Daniel, you don't have to be here. Go on back to your tent.'

'I said, let her go!'

'Or what?' Henry was losing his temper.

'This!' yelled Daniel as he walloped Henry square in the jaw.

A roar of appreciation went up from the crowd as Henry doubled over to rub his jaw and digest the fact that the puny Daniel Sherrard had actually hit him.

Robert was speechless.

Henry did not bother to straighten up. Bent double, he lunged at Daniel, grabbed him around the waist and dashed him to the ground.

'How dare you! You stupid brat!' Henry rained down thumps upon Daniel's chest and head while the crowd howled for more.

Daniel grabbed Henry's fists and managed somehow to throw him off to the side. His nose was bleeding, but he didn't care. He flung himself on top of the older boy and punched him about the face and throat, unleashing months of rage and, yes, even jealousy over Robert.

The soldiers cheered him on, though Daniel couldn't hear them.

And then, just like that, there was silence.

Always more in tune with a crowd, Henry was the first

to catch the drastic change in atmosphere. He stopped hitting back and concentrated on pushing Daniel onto the ground. The younger boy was out of breath and allowed himself a moment to make sure that Mrs Watson was still there. He avoided making eye contact with Robert but noticed Mrs Watson briefly incline her head to the people standing next to her. Even then he might have ignored this and looked to continue thrashing Henry Campsie had he not heard the widow exclaim loudly, presumably for his benefit, 'Your Majesty!'

Oh.

Standing beside King William, Reverend George Walker looked very much like he wanted to throttle both the Sherrards, Henry and the rude crowd. He asked in a shrill voice, 'What, pray tell, is the meaning of this shameful scene?'

Looking thoroughly miserable, Robert tried to make sense of it all. 'Your Majesty, Reverend Walker, I must apologise for my brother. He's just nervous about the battle. It's his first one, see ... and so he lost his temper.'

King William exchanged a puzzled glance with the clergyman.

Henry, delighted to be finally addressing the king, jumped to his feet. 'My apologies, sire. We caught a spy and Private Sherrard, here, well ... he sort of disagreed with us.'

That didn't make much sense either.

Reverend Walker shook his head in disbelief while the king turned to the boy who was still lying on the ground. Not knowing what else to do, Daniel stayed where he was. He had never been this close to the king before and, furthermore, whenever he did see him, William was usually sitting on his horse. Daniel was vaguely struck by how short the king was; he hardly reached Mrs Watson's shoulder.

Meanwhile, William found himself thinking back to the young boy and his scruffy dog that he had met outside Belfast. It had been his own idea to make a second brief tour of the camp in order to encourage his newer regiments for the following day. He had expected to be greeted with smiles and cheers, just as he had earlier, and was much disappointed to find a common brawl commanding his soldiers' attention, having believed that this sort of behaviour was more typical of the Jacobites. He allowed Reverend Walker to ask the questions, hoping that it would not be necessary for him to make a comment. He had enough on his mind without this.

'Your Majesty, might I speak?'

The woman had decided that it was time to take charge of the situation.

King William had hardly noticed her, assuming she was just one of the soldiers. Only now did he see her for what she was, a rather tall, weary woman in men's attire. Yes, he thought, he would like to hear whatever she had to say. He nodded his head.

As a mother who preferred well behaved children, Mrs Watson began by chiding Daniel. 'Have some respect. On your feet, now, this is your king!'

Daniel got to his feet immediately, blushing madly. 'Forgive me, ma'am.'

She stared at him until he got the hint and added, 'Oh, of course, forgive me, Your Majesty!'

The king nodded his acceptance.

'Sire,' Mrs Watson began, 'I mean no disrespect in coming here, but I am a widow and a mother to six young children.'

William listened as she explained about her two horses being taken from her, leaving her frantic about how she would meet the rent and feed her family in the coming months.

'Your Majesty, I know this is presumptuous of me, but I believe you are a fair man and I thought that if I presented my case in person you would understand my plight.'

Reverend Walker hardly moved as she spoke, but his expression was one of incredulity. How could this happen just as the king allowed him to accompany him on his final tour of the camp? First, an ignoble fist fight and now this strange woman blethering on about her horses. *Goodness, he must think we are a backward lot.*

Fortunately the widow held the truer opinion of the king.

When she finished making her plea, she bowed her head and waited. The crowd waited alongside her, some of them believing that she was about to be hauled off in chains for her impertinence.

'Reverend Walker,' said the king, 'have someone accompany this woman to the herd so that she can identify her horses.'

There was a gasp from the crowd. Mrs Watson kept her eyes trained on the ground until William addressed her, 'Madam, I am releasing your animals back to you and, if you want, take your neighbours' horses too and please make my apologies to them.'

Daniel saw the reverend's mouth fall open.

William thought for a moment before saying, 'I wish to write a letter.'

There was a pause, obliging William to be more specific. 'I need paper and a pen.'

The reverend began to pat himself up and down in search of anything that might suffice, but he needn't have bothered.

'I have paper and pen, Your Majesty,' Daniel shyly held up his unfinished letter, 'though the quill has probably dried out. Let me fetch some ink.'

Without waiting, he turned and sprinted towards his tent

and bag, snatched up his chipped ink pot and returned to see the king reading the letter.

'Are you sure I can use this? What about your parents?' William asked.

Daniel bowed. 'Oh, yes, Your Majesty, it ... well ... it would be an honour.'

William smiled in agreement, dipping the pen into the pot that Daniel held out in his hand and scribbling quickly on the back of the letter. He folded it in two and had a soldier rush to his secretary to have it sealed in wax.

'Make sure you take the letter with you,' he told Mrs Watson. 'I wish you well.'

With that, he walked off, leaving everyone staring after him in wonder – that is, everyone except the widow who did not seem the least bit surprised.

She made yet another request. 'Reverend Walker, could I ask for Private Sherrard to take me to where the horses are kept?'

CHAPTER EIGHTEEN

The Battle Begins

Tuesday morning was a beauty. The chilled air was pure and full of promise of the heat that was to follow. Summer was here even at this hour. The glistening dew that dotted the individual strands of grass would soon disappear, and the silvery mist that lingered across the River Boyne was enjoying its last hour or so, before it too would disintegrate beneath the golden blaze of the sun that threatened to break through at any moment.

Insects marched out in search of food as the birds competed with one another in song. Field mice were growing drowsy after their night's work and returning home to sleep the day through.

Somewhere a dog howled while not too far away was the sound of thousands of footsteps on the move.

It was time.

The two kings had to manoeuvre their men into place, in a bid to outsmart the other, as if they were playing a game of chess using the most spectacular chess board and real, breathing figures.

Two kings with their bishops, *or generals*; their proud knights, *or cavalry*; the kings had earlier set out from their two respective castles in France and in London which housed their two queens, *or Marys*; and last but not least, their plucky little pawns, *or infantry*. Every piece was vital, with its own steps to take in order to win this particular game of life and death.

The pieces were moved around the board in response to each other, with the bishops, the knights, the pawns and, of course, the absent queens (who were praying hard) all doing their best to keep their kings safe while gaining as much ground as possible. Keeping a king safe in battle was no mean feat, but it could be said that the Jacobites had an easier time of it.

Of the two main players, James was the most cautious; his concern for his good self obliged him to hang back as he sent out his pieces this way and that to knock the Williamites off the board.

William, however, was different. He favoured leading his army from the front, on horseback, encouraging them to keep up with him and make a strike for victory.

Furthermore, it was he who opened the game by making the first move.

William had devised his own battle plan, in the belief that a wise leader selects the best of his advisors' ideas to entwine with his own: *I will use some of the Duke of Schomberg's proposal and send a strand of my army off to distract the Jacobites.*

And, so, at six o'clock that morning, Meinhard Schomberg and just over seven thousand soldiers set out, according to William's orders, to make their way towards Slane to cross the River Boyne at the ford at Rossnaree. Once they crossed the river they were to head southeast, or as far as they could get before being confronted by the enemy.

'You will be my sneaky surprise,' said William. 'Therefore, I do not want you to make an attack until the rest of the army has launched its offensive.'

The Duke of Schomberg was not pleased with this plan but had given up on ruling William's mind ever again, although the king had used some of his idea which was to move men into place in order to hide the real attack from the enemy. However, the old duke worried for his son and maybe this alone prompted him to say to William, 'My Lord, do you think that Meinhard has enough men to make a stand?'

William bit his lip. The truth was he did not know the

answer to the question. He had worked out plans for three crossings to take place at different times. Meinhard was taking the right side of the army on a six-mile trek to cross the river at Rossnaree. From there he was to march east and attack the Jacobites in the flank and the rear. His father would lead the main body across the river at Oldbridge while William would lead off the left to make their crossing at Drybridge.

The duke's son knew that it was only a matter of time before they were spotted by the Jacobite lookouts, thus it was important to reach Rossnaree as fast as he could. His father was of the opposite persuasion, though he kept that to himself. He preferred that Meinhard take his time so that he and his troops would be able to cross the river while the Jacobites were already busy fighting the rest of the Williamite regiments. Otherwise, well ... otherwise the seven thousand might well find themselves facing the bulk of James's army. The duke sighed to himself. *Why didn't William just accept my plan and keep things simple?*

William watched them disappear into the mist, after warning Meinhard to be as quiet as possible. 'You know how noises carry at this hour. I need your men to be like a snake slithering on its belly towards the water's edge.'

Meinhard bowed his head. 'Yes, Your Majesty.'

Ordinarily this reminder to be quiet would have irritated

him, but this was not the time to give into his usual whim for wanting to be independent from unnecessary instruction. His mother always used to say that one of his very first sentences had been 'I do it myself!'

Meanwhile, William turned his attention to the remainder of his thirty-six-thousand-strong army. How long would it take for thousands of men to cover such a stubborn territory of forest, crevices, hills and narrow paths? As he tried to focus, a little anxiety persisted in niggling him. William did his best to imagine the next two or three hours. Perhaps now would have been a good time to admit that he was not an expert when it came to planning a battle on such a scale as this. Timing was all important. For instance, if Meinhard reached his destination too soon he was vulnerable to an all-out attack by James. Alternatively, if he arrived much later than expected he would be of little help to his father's troops who – if all went according to plan – would be dealing with the brunt of the Jacobites at Oldbridge.

True, William was comforted by the fact that he had more men than his father-in-law and far superior ammunition, but he found that his general's question would not leave him be. *What if Meinhard's forces are completely overwhelmed because I did not give him enough men?*

William was feeling guilty over his treatment of his most loyal and trusted general. It would be madness to ignore the potential danger as hinted at by the duke, especially in relation to Meinhard. Oh, it was foolish to try to worry over everyone's safety but, at the very least, William understood that he had to give his men a fighting chance.

Accordingly, the king sent out one of his English commanders, along with five battalions, after Meinhard, to support his crossing of the Boyne. As soon as he did that, William felt a lot better.

The next task was to have several cannons lined up with orders to start bombarding Oldbridge. This village, or hamlet, consisted of a few stone buildings whose occupants had made themselves scarce. William wanted to prevent the Jacobites from taking up defensive positions within the abandoned homes and cowsheds.

The cannons were pulled into place with their respective teams who set about ramming powder and shot into the barrels. Next, the captains inserted fuses and stood ready for the order to fire. This, William knew, would signify both the end of the peaceful morning and the beginning of whatever was going to happen.

The noise was tumultuous, and several people in Drogheda must have toppled out of their beds thinking that either the world was ending or God was in a rage.

BOOM!

BOOM!

BOOM!

Each cannon exploded, jolting sharply backward on its wooden wheels, with the effort of sending a ball of lead shooting across the river to crash into the opposite bank. Muck and water spewed up at the onslaught. The Williamite soldiers, all professional and experienced, worked together in near-perfect synchronicity, to re-load and keep firing. They wanted those cannonballs raining down on Oldbridge, sending every individual Jacobite scarpering, thereby making it easier to cross the river when the time came.

Hundreds of birds took flight as the first gun sounded out. They would not return for several hours. Rabbits shuddered in their burrows, while petrified squirrels clung on to their branches for dear life as the very roots of the trees shook within the ground.

The next to move out was the Duke of Schomberg, with almost twenty thousand men, including William's personal favourites, his Dutch Blue Guards. This was the main body of the army, the centre, which would perform the frontal attack on Oldbridge. The various drummers and trumpeters sounded out the reveille, signifying that it was time to get into their lines and make their way down to the banks of the Boyne.

Their shift was determined by Mother Nature, obliging them to wait for the low tide at ten o'clock, when the water level would drop in front of Oldbridge and the mist would clear. In truth, the duke was far from happy at the prospect of making their crossing in full view of the Jacobite camp but, as the king's second-in-command, he accepted that his duty was to follow orders and trust to William's determination that this was the best approach possible.

With so many men, progress would be slow, maybe even an hour or so – as wave upon wave of marching men made their way down from the glen where they had camped. From a distance they must have looked, in their different uniforms, like colourful ants who would not be distracted from their chosen path. Left, right! Left, right! As one line appeared over the ridge and continued downwards, it was immediately replaced by a second line and then a third and fourth … and so on.

'Keep your muskets out of the water! Keep your powder safe!' The duke knew that his words were unnecessary, but it gave him something to do, and he wanted to be recognised by as many as possible as their leader.

Meanwhile, Meinhard led his men on a winding, twisting route that took them several miles off to the far right of the two armies at Oldbridge, from where they could plainly hear the cannonfire.

Meinhard could not help but enjoy the morning sun, though he wished he was not wearing so many layers of clothing. It was going to be a hot day. He was not a man given to idle chat with his colleagues so he mostly rode in silence, ignoring the men nearest to him, who wisely left him alone to his thoughts.

I wish Father did not look so worried for me. Why isn't he more confident in my leadership?

At the same time he shared his father's anxiety. When an army is broken up into different groups, to perform individual attacks on an enemy, timing is probably the most crucial aspect of the entire undertaking.

At least the ground is not as bad as I feared.

He took a quick look behind him as if to check his army of English and Dutchmen were still following him.

It was easy to be lulled into drowsiness by the clip-clopping of the horses' shoes on the grass. A more imaginative man might have closed his eyes for a minute or two and pretended that he was out by himself for a morning ride where the only requirement was to enjoy the countryside.

William would wait for the duke and his battalions to perform a successful crossing before leading the remaining two thousand soldiers a couple of miles downstream to cross at Drybridge. So far everything was going according to his plan. For now, he could keep watch as the main offensive smartly penetrated the Boyne and think to himself, *what a wondrous sight!*

Schomberg's regiments slid their way down the banks and steadied themselves against slippery rocks and their neighbour's feet. Moses himself would have been proud of how those soldiers, staying in their lines, raised their guns over their heads and boldly marched into the water, almost creating their very own walkway, using their body mass to part the river.

Naturally they found themselves immediately under fire, from the Jacobite infantry that were close enough to heap as many curses as bullets upon their heads.

The duke continued to roar in as many languages as he knew: 'Keep going forward and get into formation as soon as you are out of the water.'

He could only hope that the different captains and sergeants were relaying the same message to their own squadrons. His voice could not possibly carry to every soldier as their entrance into the water was about a mile long. Also the air was full of gunshot and cannonfire. How he disliked having to deal with the Boyne before the enemy could be properly confronted, although he had to admit that the low tide was proving rather cooperative. The men would have puddles in their boots, but at least they would be cool in the heat of the sun.

Jogging his horse back and forth, the duke kept an eye on the enemy. The cannons had done their job and cleared the south bank of the Jacobites who, he knew, would be ordered back to meet the Williamites clambering onto what had been their territory. Briefly the duke wondered about his son's progress as he took in the impressive sight of so many men moving in formation together, the drums beating a steady rhythm and the different flags waving to signify those brave men and boys from Derry, the Dutch guards, the French Huguenots and the Danish boys, all bound together by their hatred of the Papist James and the tyrant King Louis of France. As they marched, they belted out their own battle songs, providing a gloriously chaotic chorus of different words and harmonies.

The Huguenots, those proud French Protestants who had been forced to leave their own country because of Louis, the dogmatic Papist king, hardly noticed that amongst their own commanders was another man who had moved in front of them, brandishing his sword and a pistol. Maybe some of them recognised him as an army chaplain, but all would have been ignorant of his identity as the best-selling author of *A True Account of the Siege of Londonderry*. The Reverend George Walker looked positively thrilled to have involved himself in leading those noble Frenchmen down to the bank of the river. Every so often he stepped out to roar at those soldiers in the Derry regiments that had survived that dreadful siege: 'Come on, boys, let us go and do the Lord's work for him! I see you Sherrard lads, and Henry Campsie too!'

The boys that had closed the gates against James's army cheered their Anglican minister and former governor. How thrilling it was to march together with all of these different nationalities.

Some of the battalions were obliged to hang back to allow the others to cross. They stood in their square formation – ten men wide and eight men in length – and began firing at the enemy over their colleagues' heads, warning the Jacobites to leave their friends – who were in the water – alone.

Again the Duke of Schomberg fretted as the minutes passed. *How long before the water level rises again?*

And again he cursed the river for its messiness. Grimly, he congratulated James for forcing it upon them as he watched the Williamite approach start to stumble under fire. The men in the water were stuck in limbo since they could not use their muskets or pistols and risk getting them wet. The duke scowled. *They are as helpless as ducklings*! However, it had to be said that the Jacobite infantry were inflicting little actual damage because their muskets and pistols were too far out of range.

Once the men had crossed and got themselves out of the water they had to get back into position again, but this time in range of enemy fire.

This is a numbers game, thought the duke. *I need all of them over there as fast as possible.*

The landscape began to change, and Meinhard quickened his pace, worrying that they were slowing down because of the broken ground. He had sent his scouts ahead, which was how he knew that the bridge at Slane was smashed up, no doubt by Jacobites to prevent them from using it.

Interesting, thought Meinhard, *James must have been concerned about an attack from the side.*

The destruction of the bridge was a reminder that they were now in enemy territory. A long time ago his father had taught him that, in a situation such as this, caution was a soldier's best friend and so Meinhard sent out scouts to scour the surrounding area, searching for signs of Jacobites. He would not risk leading his men into an ambush, even if that meant calling a halt while the scouts galloped off to check that they were safe for the next few miles at least.

Meinhard was scarcely aware of the land they were pass-

ing through though he did notice a collection of odd-look-
ing hills, or burial mounds, representing *Brugh na Bóinne*,
the Palace of the Boyne, comprised of Newgrange, Dowth
and Knowth. One of the English commanders smirked as
he said, 'We must watch out for the fairies, sir. The Irish
believe that this area is haunted by them.'

If he had expected this to start an interesting conversation with his stony-faced general, he was wrong. Meinhard turned away from the man, ending the discussion right
there and then.

The terrain was starting to cause problems for the wagons
that carried their large artillery. Meinhard could not allow
a gap to open up between the men and the cannons so it
was necessary to keep sending scouts backwards to check
on the progress of the wagons as their horses dragged them
over the various bumps and dips.

On hearing that the next few miles were clear, he sent an
advance guard ahead of them, fearing that they were taking
too long on account of those heavily laden wagons. What
was uppermost in his mind, apart from wanting to prove
himself to William, was that he was leading the charge to
help his father's offensive. While the Jacobites were preoccupied with fighting the duke's massive force, his son would
sneak up behind those Jacobites and bite them in the rear
and the side. At least this is how he would have described

it to his son, Charles, who, at seven years of age, had been bitterly disappointed not to be allowed to accompany his father and grandfather to Ireland.

It was nearly nine o'clock now; in other words they had taken three hours to cover almost four miles. At long, long last the advance guard reported back that they had spotted the windmills that proved that they were almost upon Rossnaree, where they would finally cross the Boyne.

That was the good news.

The bad news was that there was a welcome party, waiting on the other side, only they weren't so much welcoming as utterly murderous.

CHAPTER NINETEEN

James's Hasty Response

James had hardly slept a wink all Monday night and as soon as he managed to doze off he was roused by an anxious Lauzun. 'Sire, we have received the most alarming news from our sentries!'

The king did not feel ready for the day ahead and craved to be allowed to sleep for another few hours at least.

'It appears that William's army is on the move!'

'WHAT?'

James was wide awake now.

'Our sentries heard them set out about thirty minutes ago. You can still hear them marching outside: thousands and thousands of feet along with wagons carrying cannons, heading off to their right – that is, our left.'

James threw off his blankets and jumped out of bed, pointing at his clothes as he roared, 'You know what this means, don't you? The scoundrel is probably leading his entire army to that damned ford at Rossnaree – the ford that the Irish claimed to know nothing about. This nation may prove to be my undoing yet!'

Lauzun was busy grabbing at tunics while searching for James's left boot. He had little sympathy for the panicking king. *How long were we here before William arrived? William, who within moments of his arrival, set out to make a proper reconnaissance of the area, unlike us who just sat on our behinds and waited?*

Lauzun kept his true opinions to himself. When he realised that James was looking at him, he quickly said, 'Er, yes, sire. That is what we believe, that he's making his way to the ford. He must hope to surprise us with a flanking attack.'

'Well,' said James, 'it is we who will surprise him.'

There was a flurry of movement just outside the tent. Richard Talbot poked his head through and then bounded inside as soon as he saw the Frenchman. There was hardly enough room for the three of them.

'So, you have heard the news, Your Majesty. It is a bold move, to be sure, but how could he hope to get away with it? The noise of those Protestant feet is remarkable and can surely be heard for miles around.'

He was free to continue while Lauzun stood by with the king's trousers and James fixed his shirt into place. 'I suppose the question is how many we should send to meet him. Neil O'Neill and his dragoons number about five hundred in total. It is they alone who are guarding Rossnaree so we must send reinforcements as fast as possible, although we really should leave some battalions in Oldbridge just in case an attempt is made here.'

The king snapped, 'Really, Richard, of course I am sending reinforcements and I shall lead them myself.'

Turning to Lauzun, he ordered him to have his horse saddled and brought immediately, adding, 'You are coming with me.'

Lauzun inclined his head. 'Yes, Your Majesty!'

James gulped down some coffee, while Talbot waited, not daring to venture another word until the king's mood had improved. Outside he heard Lauzun shouting the king's orders.

James thought quickly. 'Fine,' he said, complimenting himself on his plan, before he said it aloud to Talbot. 'I will take sixteen thousand men with me. We have thirteen hundred holding Drogheda so that leaves two thousand cavalry and five thousand infantry to stay here with you and guard Oldbridge.'

Talbot quickly digested this while James added, 'We can assume that William is leading most of his – if not his entire – army to Rossnaree. We must appear more impressive than some of us think we do.'

His commander felt a little queasy as he wondered if Queen Mary Beatrice had informed her husband about his lack of trust in the outcome of the battle. *Why oh why did I send that stupid letter?* The truth was he had hoped that the queen might convince James to leave Ireland and return to France. Squashing down his guilt, Richard stood up and looked his king in the eye, saying, 'I agree, sire. Take the majority with you to Rossnaree. Nobody, including – I'll wager – his own men, has ever been heard to describe William as a gifted general. He has made a most obvious choice, and a poor one.'

James gazed coolly at his second-in-command as he asked, 'Are you sure about that, my friend, that you have *no* doubt?'

Talbot bristled at the question but only because it hit a nerve. In any case, it was much too late to admit that – yes – he, the Lord Lieutenant of Ireland, did doubt his king and friend. Of course Talbot would not prevent His Majesty from leading away two-thirds of the army to meet William in Rossnaree – that blasted ford. *God knows he needs as many as possible to compensate for the fact that most of those Irish boys have yet to fire a gun in battle and will have to wait a while yet since they only carry daggers and scythes.*

Richard struggled to hide his feelings. *Oh, wouldn't it be a grand thing altogether if I just said it out, just asked him how he thought that farming implements were going to fare against the latest in weaponry? Sure, he may as well have them plant some seeds at Rossnaree while they're waiting for the Williamites!*

Well, it was not like he was being asked to place his hand on the Bible and swear to tell the whole truth. He opened his mouth to make a strong, positive reply, but James interrupted him to ask quietly, 'Tell me honestly, am I leaving you enough men to hold Oldbridge?'

Richard Talbot was relieved to be able to say quite truthfully, 'Yes, sire, you are. Thanks to Louis' generosity we have the finest cavalry in Europe. If there is an attempt to breach the ford in front of the village, we will be more than able to hold our own.'

James nodded, warning his commander, 'It is as well to expect an attack at Oldbridge. It makes sense for William to try to distract us from the fact he is taking most of his men to Rossnaree. At least if you have any trouble, it will only involve whatever few men he has left behind.'

Outside, the men were gathering their weapons and finding out who was staying and who was leaving right now with James.

James had asked for the best of the cannon, the French cannon, to be loaded onto wagons and brought with them. Horses were led out of their pens to be either yoked up to the few wagons or else saddled up for their riders.

Every passing minute was like a jab in James's side. The Williamites were already out of sight of his telescope; he had pointed it in the direction that the sentries had indicated but failed to see them. *Goodness, all those thousands of men, they move speedily enough*, he thought.

His nerves were jangling and he decided to take refuge in his tent until the men were ready. Sensing a familiar dampness, he prodded his nostrils to make sure that he was not having one of his nosebleeds. They almost always happened at the most inopportune moments. It would do his Irish and French generals no good to see blood spurting from him before he even got on his horse.

He paced the small interior of his tent, dabbing at his nose until Lauzun stuck his head in to tell him that his horse and the men were ready.

'I'll be out shortly,' said James, dismissing the Frenchman with a curt nod.

So, this was it.

He gazed about him as if his tent was suddenly the most precious home he had ever known. This had been his substitute palace. There were his good blankets and pillows and there were his Bible and rosary beads, sitting on the stool beside his bed, along with the miniatures of his wife and father.

Fixing his sword and picking up his pistol, James steadied himself and prayed: 'I do this in the name of my father, brother and my baby son. Dear God, I ask You to guide me to victory today, but if I should be defeated, I beg you to look after my family in France ... and in England too.'

A drummer boy began to lightly tap out the heartbeat of the army that awaited their king.

James pulled back the canvas door of his tent and stepped out into the July morning.

CHAPTER TWENTY

All is Revealed

For the fifth time that morning, Gerald checked that Cait's drawing of their grandfather's castle was tucked into his breast pocket.

The morning had begun rather unexpectedly as the camp emptied out with thousands leaving for Rossnaree. He and Jacques had stood watching most of the army march away.

Jacques asked him, 'So, you understand what is happening, yes? James is off to meet William while we stay here minding the smallest village in the world.'

Gerald scrunched up his face. 'Did you mean to say "minding"? It's an odd way to describe it. We are *guarding* the ford in front of us.'

His friend shrugged. 'We are the finest cavalry in Europe. What is "odd" is that we are *not* accompanying your king to help defeat his rival. Did I leave France to sit here on my backside?'

Moments earlier, Michael and Joseph had passed by on their way to take up position in and around Oldbridge with the infantry battalions. Michael had lifted his scythe in a cheery salute, 'See you boys later!'

Joseph had given his customary laugh, though he looked as nervous as Gerald felt.

'It is a bit strange,' agreed Gerald, 'watching them all leave but we have a job to do here that is just as important.'

A dog was nosing its way around the various tents. They both watched it as it scrabbled at the ground, wondering how to get inside one. Finally it looked over at them and whimpered.

Jacques declared, 'No, I will not help you to steal another man's food!'

The dog whimpered again and looked at Gerald who was packing up the bullets and cartridges of gunpowder that he had made the previous evening. His gun was polished and ready, as was his sword.

Jacques was doing the same but at a much slower rate. He carried on talking to the dog. 'But you see, I would not wish our awful bread on you. Please believe me when I say that I am saving you from a dreadful fate.'

The dog sniffed the air, while Gerald rolled his eyes. The inferior quality and bland taste of the Jacobite bread was a favourite topic for the picky Frenchman. As he said himself, 'Ah, *oui*, how I miss the pastries at home … the lightest dough that is crisp to touch yet melts on your tongue. Gerald, you poor Irish boy! You have no idea of the bounty that awaits you. I will introduce you to pink icing, chocolate croissants and fruity tarts. Trust me, your mouth will water so much that you will have to hold a cup beneath your chin.'

'I can't wait!' muttered Gerald.

Actually he couldn't. Ever since Jacques regaled him about the beauty of France with its months of sunshine, sandy beaches, Roman ruins and hundreds of grand churches, he was curious to see it, telling his friend, 'I cannot even begin to imagine what it must be like to live openly as a Catholic in a Catholic country and be able to speak your own language without any fear of punishment.'

It was Jacques' idea that Gerald follow in his father's footsteps and take a boat to France; it took the young Irish soldier a while to commit to it aloud. Even the idea of being in the middle of the ocean, onboard one of those magnificent sailing ships, was enough to excite him. This was not to say that he had forgotten about Offaly. He had already warned Jacques that he wanted to go home first before he left it again.

Jacques had understood but told the boy, 'When you are

standing under your mother's roof, with her eyes upon you, you may need to remind yourself how big the world is.'

Jacques had never met Mrs O'Connor but suspected that she was a woman of unaccountable will and might. He even offered to go with Gerald to Offaly, for the sake of ensuring that the boy would be free to leave again, although he did not admit this to Gerald. Instead, he said, 'I would like to visit this famous Offaly and compare her to my town to see then which one is the best.'

Gerald had thought this a splendid idea. He was anxious for Jacques to see his grandfather's castle, or what was left of it.

This was the first time that he had made a decision about his own life. *I hope Mother and Cait will understand.* He thought they might accept his decision, but he did not hold the same confidence about his teacher. The priest had never said anything, but Gerald had sometimes felt that Father Nicholas nursed a hope that Gerald might follow in his footsteps and join a monastery. Even though Gerald wanted to see France, he could not imagine staying away from Ireland forever.

In the camp, the dog jerked its head up and swerved sharply away from the soldiers' tent before breaking into a full sprint. Gerald watched it in amusement and turned to make a comment to Jacques who put his hand up to silence him, whispering, 'Wait!'

And there it was, a thunderous blast that erupted in the near distance, followed by another and then another and another after that. It was the end of silence; each mighty crash was immediately followed by an echoing one so that there was no pause in the explosions.

Gerald froze and waited to be told what to do. Soldiers spilled out of their tents, including Richard Talbot who looked positively enraged.

One of the infantrymen came running towards them, shouting, 'They're firing on Oldbridge – a line of cannons set up on their side of the Boyne!'

'How many?' roared Jacques.

'Don't know, five or six!'

Richard Talbot took command, placing both hands around his mouth to shout at the messenger, 'Tell the men to fall back from Oldbridge but not to clear the area! I repeat, they are not to clear the area!'

The man bobbed his head forward and his 'Yes, sir' could not be heard by anyone, including himself.

Talbot grabbed the soldier nearest to him and bellowed in his ear: 'Tell them to move the rest of our cannon into position. We'll give them as good as we're getting!'

The man sped off to carry out his order. Talbot swallowed hard as he remembered the king had taken the biggest and best cannon with him. Well, they were just going to have to make do with what they had.

Meanwhile, down by the riverfront, Michael and Joseph were cowering behind one of the buildings, wondering what on earth they were expected to do. The noise was deafening and they took no comfort from the brick wall that trembled with every cannonball. Joseph's face was bleeding, though he could not fathom why; he could only taste his blood as it slid into his mouth. He stared in bewilderment at Michael, trusting him to make the necessary decision, whatever it was.

All around them they could see their comrades doing exactly the same thing, keeping their heads down in the shadows of the few houses. Michael, who had absolutely no experience of being trapped by several cannons, did, however, guess that they needed to move out of their range. He'd hardly had the time to appreciate the size of the Williamite artillery but, my God, they looked enormous.

'We need to move farther back!'

Joseph, who was practically leaning on top of him, looked blankly at his friend, not having heard a single word.

The ground was being pummelled around them with stones and grit flying up into their eyes and mouths.

Michael slapped Joseph's shoulder and pointed backwards, hoping to attract the attention of the others. He shouted,

'Move back out of the way. It's our only chance!'

Joseph thought that was an extremely sensible idea. About twenty feet from where they stood was a narrow trench that he and Michael had helped to dig. Surely it had been built for this very situation. Some of the cannonballs were whizzing past them so they would have to run fast and as far as they could before they would be out of range.

Michael waved his arms around until he had the attention of the fellows at the next building who all began to make the same gesture. Just to be sure, Michael yelled, 'Move back!'

He held up one fist and stuck up one finger and then two fingers and then three, shouting, 'Go! Go! Go!'

There was no doubt they needed to move and it made no sense to wait for a break as the guns followed one another up and down the line.

So, the Jacobites, clutching their weapons with clammy hands, had to run while the ground was pelted all around them. They heard musket fire but most of them understood that they were out of range from individual shooters. On reaching the trench, they flung themselves into it, to wait it out or until they received orders to do something else.

About eight of them huddled close together, giddy from their narrow escape. Michael felt rather proud and wondered had he actually saved their lives. Joseph certainly seemed to think so; he beamed at his friend in gratitude.

One of their companions, who bore a scar down the side of his cheek, was enraged. He shook his head and demanded, 'Where is James? Did he go back to Dublin – that's what we heard?'

Joseph shook his head and shouted, 'He's gone to Rossnaree.'

Only Michael nodded in agreement but then stopped when he saw the scornful expressions on everyone else's faces.

'Yeah,' said the man with the scar, 'and you believe that, do you? I'd say he's run back to Dublin along with those haughty French infantry and their fancy cannon. And we're the fools for staying put.'

Joseph was shocked to the core and stuttered, 'No! He couldn't have.'

And so this conversation might have continued in spite of the explosions, for what else could they do while they waited, except for the fact that Michael suddenly had an urge to check the opposite bank. He couldn't have explained why but something came over him, prompting him to peek out to see what he could see.

'Keep your head down!' warned one of the others.

Michael turned back to his fellow Jacobites in bewilderment. His face had lost its usual colour and his eyes bulged with horror as if he was still looking at whatever he had seen.

Joseph reached out to him and then stopped, deciding instead to get to his knees and look across the Boyne. They didn't need to hear him say 'Oh, my God' because they could plainly see his lips make those sounds.

Oh, my God.

The cannon kept firing as one by one the soldiers popped their heads up and saw a sight that utterly confused them, each man needing a moment before he could understand what he was looking at, which was this: thousands and thousands and thousands of Williamites were appearing out of the leafy glen and taking up positions all along the banks of the Boyne.

Oh, my God.

Nobody moved. How was this happening? Their sentries had reported hearing the Williamites march away at dawn. Who were these men? How many were they looking at and how many more were there? There seemed to be no end to the rows of colourful jackets pouring out of the glen. And there, *there* was William himself on his black horse looking hale and hearty in his fine regalia. But he should not be there at all because he had gone to Rossnaree which was four miles away.

Or had he?

The sun continued to blaze away while each and every one of those Jacobites only felt a prickly chill that made them tremble.

Michael was the first to react. His mouth was drained of every drop of moisture, therefore his voice sounded scratchy and dull when he said, 'Someone needs to run back and tell Richard Talbot.'

Joseph looked dazed, only saying, 'I don't understand. I don't understand!'

The man with the scar turned and started running even before he had properly got his two feet beneath him.

A few minutes later he was in the middle of a puzzled crowd who tried to understand what he was saying in between taking big gulps of air. 'The Williamites … they're not gone, they're there! Over there!'

Richard Talbot snarled impatiently, 'What?'

The man took a deep breath. 'Sir, we've just seen thousands of Williamites – too many to count, and William too. They're all over there.'

His listeners gaped at him and then turned to jog together towards the pathway that led down to Oldbridge, with Talbot calling for his telescope, to which the man with the scar felt desperate enough to say, 'You won't need no telescope to see 'em. I promise you that!'

He was right.

Talbot stopped still in shock. Gerald found himself stand-ing next to him and distinctly heard the Lord Lieutenant gasp, 'Mother of God!'

The scene had continued to unfold since Michael had first registered it because that first battalion of Williamite soldiers, wearing gold and blue, were now walking into the Boyne.

Richard Talbot shook his head as if to deny what was happening. They had made the most dreadful mistake, in actual fact the very worst mistake that any general could make. James had ridden off with most of their army, doing exactly what William had wanted him to do. The Dutch-man had played them as if they were puppets in a play he had written. *Why did we assume that it was all of them going to Rossnaree? Why didn't we check?*

Someone else called out, 'They outnumber us by what … maybe three of them for every one of us?'

There was no reply to this.

Even as they stood there, the Williamites were making their way across the Boyne. Talbot grimly declared, '*They're* the Dutch Blue guards, William's elite force of professional gun fighters.'

'Pah!'

More than a few heads turned in the direction of the man who had made such a disrespectful noise.

'What do you mean by that, soldier?' Talbot looked ready to thump Jacques simply for the sake of doing something.

Appearing surprised at such an unnecessary question, Jacques gestured towards the occupied Boyne and explained the obvious. 'It does not matter how good they are with guns that they cannot use while they are in the water.'

Just then there was a volley of fire from somewhere below them that resulted in at least two of the Dutch soldiers dropping with a splash into the water. This was followed by cheering and then more gunfire.

In spite of himself Talbot smiled and then jumped into action. Standing tall, he shouted loud enough to be heard by as many as possible, 'That's our side starting the fight. All infantry get yourselves down there and start shooting as if it's the devil himself who's coming to get you.'

Suddenly remembering the absent king, he said to the fellow beside him, 'Get a messenger to James and tell him what has happened.'

Then he called out again, 'I want all cavalry to ready their horses and stand by them until I give the order to mount. Now everybody MOVE!'

The crowd scattered to follow his orders. Trumpets rang out as any infantryman that was not already in place behind Oldbridge collected his weapons from his tent, before tearing down to join their colleagues.

Jacques led the race towards the horses that were already stamping their feet with impatience to be let out. Those who were rich enough to employ groomsman had only to shout for their animals and they appeared already saddled. There were plenty of young boys, from Drogheda, to help out too, getting involved in leading the horses out, without colliding with one another in their excitement. One young lad, under Jacques' terse instructions, led Paris and Troy over to their masters.

Gerald and Jacques quickly saddled their horses, Jacques irritating Gerald by checking he had pulled and buckled his straps correctly. He was not taking any chances that Gerald, in his haste, would end up toppling from Troy in front of the enemy. The order went round that the French and Irish cavalry would descend upon the Williamites from the hill behind Oldbridge. Everyone was to assemble there but were not to mount their horses until the last moment, in order to keep them fresh.

Jacques told the boy to follow behind with the horses and he gratefully complied. This was the most excitement the lad had ever witnessed and he did not want to be dismissed just yet.

Naturally the cavalry wanted to see how their infantry was faring. Jacques and Gerald were just two of hundreds who, keeping low, headed uphill on foot to watch the action.

The horses were kept a short distance away by the grooms-men and the local boys that were almost overwhelmed by the temptation to climb the hill after the horsemen and see what was going on at Oldbridge.

Down below, Michael, Joseph and the others prepared to charge the first of the Williamites climbing out of the water. It was only now that Michael was horrified at the fact that he did not own a gun. Up to this point, he had not ques-tioned his weaponry – his knife and his scythe –believing they would be enough along with his courage and rage, but looking out across the Boyne at that mighty army, whose guns and swords seem to glow in the sun, he immediately lamented his naivety and, yes, utter stupidity.

As usual, Joseph was gazing at him for guidance while the Jacobites who owned muskets started shooting, picking out unlucky individuals for a watery grave.

'What do we do?' Joseph's voice rose in panic.

Somehow Michael had assumed leadership of the group in the trench but had no time to appreciate how or why. Scanning the area around him, he instinctively made a lunge towards a large rock, scooped it up and then stood and took aim, flinging it with his might. The others immediately imi-tated him for this was something they had learnt to do as soon as they could walk, throw stones, and the ground was full of them.

'We're going to have to fight them when they come up on the bank!'

The others nodded at Michael. Well, this was the kind of fighting they had expected. The noise of the booming cannons and long-range muskets had been unexpected, but to get a chance to fight with one's fists, daggers and scythes, now that was more like it. Nevertheless, it was difficult to ignore the superior numbers of the enemy. From the corner of his eye Michael saw Joseph wipe sweat, or tears, from his face. He kept his own eyes on the ground as if to stop himself thinking about numbers. In any case, Joseph was not the only one who was frightened. Plenty of fellows were blessing themselves and mouthing off anxious prayers to God above.

Briefly Michael wondered about his family. He had not told his wife that he was joining the army. How could he have behaved so badly to those who depended on him? He had sneaked away just like his brothers and just like his parents who had gone and died on him when he was still a child.

He had been unable to admit in the tavern that day, that he had run off on Kathleen and the boys while they were sleeping, not that it was anyone's business. In any case, any money he received was being sent back to them and, please God, this would be over soon. *I'll make it up to them, I swear.*

Just get me through today, God, for their sake if not mine.

They numbered about five thousand, those brave Irish infantrymen who would provide the front-line that day while their French and Irish colleagues watched from the hill behind them.

Gerald scanned the backs of the infantry, asking Jacques, 'Can you see them, Michael and Joseph?'

Jacques didn't even bother trying to find them; he just shook his head. Brandy rations had been speedily doled out to fortify the cavalry with fire and courage. Gerald did not like the taste but at least it proved a bit of a distraction when it burned his mouth, throat and then stomach.

'Why must we wait here? Why can't we go down and help them?'

It was an obvious question.

Jacques replied quickly, 'There is no use in us riding down there while the Williamites are still in the river. The only way we can make a difference is to wait until they have lined themselves up on the bank and then our job is to sprint our horses down this hill and smash them back into the water.'

He made it sound so easy.

He pointed out someone to Gerald. 'See that fellow on the horse in the river, that's the famous Duke of Schomberg!'

Gerald watched the duke ride back and forth, his sword in hand as he urged his men to keep going forward. There were a few more dead bodies now, and the duke called for some men to jump into the water to drag the corpses back to the northern bank and out of their neighbours' way. Only for one body it was too late. Gerald saw how the dead soldier was taken by the water and carried downstream. Goodness knows where he'd end up, a stranger in a strange land.

The moment finally arrived when those Williamites reached the other side and the Boyne began spewing them up in threes, fives, tens, twenties and more and more, exactly as if a dam had burst and, instead of water, there were only enemy soldiers.

A roar sounded out from the Jacobites and while there were still navy coats busy with getting onto dry ground, the red-coated Irish infantry sprang at them. The cannon had eased up in case they killed their own but the Dutch Blue Guards would start shooting as soon as they had the opportunity to take aim and fire.

Born fighters such as Michael recognised that they had to prevent this from happening, even if it meant using their own bodies to block them. The air crackled with gunfire and smoke. Sunlight found a multiple of mirrors in the blades of the silver swords and daggers, while screams of pain mingled with the cries of triumph.

Gerald tried not to be reminded about that night outside Derry when his trench had been attacked and the Jacobites had been ordered to flee. He'd had to block out the moans of the wounded comrades that he climbed over in his haste to save his own skin. Watching the carnage below, he found it bizarre to think that he would soon be amongst it and hated himself for feeling so suddenly afraid

CHAPTER TWENTY-ONE

The Ford at Rossnaree

A few miles south of Oldbridge, Rossnaree was easily fordable, that much was true, though in order to reach it Meinhard and his men had had to first deal with a steep descent. Really, the only problem was the Irish regiment that was waiting for them on the other side of the river.

'What shall we do, sir?'

Meinhard gave the man a scornful look. 'Is that a serious question, sergeant?'

'No, sir, I mean, well, are we going to cross or would you prefer that we wait for the cannon which is still a mile or two behind us?'

Meinhard did his best to size up their opponents from where he was. Well, unless they were hiding men else-where, the Jacobite regiment was pitifully small, maybe no more than five or six hundred. They all appeared to be armed with muskets but Meinhard was prepared to take his chances. The river was wide but the tide was low and he ordered his dragoons and grenadiers into the river, warning them to be prepared for coming under fire.

The Jacobites lined up on the southern bank and aimed their muskets at the Williamite riders approaching the water. Their commander, who Meinhard did not know, told his men to hold their fire until the first batch of Williamites went into the Boyne. Meinhard urged his men to steady their horses. They had to reach the south bank as quickly as possible in order to overcome the much smaller regiment. Until they reached the bank, however, it was going to be tricky.

Shots rang out immediately, the unholy noise puncturing the air, shocking even those who were prepared for it. Within moments, there was a second mist over the Boyne, but this one was created by the muskets and the gunpowder while the heavy smell of sulphur clogged up nostrils and irritated the backs of throats.

Just like his father, Meinhard needed his men out of the water as fast as possible, but Sir Neil O'Neill and his five hundred dragoons were not going to make it easy.

Back at Oldbridge, the Duke of Schomberg was more

than a little surprised by the ferocity of the Jacobites defending their southern bank. The Dutch Blue Guards had managed to cross the river but had been immediately set upon by the Irish infantry. Fighting was up close and fierce. Bodies were down on both sides as soldiers were shot at, stabbed or stunned from rocks to the chin. If there wasn't time to reload a musket, it was turned upside down and used to try and bash out the brains of the on-coming assailant. The more modern muskets of the Williamites allowed their owners to shove the bayonet's spear head into unprotected chests and necks.

The duke signalled for reinforcements; that is, the second wave of battalions now approaching the Boyne: the French Huguenots and the Irish Protestants. He spied the Reverend George Walker in the mix but did not pay him any heed. The duke found it odd that a clergyman wanted to go out and kill. Besides, the fiery reverend was not a favourite of the king's, but the duke could not deny the man's courage and passion for William's cause.

The beat of the Lambeg drums accompanied the Derry men, though they could hardly hear it. Daniel Sherrard wondered if the guns could be heard back in Derry. His feet thoroughly soaked through, he kept in step behind Robert and reckoned that Henry Campsie had never looked as happy as he did now in storming the river to attack the

Papists. He and Henry sported a few bruises as proof of their fight, but that was all forgotten about now. Now they united against the Jacobites. Daniel briefly wondered whether he, Robert and Henry had caused all of this since it was they and their friends who had closed and locked the city gates against Richard Talbot's Catholic army.

Oh well, no time to ponder that now.

'Ha!' roared Henry. 'Now's our chance to get them back for what they did to us.'

It was starting to get rather chaotic on the bank as the Dutch did their best to hold off the Irish infantry, while the French and Irish Williamite soldiers needed time to get themselves out of the water and space to fire their guns.

The Jacobite Irish were doing their damnedest not to allow the enemy to step any further beyond the Boyne. Apart from anything else, one had to be careful against accidentally harming or killing a friend due to the thick smoke that stung men's eyes, blurring their vision. The Jacobites were the ones with white paper in their hats, while the Williamite regiments, who also wore red coats, dressed their hats with small sprigs of greenery. It was not, as you can imagine, the easiest distinction to appreciate during the hysteria of battle.

Behind him, on the northern bank, the duke knew that William was watching his progress through his telescope.

They had plenty more fighting men yet to cross, but William was biding his time, wanting to tire out the Jacobites, while drip feeding them even more soldiers to contend with.

William checked his pocket watch, a gift from his queen, and found that the fighting was into its fiftieth minute. Instinctively glancing to his far right, he wondered how Meinhard was getting on. It was obvious that James's army were not all engaged on the far bank, holding off his guards.

So, where were they?

Four miles away, the Williamites had made little leeway and Meinhard had developed a hatred for the Boyne: *If we were in the middle of a field, there would be no contest between them and us. The river slows us down by demanding my men's attention and allowing the enemy to open fire on them with as much time and care as they need.*

Certainly these Jacobites seemed well armed with no shortage of bullets. Their young commander was everywhere, championing his men. At some point, he cried out an order and their horses were brought to them. Dragoons were mounted infantry, that is, they travelled on horseback but fought on foot. Meinhard was surprised at their change in tactic: *Why bring in the horses? Are they preparing to retreat?*

He waited, but there was no sign of the Jacobites leaving. Mounting their horses gave them some height from which to fire down on the Williamites in the river. It also lent them speed to charge up and down the bank, lest Meinhard's men thought they could avoid an immediate clash by crossing further down the Boyne. The Irish dragoons worked hard to cut off every conceivable part of the river bank.

Meinhard was conscious about time: *surely it has nearly been an hour now*. Furthermore, he did not want to lose any more men.

Turning his horse away from the Boyne, he galloped back the way they had come, suddenly knowing exactly what he needed to do. *By God, they had better be here by now or I will personally lash the drivers myself!*

On the Jacobite side, it was Sir Neil O'Neill himself that first spotted the Williamite monster guns in the distance. How proud he was of his men who were putting on such a glorious show against God only knows how many Dutchmen. But where was the support that was promised to him? He had thought the plan was for his men to position themselves here overnight in case William tried to breach the ford, but he had been assured that another regiment would be sent out to help them. *I'm like Robin Hood here with his bunch of merry men, facing down the armoured legions of bold King John. We've got the heart, but it is they who have the might.*

Even faced with the superior might of Williamite weaponry, he did not consider the possibility of retreat, and he knew that as long as he stayed not one of his men would leave either.

Nevertheless, within the next moment or two, everything was about to change.

Well, so be it, he thought, as he re-loaded his pistol to fire again.

Perhaps it had been foolish to think they could have held off the bigger army as long as they had gunpowder. But hadn't they done well?

The shocking blast of the cannon made the inexperienced horses rear up and attempt to flee. The lead ball smashed through his men and their terrified animals, battering the bank beneath their feet. Water, mud, rocks and torn limbs sprayed in all directions. *Maybe*, thought *O'Neill, it is time to go. I'll not martyr my men for James; he is not worth that!*

Alas, it was too late.

A second cannonball shot out across the river and caught him full on the leg, smashing his thigh wide open, before ripping the flesh from his horse's side. His body crumpled helplessly over the horse's neck as blood spurted from both of them. His dragoons were instantly weakened at the sight. Only his high saddle prevented the Irish commander from toppling into the river. One of his men grabbed his reins, and they all turned and let their horses fly as fast as they could, leaving the cheering Williamites free to finish that all-important crossing in peace.

Meinhard Schomberg was feeling rather smug as he led his battalions on from Rossnaree. A messenger had been despatched to tell William the good news. The duke's son lifted his face towards the sun and thought to himself: *it was a pity to lose a whole hour, but no matter, it is done now.*

He sent his scouts on ahead and made sure that the wagons would be kept up to speed, hinting at dire punishments for those responsible. However, his men were eager to fight again, so relieved were they to be finally finished battling the Boyne.

Now, it was time to find James and his army.

CHAPTER TWENTY-TWO

Checkmate!

James heard the exploding cannon in the distance but was not unduly worried about the remains of his army at Oldbridge. *Of course William will try to distract us from Rossnaree by firing cannon at us.* It only confirmed his belief that he was going to surprise his son-in-law who had hoped to surprise him.

To silence the fretful voice in his head, he decided to hand himself over to God. In other words he made God responsible for his immediate future, silently asking Him to *give me a sign either way and I will accept my fate.*

If God meant him to be king once more, so be it. If God meant him to return to France and settle down to a small but quiet life, so be it. The third option was not as attractive as the others: *but if God means this to be my last day on earth, so be it.* If he could choose for himself, he would definitely pick one of the first two. He did not want to die just yet. After all, who would want to die on such a beautiful day as this?

The shrubs and hedgerows were alive with flashes of oranges and reds as the butterflies danced their way from flower to flower, unbothered by their large and sombre audience. Buzzing bees mistook the plumes on James's hat for a blooming flower, but he didn't try to wave them off. When he was seven he had been stung by a bee that he had flapped at with his hands. His nurse explained that had he just stood still, the bee would have realised its mistake and continued on its way. According to her, insects were only concerned with surviving their day and had no interest in tackling the impossible.

His horse's tail swished cheerily at the flies and really if James did not dislike the countryside so much he might have been able to appreciate that, for the moment, he was surrounded by perfection.

'Sire!' Lauzun gestured ahead.

In the distance was an approaching figure, one of the scouts who had been sent out to look for the enemy. They were surely halfway to Rossnaree and should expect to see William's army within the hour. Because the youth had his horse at a gallop, James assumed that the news was impor-tant and sat up a little straighter in the saddle, feeling the old tension stretch across his shoulders.

The scout drew his horse up in front of him and saluted. 'Your Majesty!'

James flicked his hand. 'Well, have you spotted them yet?'

'No, sire. Not yet.'

'Really? How far did you go?'

The scout, a boy of seventeen or eighteen years, looked worried. 'I rode as far as I could, My Lord. I mean, as far as it was possible.'

James did not appreciate vagueness in wartime. 'What do you mean? Explain yourself and be quick about it!'

'Yes, Your Majesty' was the obedient reply. The young man pursed his lips and continued, 'Sire, I am not from these parts. I come from Tipperary.'

He was interrupted by his nervous king who cried out, 'What on earth are you talking about? What has that to do with anything?'

The scout decided against any further delay in presenting his bad news. 'Your Majesty, about a mile from here I encountered a deep, overgrown ravine that looks … well, it seems just about impossible to cross.'

One look at the bewilderment on his king's face prompted the scout to hurriedly suggest, 'But, sire, I'm not from these parts. Maybe there is another way around. That's all I meant.'

'Well, then,' said James. 'There's your solution!'

'Sire?' The scout was keen to understand what he was being asked to do in order to bring this unpleasant interview to an end.

The king rolled his eyes and said in a weary tone, 'Why don't you go and get me someone who is from this wretched place and send them to find me another approach to the ford?'

'Oh, yes, Your Majesty. As you wish, sire. Right away!'

The young man made good his escape, galloping down the lines of French Jacobites in his quest to find a local soldier who knew the landscape. It was a simple request and James was right, an obvious solution to their predicament. So, how was it that he could not find a single soldier that knew his way around the area?

The scout kept going, partly because the further he went down the army the more distance he created between the bad-tempered king and himself. If he could, he might have continued until he reached his home county. He knew what he had seen and he alone knew what it meant. James would simply have to see it for himself.

And so he did, about forty minutes later. He saw it all. There were the Williamites about a mile away from him and there, in between them, was a steep drop into a valley that was crammed with huge thorny bushes, tall mounds of nettles and trees packed in tightly, as if protecting a secret gateway to another world.

It was embarrassing, maybe even comical. Two armies wanting to get at each other and all they could do was make obscene gestures that could barely be seen from a distance and issue threats of violence, at the top of their voices, that they could not make good on.

The onus was on that young man from Tipperary to inform James that there was no one from the area in their ranks and that he had tried and tried but could not find a way either down or through the thorny jungle of the ravine. 'Sire, there is no way for a horse to get through that bramble; it is as solid a barrier as the walls of Derry were.'

Stung by this thoughtless reminder of his earlier failure, James yearned to whip the scout and welcomed the distraction of a messenger from Oldbridge.

He gazed across to the colourful figures in the distance and wondered what his son-in-law made of this bizarre episode. Perhaps William believed that James had planned this clever usage of the landscape. First there was the fast-flowing and expansive river to be dealt with and now there was this gaping hole in the ground itself that no animal, wagon wheel or man could penetrate.

Maybe I should build a palace here, thought James. *It is prov-*

ing safer than my old nursery where I had not a care in the world.

The messenger bowed and said rather quickly, 'Your Majesty, the Lord-Lieutenant Richard Talbot sent me to tell you that William, along with most of his army, is attacking Oldbridge.'

James showed no change in his expression.

Not a sound was emitted from any of the listeners that had gathered around him. The silence was unnerving. It was as if everyone present had turned to stone, including the horses.

Lauzun suppressed an urge to shout out something vulgar. Unable to look at James, he focused on the space between his horse's ears, spying a tiny insect scurrying along the hairs, disappearing suddenly only to reappear again.

Feeling obliged to explain himself further, the messenger tried again: 'Your Majesty, I am told to inform you that our sentries were mistaken; that William made it seem that his entire army had marched away this morning. But they are still there and are attacking us hard.'

The messenger wiped the sweat from his brow and made his own confession: 'As I was leaving I saw Williamites approaching the bank at Oldbridge.'

Turning slowly, James peered at the enemy in the distance and summoned his telescope. He lifted it to his right eye and through that tiny, circular window he recognised the figure of Meinhard Schomberg who, at that moment, was positioning his own telescope to his right eye and staring right back at him in dismay.

Checkmate!

It seemed that the game was over.

You see, in a game of chess the king does not need to be actually captured in order to be defeated. He just needs to be held in 'check' with the *threat* of capture and for there to be absolutely no possible way of removing that threat.

The crowd around James faded from his sight and he was left dazed, listening to the summer breeze tangle with the banners behind him. After a few minutes of standing still, the horses, including his own, dipped their heads to discreetly nibble at the grass; it seemed to them that there was nothing else to do. And it seemed that James agreed with them.

A weight had been lifted from him and it was not of his own doing.

I asked God for a sign and here it is.

One of the French infantry whispered to his friend, 'Is he talking to his horse?'

Indeed, it did look like James was doing exactly that.

Lauzun moved away from the king to give them both space to think.

James continued on mumbling to himself, 'How could I have been so blind? First I am nearly murdered at Derry and now this … this obstacle that surely did not exist before today. I cannot cross this and there is no way to return to Oldbridge in time to do anything.'

His horse continued to munch, while James took a breath and released it, saying, 'To continue would be against God's wishes. He has kept me safe from harm and I owe it to Him to cease this useless campaign.'

The French soldiers shifted from one foot to the other, raising their eyebrows, afraid to breathe a sigh of relief just yet. One of them whispered, 'They say at Derry that he went into shock and sat motionless on his horse for hours. Do you think that this is what is happening now?'

A second soldier asked, 'Should we not be heading back to Oldbridge? They are probably being overwhelmed without us.'

No one bothered to agree to this. The first man shrugged. 'Perhaps he should just give up?'

Oh, just about every man agreed with that idea. As far as they were concerned, James could take all the time he needed if he was going to forget about a battle and let them go home.

The birds struck up a joyous chorus, the sun dazzled, the horses relaxed while the bees buzzed around and around. If this wasn't Heaven it was as near to it as you could get in the whole of County Meath.

One man, however, wished for a little more. 'Just a pity we can't sit down for a bit.'

'Hear! Hear!' said his friends quietly.

CHAPTER TWENTY-THREE

Here Comes the Jacobite Cavalry

Back at Oldbridge, Richard Talbot was calling out instructions to the cavalry troops who gathered together at the bottom of the hill from where they had watched their infantry do their best to hold off the attack.

'I didn't hear him. What did he say?' Gerald's voice was high and thin.

Jacques held him at the elbow. 'Come on, Gerald. Master your panic, do not be lead by it. You know better than that.'

'But Jacques … I don't know … I …'

Jacques held the boy still and kept his voice low. 'Take a deep breath, and then another, and another.'

Gerald did as he was told, grateful that his friend ignored his trembling limbs. An icy cold sweat trickled down the side of his face, and he wished with all his heart that Nancy might suddenly appear with his handkerchief because he needed it more than he had ever expected to need a small square of linen cloth.

Below them the fighting was growing more desperate. The Williamites were positively swarming the Jacobite side of the Boyne, but the Irish infantry kept plugging away at them. However, much worse than that was the sight of thousands of extra Williamites hanging around until it was their turn to step into the water. Gerald tried to silence his fear, but how could he pretend not to see the facts: *we don't have enough men.*

And neither could he fail to notice the dismay in his friend's eyes. The Frenchman rolled his lips inwards and Gerald plainly saw him clench his jaw. Also, Jacques' skin was shiny from sweat, though he did try to blame that on the warmth of the morning.

The order came through for them to mount their horses, but Jacques was not letting Gerald go until he was sensible again.

'What you are going to do?'

Gerald did his best to concentrate. 'Stay beside you and Paris.'

The two soldiers had watched as the Williamites exited the Boyne and began to step into their square formation.

The war-torn Jacobites had fought valiantly but, in the end, they found themselves overrun. Where possible, the Irish infantry began to edge away from the river.

Among them was Michael, whose adrenaline was beginning to flag, making him aware of a multitude of aches and pains throughout his entire body. His clothes were splashed with blood that he could not be sure was his. One thing was certain and that was they needed more weapons. Michael kept up the same cry throughout: 'Take any muskets and swords!'

He did his best to look out for Joseph but had lost sight of him a while back. He saw the wounded being dragged away and tried to see if the boy from Trim was amongst them.

Keeping an eye on the hill behind them, he waited for his men to be relieved. He had guessed what was going to happen next. In between all the noise, he just about made out the blast of the trumpet and thanked God for it.

The infantry had done all that they could, but now they must step aside, to allow the French and Irish cavalry take their turn.

'Soldiers, mount your horses and wait at the top of the hill for my say-so!'

Gerald shook off his friend's hand and planted one shaky leg in front of the other until he reached Troy, who greeted him with a nod of his head. The Drogheda lad gave him a boost up onto his horse's back and ran to do the same for Jacques who was already sitting on top of Paris. Jacques threw the boy a silver coin. 'Don't hang around here. You understand me? It could get dangerous. Go on back to Drogheda or wherever you came from.'

The boy nodded vigorously as he stared in reverence at the coin in his mucky hand.

The trumpet sounded and the riders spurred their horses back up the hill. All in all there were two thousand of them, and they stretched themselves across the length of the hill, maintaining their columns as steadily as they could. They would make runs in groups of sixty.

Gerald began to quietly recite the words of Saint Teresa to keep himself calm and focused: 'Let nothing disturb you.' *I can do this.* 'Let nothing frighten you.' *I can do this.* 'All things are passing'. *I can do this.*

The various generals were all taking their places, Patrick Sarsfield muttering to his peers, as he spotted William in the middle of his soldiers, 'I wish to God we could swap kings!'

They wondered if James might suddenly reappear with their cannon and the badly needed men. *Surely he will,* thought Richard Talbot. *Aren't we doing all this for him?*

There was no time for speeches. The Jacobite infantry were being crushed and badly needed help. Therefore

Talbot raised his gun and cried out, 'Knock them back into the river and keep them there.'

The cavalry roared while their horses shucked their heads and prepared to run. Gerald felt his nostrils would never be rid of the smell of the animals, thick and musky, neither pleasant nor unpleasant. Before him, he saw the ruin of his grandfather's castle, the broken, fragmented palace that hid him, as a child, when he was frightened or in trouble. It occurred to him that the ruin could well be Ireland herself. Today she was the one in trouble and it was up to him to protect and shelter her within. What was the next line of the saint's prayer: 'Patience gains all things.' Well, the people of Ireland had waited long enough, hadn't they?

Father Nicholas' student reached inside himself and found his courage, in that moment seeing himself echoing his proud ancestors who had believed that Ireland could be freed from foreign rule.

Jacques remembered something and shouted at his friend, 'We are the sleeping army, yes? Only we are awake now!'

A shot rang out and the cavalry were released. Gerald dug his spurs into Troy's side and hollered as loudly as his comrades. It looked like each and every horse jumped an imaginary fence, just for the fun of it, before hurtling themselves down that hill towards the Dutch Blue guards who watched their approach. All Gerald could hear were the thunderous hooves that blocked out the gunfire for a few moments at least.

This was a wondrous boost to the Irish infantry, who took off to the side, out of the path of the horses, and cheered their men on. Michael whooped in delight when he spotted Gerald and Jacques, though they were oblivious to his shouts of encouragement.

Jacques had warned Gerald to be mindful of the enemy's actions at all times. The squares of William's elite force shifted as one man for every five stepped forward holding out a long pike with the deadly spear-head. Within seconds, the Williamites were surrounded by pointed pikes as the blocks of men took on the appearance of a prickly hedgehog, whose spiky coat would keep it safe. Those pikes were for fighting an enemy cavalry … in other words those pikes were for taking down the Jacobite horses.

But these horses were no ordinary horses and had been well trained for conditions such as these.

Gerald and Troy, Jacques and Paris were in the second row of the first attack and kept at a murderous gallop. They swung down that hill and raced one another to the enemy. Gerald worried that he hadn't enough strength to pull Troy out of the pikes' range; he had his pistol in his left hand while his right held the reins. He needn't have worried. Troy merely copied the horse in front of him, veering sharply to the left, leaving Gerald free to point his gun into the centre of the Blue Guards and fire. Maybe a hundred or so pistols were simultaneously discharged. The noise was ferocious as the air filled with smoke and the screams of wounded men.

'Turn! Turn!' Gerald yelled at Troy, who was turning anyway. The Jacobite horses were moving with the instinct of the herd, avoiding the pikes, running down the side of the Williamites, before swerving to follow one another right back up that hill again.

Jacques was right; there was no time to be afraid.

The second run imitated the first. The horses sprinted down as fast as they could before turning at the last moment under the burst of gunfire. Those pikes waited to slash open the nearest animal, while the Blue Guard reloaded their weapons through the blinding smoke and all-out calamity.

Jacques showed no surprised when Gerald shouted, 'We need to hit the pikes in front to get through them!'

Gerald had grasped that in order to do real damage the cavalry would have to pierce right through to the soft underbelly of the hedgehog: in this case, the lines of soldiers behind by the men with the pikes. They were the ones shooting at the Jacobites.

'Ready?' roared Gerald.

'Ready!' roared Jacques.

Down the horses galloped once more, digging lumps out

of the ground as they went. Keeping to the middle of an attacking line would allow them a chance to attempt to force their way through distracted Williamites. Gerald focused on recognising an opening and kept the stirrups pressed up tight against Troy's flank, willing the horse against turning this time. Paris was right beside them, Jacques already reaching for his sword. Just like before, the horses in front swerved, but Troy and Paris did not follow them.

The distance between them and the pikes was quickly disappearing, allowing Gerald to register the pock-marked features of the Williamite that had guessed their intentions and was preparing to stop them. Presumably he shouted a warning to the men standing either side of him, but he did not manage to emit more than a few syllables before Jacques reached him, slashing his cheek open with his sword, causing the Dutch soldier to take an involuntary side step away from the weapon that came for him a second time. As he dodged to the left, to avoid Jacques' sword, Troy promptly bit his other cheek. Understandably, the man reached for his bleeding face with both hands, thus bringing his pike to an upright position and presenting the Jacobites with their first break.

Troy and Paris surged into a sea of swords and rifle fire, and Gerald was much relieved to see that they had been followed by dozens of comrades, whose horses lashed out at the Dutch guards with their back legs, while rearing up to dwarf the Williamites with their entire bodies. It was only now that Gerald truly appreciated the horse as a powerful fighting machine.

Meanwhile, the Jacobite riders fired their pistols and carved the air around them with their swords, maiming and killing the enemy, who now found themselves properly under pressure and already fatigued from the previous hour of fighting the Jacobite infantry.

CHAPTER TWENTY-FOUR

The Duke of Schomberg and the Reverend Walker

From the middle of the Boyne, the Duke of Schomberg spotted the Jacobite cavalry on top of the hill and drove his horse forwards, determined to be on the ground beside the Dutch Blue Guards for the first attack.

The next battalions were lining up behind them, and the duke saw William summoning his commanders to make a third crossing. Unsure as to how many horsemen made up the Jacobite cavalry, the Williamites' only option was to lengthen the haphazard battlefield at Oldbridge, thereby forcing the Jacobites to stretch their lines. The best way to accomplish this was to send more battalions into the river but have them cross a good distance away from the Huguenots and the Derry soldiers.

Meanwhile, the Jacobite cavalry launched themselves onto the Dutch Blue Guards. From where William stood, his elite force looked to be taking a brutal thrashing. He shouted out in distress, 'My guards! My poor guards!'

He roared to the nearest generals to take their men further down the river and make another crossing, though they would not have the benefit of a low tide. Once again, it meant having good fighters stuck in nowhere land because they could not fire their weapons from the middle of the Boyne. *No matter*, thought William. *I will not sit here and watch my guards be slaughtered!*

The duke silently commended his king on his quick thinking and then concentrated on getting his horse out of the river as fast as he could. All around him were the French Huguenots and he was bent on rallying them: '*Allons, mes amis, rappelez votre courage et vos ressentiments. Voilà vos persecutors!* ('Onwards comrades, recall your courage and your resentments, there are your persecutors!). Just like William, the duke had his favourites; these Protestant French were dear to him because these were his wife's kinsmen. Susanne's sudden death two years earlier was probably the only reason that he was still, at this age, on top of a horse and about to fling himself into the middle of a bloody great battle.

He felt no need to personally urge the Derry regiment

since he didn't know any of them, but there was the good Reverend Walker rousing them out of the water and that booming voice was more than enough for any battalion.

The riverbank had been transformed into a muddy bog, while fresh difficulties arose as the numbers standing on it increased. The duke saw the guards ready themselves for the Jacobite cavalry and watched the horses tearing down that hill as if nothing human could stop them. Down they came, but most of the Jacobite horses swerved to avoid the deadly pikes; the duke saw a few riders continuing the charge head on and readied himself for confrontation.

Within seconds, he was in the middle of a frantic mêlée made up of both his men and enemy soldiers. As his horse twisted this way and that, he lashed out with his sword while continuing to direct the French Protestants to a more prominent spot. Guns exploded all around him, and the smoke prevented him from seeing farther than a few feet. None of this, however, particularly bothered him as he had spent the last fifty years surviving confusion such as this. Meinhard always said that he coped better in chaotic peril than he did at fancy dinner parties. In any case, he would never allow himself to display even a hint of anxiety in front of his men. If he did, he deserved to be stripped of his post as second commander-in-chief.

Then all went quiet. To be sure the action continued

all around him, but he could no longer hear it. When he opened his mouth to shout, he found he could not speak. Slowly he looked down at himself to see if he was really here at all. He could still feel the warmth of the sun and that much was a comfort. Fascinated, he watched the men fight. He saw the swords cut through flesh and the bullets that ripped out lumps of bone and skin.

To his surprise he could plainly see the bullets being fired out of the guns; his eyes were able to track their routes as they smashed through one man and continued on their way into the next. How strange, he had never been able to see them before. He saw men claw at one another, trying to gouge out eyes and punch noses bloody, and it seemed to him a dreadfully sad thing. What was this rage that had contaminated even the horses? Those magnificent animals should be at peace not war.

He felt tired and thought of floating off to sleep on the river. The Boyne sparkled in the sun like a diamond necklace. He closed his eyes and heard the birds sing, a sound he had not heard since early morning. How he had missed it. He saw Meinhard sitting on his horse, bored and frustrated but safe. That was good news indeed.

Feeling a gentle breeze on his face, he gradually became curious about his surroundings. So he opened his eyes, bid the Reverend Walker a good day and found himself walking in a meadow where his hands were caressed by the tall grass and his mind was soothed by the sight of pink roses and wild blue hyacinth. He laughed out loud. 'When did I ever look at flowers?'

It was only when he saw his wife waiting for him beneath their favourite tree that he realised where he was … and why.

'Keep it quiet!' was William's response when he was told how the duke had been felled by two sabre cuts to his neck and a bullet to the back of his head.

When he was told that the former governor of Derry, the Reverend George Walker, was also dead, from a bullet to the stomach, William only muttered, 'That fool had no business being on a battlefield!'

CHAPTER TWENTY-FIVE

Looking after Reverend Walker

Daniel was appalled at the sight of Reverend Walker sliding from his horse into the water. Unused to such circumstances, the horse continued on without its rider. *No, no, this was not meant to happen. We have not begun to fight back. The battle hasn't started yet.*

He screamed at his brother's back, 'Robert! Robert!'

But Robert was too distracted to hear him. Bullets stabbed the river around him, a deadly downpour, and the noise was like a heavy blanket wrapped around his head.

He might not be dead; I might be able to help him! These were the thoughts that pushed Daniel to break out of his line and commence kicking the river out of his path as he headed towards the reverend who – it must be said – appeared to be sleeping soundly, aside from the blood that poured from his stomach and formed a reddish cloud in the water.

There was too much going on and Daniel felt enormous relief to be able to concentrate on this one thing. His arms were already complaining at holding his heavy rifle over his head, but he was adamant he would not lower it. That was the number one golden rule as explained to him by Henry and Robert. The river must not, under any circumstances, be allowed near their weapons.

The water sloshed up and he swallowed a mouthful, choking on it as he considered it was diluted by Williamite blood. The reverend wasn't the first man down; Daniel had seen plenty fall in the last few minutes, but he knew the reverend and had depended on the churchman, amongst others, to get his family and city through the siege. Daniel felt it was only his duty, as a native of Derry, to tend to his leader now.

He dearly wished his father was beside him but then scorned such a ridiculous thought as to desire to have his father here in what surely was the most dangerous place to be in the whole of Ireland.

'Reverend Walker! Sir, I'm coming!'

Shouting helped to release the tension in his jaw. He thought that he must have bitten his tongue or maybe it was the inside of his mouth. He could taste blood and it was all he could smell too.

Finally he reached the reverend and saw that the man's eyes were open. Daniel tugged at him. 'Sir? It's Daniel Sherrard!'

The clergyman did not stir. Daniel was reluctantly reminded of the last time he saw his friend James on the walls of Derry. He too had stared like that, obliging Daniel to close his eyes for him.

'Reverend Walker, it's Daniel Sherrard!'

Ignoring the obvious, Daniel pulled at the reverend's collar to loosen it and gingerly lifted back his jacket, wanting to see the wound. There was a sudden sharp pull at the body and Daniel realised that a second bullet had penetrated the reverend, this time in the hip.

Daniel could no longer deny the truth. He looked around him in horror, not knowing what to do. Why couldn't the reverend just wake up for a moment to give him some guidance? Out of sheer desperation he tried shouting in the dead man's ear, 'Please, I beg you, sir, what should I do? I can't leave you here and you won't help me.'

He was suddenly thumped in his side and turned to find his brother shouting at him as if he had gone quite mad, 'What the hell are you doing? You fool! Get out of the river! NOW!'

Daniel was stunned. He had never seen such fury in

Robert's face and wouldn't have believed it was possible that his brother could speak to him like this. Feebly, he pointed to the man beside them. 'We can't leave him here!'

'He's dead! Dead! Don't you get it? Come on!'

'I KNOW he's dead!' It was all that Daniel could think to say.

Robert gave him a dreadful look as he declared, 'I will not look after you!'

His expression was a mixture of anguish and fear, but it was easier to be angry so he added, 'You should've stayed at home!'

Daniel felt he had been smacked in the mouth. Only this time it wasn't by Henry Campsie but by his own brother who had never ever hurt him, even when they were children.

'Did you hear me? I wish you had stayed in Derry!' It wasn't enough for Robert to shout it once – oh, no – he had to shout it a second time.

Daniel felt his knees sag and bumped up against the reverend. He turned away from Robert because he couldn't bear such anger. Using one hand to keep his musket aloft, he seized hold of the body, his decision made.

Robert screamed, 'What are you doing? Get back in your line!'

'No!' shouted Daniel. 'I'm bringing the reverend back to our shore.'

When Robert looked fit to burst, Daniel added, 'He'd want me to, you know he would.'

As much as Robert wanted to argue with this he couldn't. Yes, of course, the last thing Reverend Walker would want would be for his body to be abandoned as if it were nothing more than a piece of dry wood.

But they were meant to be advancing on the Jacobites with the rest of their comrades. Surely the reverend would not wish to prevent them from carrying out their duty?

Robert struggled to pinpoint his decision while assailed by a hundred thoughts and, perhaps, the same amount of bullets.

'Damn you!' he yelled at Daniel.

If it wasn't for his brother, he'd be up on the Oldbridge bank simply fighting for his life and king, without having to deal with complicated matters like this.

Robert then went back on his word, not to mind his sibling, as he shouted, 'All right, take him across but I need you back here as fast as you can!'

Daniel nodded. 'I'll be a few minutes.'

Had such an ordinary sentence ever been uttered before in such extraordinary circumstances?

Robert focused on finding his fellow soldiers. He was

sure that Henry would rebuke him for releasing Daniel however temporarily, but there was no time to think about that. Then he saw something which perhaps confirmed that he had, after all, made the right decision. There, not twenty feet away from him, was the lifeless figure of the Duke of Schomberg, draped over his horse's back, the reins in the hands of a Dutch guard who obviously shared Daniel's sense of propriety that a fallen leader should be retrieved immediately and removed from further harm. The guard pulled the horse back into the Boyne, preparing to cross it once more.

William had lost two great leaders one after the other. Robert shivered as if a freezing pebble had skimmed the back of his sweating neck. Of course he had heard all about the duke's gallant career, but then had been shocked when he finally set eyes upon the famous general to see a frail, old man weighed down by his uniform.

An elderly man and a stubborn clergyman: Robert wondered if perhaps their deaths were inevitable today.

Wait! He had an idea. Surely the Dutchman could not refuse to take Reverend Walker's body too? That made sense didn't it, seeing how they were both headed back to camp. Robert worried that he was only trying to keep Daniel safe, and out of the battle, in allowing him to return the reverend to the right side of the Boyne. Well, his new solution would disprove that notion.

'Hi! Hi!' He shouted at the guard, wishing he had learned 'Stop' in Dutch.

Of course the man could not hear him. Robert's voice was one of thousands at that precise moment.

So he turned to call his brother who was somewhat nearer. 'Daniel! See there!'

Diligently keeping his gun above him, Daniel was dragging on Reverend Walker's neck, losing the battle to keep the clergyman's head out of the water. Nevertheless, he reasoned that it was more important to reach the opposite bank than to try to keep the dead man's hair from getting wet.

He hadn't bargained on such a heavy load. Certainly the reverend was not slim, but Daniel had not expected to feel like he was pulling a large, live animal that wished to go elsewhere. Several times he had had to make a grab for the body as it threatened to float back to the Jacobites. Daniel began to panic at how much time he was losing. Robert might well think he was using the reverend to miss out on the fighting. *Oh God,* he suddenly thought, *maybe I am?* How he wished the reverend would open his eyes and tell him what to do.

'D-a-n-i-e-l!'

He just about heard the familiar shout and looked over

his shoulder. Roger was gesturing frantically to his left ... wait, Daniel's right. His brother shouted something, but Daniel couldn't catch it and was too distracted to decipher the shapes his brother's mouth was forming.

'What?' he shouted in exasperation. 'What is it?'

He scanned the scene to his right and finally guessed what his brother meant. If he'd had time, he would have been dismayed by the death of the grand old duke, but he was only relieved to have understood what Robert wished him to do.

'Reverend, I have to put you on the duke's horse!'

Daniel felt reassured by the sound of his voice and so he added, 'I hope you don't mind.'

He hailed the Dutch soldier who was in the distance, urging the horse to keep up with him, 'Hallo! Hallo!'

'You see,' he explained rather proudly to his silent companion, '"hallo" is Dutch for "hello"!'

He saw the guard glance across at him, and Daniel did his best to raise the reverend's head so that the guard might recognise him as the leader of the Derry battalion. Daniel shouted, 'Will you take him too?'

The guard did not look the slightest bit interested in whatever Daniel was asking, only knowing that the boy was talking English, a language he did not understand.

Daniel felt obliged to make a promise. 'Don't worry, sir, if he refuses I'll take you back anyway!'

And he would have, of that we can be sure, only for the musket ball that forced him to let go of the clergyman and briefly watch him drift off without protest.

Daniel thought Robert had thumped him again, but this time in the back of his neck. Having freed his arm from Revered Walker, he lifted it towards his head, wanting to protect himself from another blow, but his arm failed him and, instead, led him face down into the water so that he could witness his precious musket plunge towards the river-bed. James would be so mad at him for losing it. No, no, he didn't mean James. James was dead. He had starved to death in Derry. No, he meant Robert, his brother.

How was it possible that his hands were completely empty when moments ago he had staggered beneath their weight? Daniel felt lost even though he knew exactly where he was.

Sounds were dreadfully muffled and the cold water beneath the surface stunned him. A sudden shadow blocked the light as he vaguely felt himself pulled upwards again.

'Daniel! Daniel!'

Ah, it was only Robert. Daniel wished he would let him sleep; he felt overcome with drowsiness and shut his eyes.

'NO! NO! Wake up!'

Daniel could not see the terror in his brother's face nor

could he hear the grief in his brother's cries. He just wanted to be left where he was. That was all.

He dipped his head only to have Robert clutch his chin out of the water. Daniel marvelled at how the sunlight broke in and around his brother's face and enjoyed the motion of the water's current, which rocked him gently as his brother held him close. Robert sounded so very far away, but Daniel didn't mind. He only felt love and beloved. The Boyne held him in a warm embrace and there was Robert right beside him, his tears washing away the grime and the dust.

And there were those glorious walls that had kept them all safe last year. Daniel lazily counted the bricks and reached out to touch them, thrilled to find they were still warm from the sun. The bell in Saint Columb's Cathedral rang out while Horace barked in delight and Daniel sighed in contentment. He was home at last.

CHAPTER TWENTY-SIX

The Kings of the Boyne

When he felt ready, James decided that he might as well get on the road for Dublin. *At least I can tell Louis that I tried but it just wasn't meant to be.*

He summoned Lauzun to him and displayed not one wit of emotion as he said, 'We will head for Dublin. Gather the men together.'

Lauzun was aghast, but just for a moment. Briefly he wondered how the rest of the army was coping without them at Oldbridge. Of course he was anxious about the cavalry but, like James, he promptly decided to concentrate on what he could control, thinking to himself, *surely I cannot be expected to get everyone back safely to France. Won't it be enough to get James back in one piece, along with the cannon and most of our infantry?*

He swung his horse around and began to issue orders as

loudly as he could, pretending not to see the relief on the faces of his fellow countrymen.

Thank God, we are going home!

Back in Oldbridge, Michael found Joseph crying in the trench. His trousers were sodden with urine and he was on his knees praying, his head continually nodding, like the pendulum of a large clock, with his knife lying uselessly on the ground beside him.

'Joseph! What are you doing? Come on!'

Joseph was ashamed but stubborn. 'No, I can't. I'm not like you. I didn't know it was going to be like this.'

'Nobody did! Do you think I've done anything like this before? Get out of the trench before anyone sees you.'

'I saw the old woman, Michael. I know who she was. She smiled at me.'

Michael was mystified. 'What old woman? Who are you talking about? There are no women here, only soldiers.'

Joseph scowled. 'I recognised her. She was standing in the river washing the shirts of those about to die. They were white shirts but covered in blood. She smiled at me, Michael. Do you know what that means?'

Shaking his head, Michael protested, 'You imagined her, Joseph. The banshee is just a legend, a myth, she's not real.

She's for telling stories around the campfire late at night, that's all. Please come on out of there like a good fellow.'

'Are we winning?' Joseph silently begged his friend to lie to him and Michael willingly complied.

'Yes. Of course we are! The cavalry are tearing them to shreds. I even saw Gerald and Jacques; they waved at me and asked for you.'

Joseph looked at him wide-eyed. 'Did they really?'

'Yes. They wanted to know if we'd go to the tavern after-wards. I told them that I'd have to check with you first.'

'Oh, yes, Michael. I think I'd like to do that. Can we go now?'

Michael never flinched. 'I can't go right now, Joseph. We … I have a few things to do. But perhaps you could help me and then we'll go.'

'Do you promise?'

'Yes, Joseph. I promise. Now come on, give me your hand and I'll pull you out.'

'All right, Michael. Thank you.'

Gerald and Jacques had made several runs at the Dutch guards now. Each time they had killed and each time they had managed to exit the fray and drive their horses back up the hill to reload their pistols. From their vantage point it was impossible to deceive themselves. The Jacobite position was growing more precarious. They saw the fresh enemy battalions being led down to begin crossing the Boyne and, still, there was William with his cavalry who had yet to make a move.

'We can't give up!' Gerald's statement sounded like a challenge.

Jacques' teeth shone like bright stars out of the mishmash of grime, sweat and blood on his face as he reassured Gerald, 'I'm not giving up!'

Gerald admitted, 'I'm not sure how much longer we can hold them off.'

His friend shrugged. 'If they would just stay in the river, we could shoot them down, one after the other.'

Their guns reloaded, they spurred Troy and Paris back down the hill. The battle was still raging away. Their commander, Richard Talbot, had also noticed the new arrivals and was splitting up the cavalry, sending riders down to prevent the Prussians, the Finns – or whoever they were this time – from getting out of the river.

Jacques and Gerald found themselves amongst those who were being directed down to confront the new group. The horses became preoccupied with not stepping on the bodies of the dead and wounded. Gerald trusted Troy to find his own path through the confusion. If he had had the time, he might have marvelled at his own transformation. This battle had brought out the soldier in him and it seemed that he had spent his entire life on horseback fighting an enemy army. The boy he once was had gone and, in his place, a warrior had been born. After all, he was his mother's son and an O'Connor. This was, he supposed, what people meant when they said that something was in their blood.

They reached the spot and began to fire at the soldiers in the river who were bitterly struggling with the water itself. The tide had risen and the waters were flowing rapidly once more. Really, they had been mighty brave in just stepping into the Boyne, whose temperament had continued to worsen since that first crossing.

Gerald took no pleasure from aiming his gun at fellows who barely kept their heads out of the water. In fact, those Williamites were lucky, though they were too scared to realise it. The water that threatened to drown them made it just about impossible to get a clean shot at them. One man was screaming the same line over and over again.

Gerald asked Jacques, 'What is he saying?'

Jacques took a guess. 'I can't swim?'

And just like that, the warrior was gone, and the boy in Gerald returned. 'Shouldn't we do something?'

Jacques was puzzled. 'What do you mean?'

'It doesn't seem right to let him drown. I can't kill a drowning man.'

'*Mon Dieu!* You want to save him and then kill him, yes?'

Gerald refused to answer such a question.

His friend shook his head. 'This is no time to develop a conscience. You know the saying: "All is fair in love and war"? Well, this is what it means.'

The man continued to scream, and two of his comrades tried to reach for him, but they found themselves being pulled under as he frantically latched onto their arms in order to keep himself steady. They were obliged to shrug him off, leaving him splashing and swallowing pints of river water.

'But he's not even English. He probably would have hated Oliver Cromwell!'

The Frenchman was incredulous. 'What in God's name are you talking about? He's not English? What has that got to do with anything? We're the ones fighting for the Englishman!'

Gerald was confused again. 'None of this makes sense!'

'This is war, Gerald, and it doesn't have to make any sense at all.'

Michael was in a bit of a quandary. Joseph would not

leave his side and Joseph was in no state to fight. The cavalry was stretched to breaking point and any available infantrymen were obliged to get stuck in and help them. He considered trying to lose his young friend in the smoke and the commotion. However, much to his surprise, he discovered that he could not wilfully abandon this boy who continued to tremble and cry. It was uncanny. *Trust me to wait until I'm in the middle of a battle to discover that I do have a heart.*

'I want to go the tavern now, Michael. You promised we could go.'

The sounds of Jacobite soldiers being shot and stabbed about twenty feet away from where they stood was making Michael desperate. Then he had an idea: 'Joseph, I need you to do something for me and then we can go to the tavern.'

Joseph seemed not to hear anything but Michael's voice. He nodded his head like an obedient child. 'What is it?'

Michael thought quickly. 'Em … I need you to go back to our tent and get me some bread. I meant to bring it with me but I forgot and I'm starving now.'

This seemed perfectly reasonable to Joseph, who smiled his usual smile. 'I'll get it for you. I'm hungry too so I'll fetch enough for both of us.'

He turned to go, adding, 'Hey, I'll get some for Gerald and Jacques. We should all eat before we go to the tavern.'

Michael nodded frantically. 'That's a good idea. Do you

have your knife with you? Keep it in your hand, won't you ... you know ... just in case you need to cut the bread ... or something.'

Joseph looked at him and said, 'I'll be all right, Michael. Don't worry.'

Not wanting to watch the boy leave, Michael turned away and tried to find relief in finally being alone again.

Back to work! He flung himself into the nearest group of soldiers and began slicing at them with his scythe, careful to stay out of the way of the horses that were biting and kicking any man that stood too near them, not caring what uniform he was wearing.

This is not going well, he thought. *We cannot hold out for much longer!*

Up on the ridge the Jacobite commander, Richard Talbot, kept expecting to see King James returned with the rest of the army. *Where is he? God knows we could do with the French infantry, not to mention their cannon.* Even so he had been thoroughly surprised by the men. He would never have imagined that the Irish infantry would have shown such courage, or that the cavalry would ignore the far superior numbers of the enemy and continue to give it their all, as if they actually believed that they might win. *Such a pity*

that the king is not here to see them. Talbot sighed and then it occurred to him, *perhaps it is time to stop calling him king.* But maybe he was being premature, maybe they could still win through some miracle of God.

And if we did win, thought Talbot, as he gazed upon his ragamuffin army, *it is all of them who should be called king. Not James cowardly Stuart.*

CHAPTER TWENTY-SEVEN

A King's Letter

Mrs Watson had not gone very far at all. She had decided against making an immediate start to her journey home. Actually it was Daniel who had advised her to wait until the morning. On reaching the horses' pen, she had peered at the sky, trying to determine how much light there was left to the evening.

Daniel could not believe that she was thinking of leaving that very moment. He asked if it would be better to wait until morning, but the widow shook her head and replied, 'I need to get back to the children. Marian must be desperate for me.'

He knew she would say that but he persisted, 'Ma'am, your face is so pale and you are trembling.'

She was exhausted, that much was true. Also, she was only fully realising how near she had come to being arrested, or worse. Her throat felt like she had swallowed a jagged rock, while her limbs felt heavy and swollen. She smiled at the boy and confessed, 'I don't think I've slept more than a few hours since leaving home. I'm too worried about them.'

'But they're fine.'

She looked at him in confusion while he blushed, finally admitting, 'Em, I saw them after you left. I went looking for you and Marian let me in.'

'Why were you looking for me?'

Daniel sighed. 'When Robert and I returned to camp with your horses, his friend – Henry, you just met him – convinced us, I mean, Robert, that you were actually a Jacobite soldier in disguise.'

She stared at him.

He rushed on. 'They wanted to go and search your house right there and then, but I didn't want them upsetting the children so I said that I'd go and spy on you.'

He shrugged his innocence and hers.

'I told them that I had seen you and that you were definitely a woman.'

She didn't thank him, only asking quickly, 'How were they?'

'They were fine. Really. Well, Samuel was a bit put out that you wouldn't take him with you.'

Here, she smiled sadly.

Wanting to reassure her, Daniel said, 'But Marian had them all in hand, sitting at the dinner table, waiting to be fed.'

Of course Daniel could not resist mentioning his contribution. 'I fed the baby, you know, mashed up his potato in milk, just as he likes.'

In spite of herself Mrs Watson burst out laughing. 'And did he leave his mark on you?'

Daniel smirked. 'I can still smell it on my trousers!'

They suddenly felt self-conscious about their surroundings, their voices sounded too loud, too free.

'So, tomorrow you fight?'

Daniel nodded; his smile withering as he was reminded where he was and why.

Her heart lurched and she wondered how old he was ... and what he was doing here at all. She felt a sudden urge to insist he come with her. Why, she could tell him she needed help with the horses. After all, the ten she had recognised, which belonged to her neighbours, were burden enough on top of her own two.

Bess and Star had whinnied their relief on seeing her again, nuzzling her, toppling her hat to the ground. How grateful she was to King William. If he had refused her request, it would have been too awful to contemplate.

Daniel tried to make her see sense. 'Do you really want

to be travelling in the dark with horses? Surely you will be vulnerable to wolves, or whatever else is out there at night-time?'

She struggled to be practical, but it was difficult when she wanted so much to be walking through her front door as soon as possible. Then she thought of something daft, but it was enough to convince her to stay put. She announced, 'All right, I will wait until tomorrow. And then if the battle proves to be a short one, you might help me bring these horses home.'

They had shook hands on it, Daniel grinning as he realised he'd probably have to sneak off on Robert to help her, but it would be worth it.

'See you afterwards, then!'

To her surprise, Mrs Watson had managed to sleep. Knowing that she was going home and bringing Bess and Star with her, that her children would not starve and that she would not lose their home gave her the best night's sleep that she had had in some time.

Who knows how long she would have slept on if it hadn't been for those boisterous cannons firing on Old-bridge, announcing that the battle had begun?

It was so much louder than she had expected it to be, and the horses were nervous and jumpy. She held on, just in case. She found a safe spot for the horses, fearing that some wanton soldier would take them. There, she had tied them together and breakfasted on bread and apple, too excited to eat but needing to pass the time in the hope that the battle would finish up quickly.

She wished she had learned to read. She had forgotten all about King William's letter until she saw it in her bag. Smoothing out the crumpled, folded sheet, she could only stare at the waxed seal in wonder. What would the children say? Thinking about them made her fiercely impatient to leave.

How much time had passed and how much longer should she wait? Her conscience wrestled with her heart: *I shook Daniel's hand which is as good as promising him that I'd be here when he finished. But he knows I have to get back.*

She waited some more, distracting herself by brushing down the horses with an old hairbrush that she used for Bess and Star. She hoped it might help to calm them against the sounds that carried up from the Boyne. She had not expected to hear men scream out in pain but there it was, humans being torn apart by bullets and swords. She could hear it all.

Then it occurred to her that she was in a dangerous place if William lost. What if she was listening to the Williamites being overrun and then pursued by raging Jacobites?

I can't endanger myself, risking orphaning my own children. I can't do that!

'Right!' she said out loud.

She'd ride Star to the edge of the camp, or as near to the edge as she dared, to see if she could gauge the situation below. She'd do this for the boy that had helped her so much but no more. When all was said and done, her own children had to come first.

There were soldiers everywhere, but they didn't pay her any heed. They marched in formation over the top of the hill and down towards the river. Mrs Watson had never seen so many soldiers in her life. The drums beat out a reassuring rhythm while she looked on, finding herself mightily impressed.

He saw her first, recognising the tall figure beneath that same floppy hat, atop the horse that was familiar to him. Inwardly, he thanked God for answering his hasty prayer and finding her; outwardly, he swallowed up tears, cleared his congested throat and shouted rather shakily, 'MRS WATSON! Over here!'

'Oh, thank goodness!' she muttered in relief. 'It's Daniel already.'

She pulled her hat forward to tilt the brim against the blazing sun.

And then she saw them, Robert carrying his brother in his arms, the large blood-dark patch on his tunic where Daniel's head rested against his shoulder.

Jumping down from Star, Mrs Watson ran as fast as she could. Robert stood and waited, having run out of strength to carry Daniel any further. His face told her all she need to know. Daniel stared, without seeing, at the blue sky above them. Robert allowed her to gently close his brother's eyes, and then she hesitated, unsure what was expected of her.

'I have to get back!' He spoke roughly as if expecting her to challenge him in some way. When she didn't, he relaxed a little even as he tightened his hold on Daniel, pressing the body ever closer to him. Robert was appalled to witness this silent, lifeless thing that used to be his brother. He still expected him to wake up and complain royally about being carried, being hugged and being here. It was too soon to accept his death, too soon to mourn him.

'He didn't even get to fight.'

Mrs Watson looked puzzled. 'What do you mean?'

Robert closed his own eyes for a moment, to steady himself, and replied, 'We were still in the river. Reverend Walker was killed, and Daniel wanted to get the body back to the safety of camp.'

Robert added once more, 'We were just in the river.'

Mrs Watson nodded briefly and asked, 'Where are you bringing him?'

'To you.'

She said nothing to this.

'Would you take him?' He had not considered that she'd refuse him.

'You've got horses ... and you knew him ... a little. He trusted you.'

He gestured towards the Boyne to explain, 'I can't do anything, I have to go back.'

Her silence prodded his guilt and, feeling criticised, he snapped, 'I suppose you think I should take him back to Derry, to our parents. Sure, why not! I should be a good son and dutiful brother. I mean if this was a storybook, I'd return to my father's house and be the son he was to them, to make up for his loss. A nice happy ending!'

His tone and tears were bitter and he looked away from her, dreading that she would agree with his words. Because if she did, then he really wasn't sure what he'd do. How long had it taken to carry Daniel's body from the middle of the Boyne to this spot while every step felt like another slap in his face delivered by his parents, by Daniel and, most of all, by himself?

She sighed. 'I can't take him back to Derry either. Is that what you're asking me?'

He shook his head, almost disappointed that she didn't tell him what to do.

'Do you want to put him down on the ground? You'll tire yourself out.'

Well, at least he was allowed to do that. She helped him stretch Daniel out on the grass between them.

King William's letter fluttered out of her pocket, landing on Daniel's chest. What a jolt it was to see that familiar handwriting. Robert gasped in confusion but then remembered aloud, 'Daniel gave His Majesty his letter to write on the back of it.'

The widow picked it up and turned it over, shyly admitting, 'I can't read so ...'

She handed it to him. 'You keep it; send it on to your parents if you like.'

He scanned it quickly, just a few sentences describing the upset amongst the soldiers when it was believed that William had been killed.

'No,' said Robert. 'There's nothing in it for them. But thank you anyway; it was kind to offer.'

She shrugged.

'Besides,' he added, 'surely you want to keep a letter from the king?'

She watched him run his finger over the red wax that sealed the letter and surprised them both by asking, 'Will you read it to me? It was only a few lines as I remember.'

He looked towards the Boyne again.

'Just a few lines,' she repeated. 'I feel foolish carrying it and not knowing what it says. I had planned to ask Daniel ...'

He snapped the seal and unfolded the note, for that was all it was, and read:

> As a reward for perseverance and bravery, I hereby confirm, assign and make over onto Jean Watson, widow, and her heirs male forever, free of rent, all that parcel of land she now holds in Killaughey, the parish of Donaghadee, be the same more or less.
>
> Signed:
>
> King William, July 1690

'Oh my goodness,' said Robert. 'Do you know what this means?'

Mrs Watson covered her mouth with her hand, trying to hide her smile. 'I own the farm?'

'Forevermore,' said Robert, looking pleased for her in spite of everything.

She gazed at Daniel for a moment or two, letting the news sink in. Robert gave her back the letter and waited. Taking a deep breath, she decided to make a promise. 'I'll take Daniel home with me. Now that I own the land ... well, I'll see to it that he gets a proper burial.'

Robert was both relieved and horrified because now that he had, once more, taken care of his younger brother, it was time to say goodbye to him.

CHAPTER TWENTY-EIGHT

Crossing the Boyne

It might be an exaggeration to describe William as being in awe of the Jacobite resistance, but he was certainly astonished at their show of force.

The Boyne, he could plainly see, was causing extreme difficulties for his men that were still engaged in trying to cross it. He could hear their cries and watched helplessly as one man was carried away by the rising tide, his body becoming still and gradually turning over, as if he had suddenly decided to study the riverbed. Meanwhile, whoever wasn't drowning or fighting to breathe was being shot at by the Jacobite cavalry who had nothing else to do except wait for their approach. It made for painful viewing.

At last, it was time to summon the final battalion, the Danish cavalry, and lead them into the river. It was not going to be easy but he had no choice. *I cannot be seen to lack in courage or belief in my own victory.*

He studied the river and saw it was perilously deep. The water flowed steadily and calmly, as if pretending to the observer that it was not a killer. King William pressed his lips together and continued with the conversation in his head: *Louis built his palace on bog land to show how he can lord it over nature. How I should like to see him take on this river. He'd lose his nerve soon enough*

But what if he drowned? That was not a glorious death and, in any case, he did not come here to die.

How Mary would rage if she could see me now.

He had promised his wife he would not take any undue risks and now look at him. The trumpet sounded out and he directed his horse downstream, to make a crossing at some distance from the last one.

Never had the river seemed so wide to him. He would have liked to pick up a rock and fling it into the middle to see how deep it was, but he did not want to intimidate his men any more than they were already. So he simply dug his spurs into the sides of his horse, prompting her to walk in. *That's the wonderful thing about horses*, he thought. *Once they trust you they will allow you to walk them anywhere. Poor devils! But maybe they are better off. They know nothing about dying.*

Within a few short feet, the water reached his knees. It was cold even on such a sunny afternoon as this. Time had marched on and the hours were adding up. The mare kept her head out of the water as she grunted with the effort of walking against the flow of the Boyne. She shucked her head in frustration, wondering why she could not move at her own speed. Behind her, her fellow horses were experiencing the same confusion. Their riders strained to keep pushing them forward, while some felt it would be easier on the animals if they dismounted and allowed the horse to swim, if it had to, while they hung onto the reins.

With growing alarm William understood that he was in serious trouble. He could not swim so there was no way he would dismount, but his horse was almost at a standstill thanks to the strength of the river. He kicked her sides to keep her moving. Without realising it, he was using his entire body to urge her forward, while trying to resist the current himself. After a few seconds, he was out of breath. A few seconds more and his breathing grew ragged until he could only wheeze. Now his chest ached because his heart was beating so fast and he recognised that his overworked lungs were under attack … in the middle of the River Boyne. *Please, please God, no. I beg you. Don't let me die like this.* Sprawled over his horse's neck, he panicked that he might lose consciousness, slip into the water and end up drowning anyway.

There was a buzzing in his ears and the afternoon light

was growing dim. His chin was so close to the water that he could have wetted it without having to move. All he could think about was breathing – such a simple act that most of us never question. He needed to sit up to make it easier to catch his breath, but his exhausted body refused to obey him.

He only became aware that there was a man by his side when he felt himself being dragged from his horse; he was past caring whether he was friend or foe, although, to be sure, it was a relief when he heard a thick accent declare, 'Don't you worry, Your Majesty. I'll have you out in a wee bit.'

William didn't know what a 'wee bit' was, but he didn't let that bother him. The man, or giant that he was, was using the horse to block the might of the river while carrying his king in reasonable comfort to safety. Goodness only knows how many minutes were involved until his saviour got him and his horse to the southern bank of the Boyne. William was in too much of a daze to thank his saviour, only managing to wheeze out a few words, 'Wh ... who are you?'

'Samuel McGregor from Enniskillen. Just rest yourself there, Majesty. I need to go and help some of the other lads.'

And off the giant strode, back into the river.

It took some time but the Danish cavalry were finally

across. The water spilled from them and their horses as they nervously checked that their gunpowder and muskets had remained untouched.

William's breath was returning to normal and he told the men to be ready to fight. How relieved he was that the Boyne was finally behind him. *My God, I did it!*

He fully expected a Jacobite attack of some description, but it didn't happen. As soon as he could, he got back on his horse, a sign that every single soldier was to get on theirs. The battalion was two thousand strong and he prepared to lead them upstream to reinforce the others.

'Be on your guard,' he instructed the men nearest to him. 'We could be ambushed at any time!'

He looked around in vain for Samuel McGregor. *He did exist, didn't he?*

No matter. They had to press on.

And then they heard it, the Jacobite trumpet blasting out the notes to retreat.

'Follow me!' William roared as his horse leapt forward, glad to have her four feet back on dry land.

CHAPTER TWENTY-NINE

Retreat!

'Jacques, look!' yelled Gerald. 'William's cavalry! They're going to cross farther downstream!'

Jacques scanned the bank behind them and could see no spare men to deal with yet another crossing. They were barely coping as it was and that was no mean battalion over there, it looked to be another couple of thousand men who had not been in combat for hours and, therefore, were fighting fit.

Jacques searched the sky for inspiration but got no further than thinking the obvious: *there are too many!*

Turning to Gerald, he said, 'Go back to Oldbridge and tell them. Go on, now!'

Gerald dug his feet into Troy and they took off. Oldbridge was only a mile or so away; maybe Talbot had already noticed that William was preparing to cross. A shot rang out, but Gerald took no notice; it was only one of thousands he had heard that day. He was certainly not expecting a sudden reaction from Troy who stumbled, pitching forward onto his forelegs while his hind legs were still in motion. The poor animal made a most dreadful noise, like a baby strangled by whooping cough. Gerald slid off him and saw a gash in the middle of Troy's chest. As Troy gulped for air, blood pumped out of him. Overcome by terror, Gerald merely stared. The horse rocked his head from side to side, trying to shake off the pain and the blindness which was surely falling.

'I don't know what to do. I don't know what to do!'

Who was he talking to ... poor Troy himself?

The animal was in agony. It was unbearable to watch, and yet Gerald could not move.

A shadow appeared behind him and a second shot was fired but this time from a different rifle. The horse ceased resisting and slumped forward in silence. Gerald turned to find Michael standing there with a musket in his hand and looking mortified at what he had done.

'I had to, didn't I? He was dying and it was the only merciful thing to do.'

Stunned, Gerald walked up to the body.

Michael followed him, saying, 'It isn't safe here. We've got to get moving.'

Gerald got down on his knees and patted Troy's neck.

'Where's Jacques?' asked Michael, keeping a look out for Williamites.

'Back there' was the dull response.

'All right. Let's go and get him, shall we? Where are your weapons? You'll need to take those along.'

Michael leant over Troy to reach for the sword and the musket that had been dropped to the ground. 'There you go. Is there anything else you need?'

Gerald shook his head. 'I just stood there and did nothing, like I always do.'

He looked up at Michael. 'I could see he was in pain and I didn't do anything. I should have shot him but I was too afraid.'

Michael shrugged. 'Of course I could do it. He wasn't mine, was he? I didn't know him which made it easier. Look, he's at peace now, but we're not. We need to get out of here.'

And then they both heard it, the trumpet signalling retreat.

In the next moment, they were part of a huge crowd of battered-looking Jacobites that were on the move. 'Come on!' yelled someone. 'Head for the Hill of Donore. We can make a stand there!'

'They're right behind us. Get going!'

That was enough for Michael. He put his hands under Gerald's shoulders and dragged him upwards. 'Right, you're coming with me. If you want, we can come back later for the funeral, but right now I need you to run like you've never run before!'

And with that, he pushed Gerald in front of him and then pushed him again and then again until Gerald snapped out of his daze and broke into a jog.

Michael gushed, 'That's the spirit, lad! Keep going until we reach the Hill of Donore.'

Those tired Jacobites had quite a run ahead of them. The hill was about two miles away, but if they managed to reach it, the ruin of the church and its wall would afford them some shelter. They had been fighting for hours now, but if the two miles enabled them to stay alive then it would be worth it.

Michael felt that his heart was bursting out of his chest, while his scythe and stolen musket had never felt so heavy. He did his best to keep up with the boy and had to fight the temptation to stop and take off his red coat … and his boots, if it came to it. He'd much rather be running in his bare feet.

The way to the hill lay through a forest and the redcoats disappeared into it, shooting off in all directions. All the while they could hear the triumphant shouts of the Williamites that were not too far behind them. Michael simply followed Gerald since there was no time to stop and debate the direction they should take. Surely, all that was required was to keep heading south.

As he ran, he repeated their destination to himself: *The Hill of Donore. The Hill of Donore.* In between that, he admonished himself against thinking of anything else. Yes, it was best not to dwell on the perilous fact that they were now being chased by all those thousands upon thousands of Williamites and there was no longer a river between them. What would happen if they were caught?

He was concentrating so hard that he smashed right into Gerald and then was quickly obliged to grab the boy to stop him from falling into a clump of thorny bushes below them. Without realising it, they had run up some sort of mound or slope and there was no way down that did not involve a wild jump that might well break one or both legs before those thorns ripped them to shreds.

Because they were forced to stop running, they suddenly realised that they were in quite a state. Michael said nothing when Gerald collapsed to the ground pleading, 'Just for a minute. Just let me get my breath back.'

Michael nodded and flopped down beside him, dropping his weapons to wipe his clammy hands against his now filthy coat. He would have to wait until the blood stopped roaring in his ears to judge how close or far away the Williamites were. He had lost his bearings, but it would be a minute or two before he could care about that. Gerald looked so miserable that Michael was prompted to say, 'If it's all right with you and Jacques, I promised Joseph that we'd go to the tavern later.'

Gerald looked at him in bewilderment until Michael winked at him and then, in spite of everything, Gerald dissolved into laughter, shoving the cuff of his coat into his mouth to stop himself from making any noise.

Until then, Michael had all but forgotten about Joseph and was suddenly so overwhelmed with guilt that he could not tell Gerald about sending the boy back to the tents. He put a finger to his lips for silence, and they both listened. There is something magical about a forest, where crowds of people can be swallowed up out of sight, while sounds are magnified but hard to pinpoint exactly where they are coming from.

Gerald could feel his heart thudding against his chest. He strained to decipher the shouts in the distance, wondering where Jacques was. *Will he find Troy's body and be angry with me?*

At least, thought Michael, *the Williamite cavalry can't come in here, the forest is too overgrown for horses*. However, they could not stay here. He whispered to Gerald, 'We need to get going if we're to make it to Donore in time.'

'In time for what?' asked Gerald.

'You heard them. We're making a stand there.'

Just then, they heard a rustle coming from somewhere behind them or was it in front of them? They froze and waited to hear something else and were in no way prepared for the giant shadow that silently swooped just over their heads. Gerald clamped his mouth shut to stifle his scream. It was a hawk and appeared to have vanished in an instant. Michael blessed himself, not caring if it made him look weak in front of the boy.

Gerald shrugged. 'At least it wasn't a raven. For a moment I thought it was the banshee.'

His companion groaned. 'Oh, not you too. Joseph was blathering on about seeing an old woman washing blood-stained shirts in the river. I mean, for God's sake!'

Gerald blessed himself, and Michael wished he could swallow back his words. The forest was spooking him too; it was like the foliage was reaching for them and he feared that if they did not leave now they would never be allowed to. He stood up and asked Gerald, 'Well, are you coming?'

The boy only nodded.

How loud their footsteps sounded, as they made their way back down to solid ground. Sunlight pierced the tiniest of cracks in between the trees and Gerald remembered

Father Nicholas telling him that he felt nearer to God in a forest that he did anywhere else. However, this forest was full of Williamites and neither Gerald nor Michael could allow themselves to forget that.

They crept along, wincing at dry twigs that snapped beneath their feet and untangling themselves from branches that snagged their clothes. Michael led the way, while Gerald fought against imagining that he could hear lots of worrying sounds until neither of them could deny it anymore. There were Williamites all around them. They could hear the grunts of running men and shouts in foreign languages. Michael cursed himself silently. They should never have stopped running, now it was too late.

And then, just like that, they stepped out in front of one of the enemy.

It took the Williamite a moment to realise what they were. For a second, no one moved. Then the man smiled unpleasantly as he raised his musket, saying, '*Je suis désolé!*' ('I am sorry!')

Gerald felt something tiny hit his hat and glanced upwards to see a grinning Joseph, his mouth bulging with food, sitting on a thick branch in the tree beside them. Michael must have spotted him too because he stared back at the Frenchman while saying, 'Joseph, stay where you are. Unless you have a musket up there, just stay out of sight.'

'Are you mad?' Gerald was baffled. 'He has to do something or we're dead!'

The soldier seemed surprised by the sudden burst of conversation. The Jacobites presumed he could not speak English and as long as Joseph kept quiet, he was safe.

Drops of sweat stung Michael's eyes and he sounded defeated. 'Leave him be, he can't do anything. It's not his fault. His mind ... it's gone.'

'But we need him!' said Gerald. 'You hear that, Joseph, we need you!'

'*Soyez silencieux!*'

All this talk was making the Williamite edgy. Michael knew if the man shouted out for help they were goners. Therefore, he slowly reached down to place his own musket and sword on the forest floor and then held up his empty hands.

'Now, Mister Frenchman, you wouldn't shoot an unarmed soldier, would you?'

Apparently he would. The soldier pulled back the trigger and yelped in surprise as someone rushed out at him, knocked him over and began punching him.

'Jacques!' shouted Gerald in heady relief, before being promptly thumped by Michael for making so much noise.

The two Frenchmen were well-matched as they struggled for the upper hand. Keeping his sword at the ready,

Jacques had one free hand to deliver punches. He needed to finish the man off quietly and quickly. The forest was positively crawling with enemy soldiers. Fortunately, they were not actually searching for Jacobites. Instead, they were more concerned with chasing after the retreating army.

Michael focused on trying to get Joseph out of the damned tree, while Gerald wondered how he could help his friend. This was one situation where he would not simply stand and stare. With dagger in hand, he watched the two fighters intently and waited for his moment. Finally it came when the Huguenot rolled over on top of Jacques to pin him to the ground and Gerald was able to plunge his knife into the man's back. Gerald had meant to stab him a few times; he knew that one stab might not be enough through the man's bulky coat, but the angle was awkward. What he had not allowed for, however, was that the man would cry out in pain before releasing an anguished yell for help. And yell he did, until Gerald grabbed a rock and smashed it over the man's head, knocking him unconscious or maybe killing him. He had no idea as he shoved the now-silent body off Jacques.

All he did know was that the man's shouting had succeeded in attracting his fellow Huguenots. Jacques hissed, 'They're coming. We've got to get out of here.'

Michael looked up at Joseph, feeling utterly helpless.

'Please, Joseph, please come down now.'

Joseph merely smiled, and Michael suddenly remembered the magic words: 'We're going to the tavern, Joseph. Aren't you coming with us?'

'What's wrong with him?' whispered Gerald.

Jacques had no idea what was going on with Joseph, but he grabbed Michael and began herding him and Gerald away from the excited voices that were calling out for their fallen friend. He would have preferred to cover up the body, but there was no time. The three of them broke into a disjointed run as they climbed over tree trunks and got scraped by brambles, almost losing their hats. To their despair, they found themselves forced to a stop as the brambles thickened and trapped them.

In no time at all they heard exclamations of horror. Jacques whispered, 'They've found him.'

The three of them crouched down. Michael wondered if it was better to split up and take off in three different directions. Jacques listened to the French soldiers and translated, 'One of them is suggesting that they keep going and come back later for him.'

Gerald was grateful to have Jacques beside him. It was a huge advantage to be able to understand what the enemy soldiers were saying. He and Michael were lucky to have Jacques because if they didn't, they might do something unnecessary, not realising that the French soldiers were not going to take the time to avenge their comrade's murder.

Yes, they were lucky to have Jacques right beside them.

However, neither of them needed Jacques to translate the voice that was speaking now. Instead they just stared at one another in fright as they heard Joseph call out to the Williamites, 'Look at me, I'm up here. I'm the one who killed your friend!'

Michael jumped up only to be pulled down immediately by the other two. He pleaded with them, 'He thinks he's saving us. We have to do something.'

Jacques shook his head, while Gerald put his hands over his ears. If they moved, they were all dead.

'Ha! I'm not scared anymore!'

Joseph had barely finished before a volley of shots silenced him. The three Jacobites could not look at one another while Jacques leant over to fasten a grip on Michael's arm, fearing he would make an enraged dash to confront the boy's killers. They sat there until they could no longer hear the Williamites. Gerald stole a glance at Michael and, on seeing tears running down the man's face, said, 'He saved our lives. He was very brave.'

'No,' spat Michael. 'He was bloody stupid!'

Jacques waited a moment before saying, 'No, it is war that is stupid.'

He and Michael stared at one another for a moment or two before Michael quietly agreed, 'Yes. Yes, you're absolutely right. War is stupid.'

He held out his hand to Jacques who gave it a firm shake. Gerald looked from one to the other, not understanding what was going on.

'I wish you all the best, my friend. Gerald, say goodbye to Michael. He's going home.'

'What? Really?' asked Gerald, not wanting to cause a fuss but needing an explanation all the same.

Michael took Gerald's pre-offered hand. 'I must go back to my wife and children. If I die, they will be turned out of the house to starve. It's funny. I did not really consider the possibility of being killed until Joseph … anyway, my family cannot afford to lose me. I'm all they have.'

Jacques warned him to leave immediately, saying, 'You could take the Williamite's coat; it might keep you safe if you run into any of them.'

Michael smiled sadly and shook his head; he did not want to see Joseph who was probably lying mere feet away from the French soldier. 'Good luck, you two. I better get going in case they come back. Stay safe!'

The two friends walked for a minute or two in silence until Jacques asked, 'You don't agree with him leaving?'

Gerald found it a difficult question to answer. 'I don't

know ... maybe. Isn't it like giving up, or being a coward?'

He felt guilty talking like this. 'But he's no coward. He looked after me earlier, and he tried to look after Joseph.'

Jacques nodded. 'True and why should his family suffer for King James? Sometimes courage is knowing when to stop.'

CHAPTER THIRTY

The Hill of Donore

It had been a long day and it was not over yet. The Jacobites ran the two miles from Oldbridge, and when they had done that they had to run up the hill of Donore itself. And when they had done that they had to fight an army that was four or five times the size of theirs and right in front of them.

But fight they did.

William was on the ground in the midst of his men, using swords, pistols and then his fists. His clothes were still damp from the Boyne, but he sensed that they were almost done and this helped him to ignore his nagging hunger and exhaustion. Those Jacobites were battling to survive and this lent them a great spirit born out of desperation.

Once again, the noise from the muskets was tumultuous, and the billowing smoke was blinding. Red coats mingled with blood and each other. By this stage, those tiny sprigs of Williamite greenery and bits of Jacobite white paper had just about disappeared from sight, thereby rendering the conditions as treacherous as they could be.

Having just finished off a Jacobite, William was looking about for his next victim when he became aware of a big man who was quickly bearing down on him. The man, who had recently lost thirty of his comrades, had become maddened with grief and rage. He searched and found a redcoat to take his revenge upon. With his sword and bayoneted rifle raised in each hand, he bellowed out some sort of battle-cry and drew himself up to his full height, intending to cut the Papist into several pieces. Just at the last moment, William found his voice. 'What are you doing Samuel McGregor? Are you angry with me now?'

The man froze, appalled as he recognised the man he had carried out of the Boyne. 'Sire! My God, forgive me!'

William forgave him immediately. 'Go find another redcoat to take care of and be sure that he's your foe not your friend!'

Samuel disappeared, leaving William to reflect on what might have happened had he not noticed the man in time to stop him. *Imagine to have survived this far and then be murdered by one of my own.*

The smell of blood was everywhere, and men were dying

in their hundreds on both sides. Because the fighting was up close it was especially brutal and vicious. The closer you are to a man, the more complicated it is to extinguish his life. Therefore, the soldier is forced to be creative and determined. Skulls were smashed, throats were impaled and arms were snapped in two.

William allowed himself to back away from the ruins of the old church, which was the hub of the battle, and be escorted to his horse by a variety of Europeans. Time was marching on, and still those Jacobites stood their ground.

Earlier, Meinhard Schomberg had sent a messenger to describe his situation, being stuck a mile away from James and unable to get near him. William had ordered the duke's son to stay put and keep trying to find a way through. If the worst came to the worst and it was impossible to get at them, then at least Meinhard was keeping James and the best part of his army tied up. Thinking about Meinhard reminded William that the general would have to be told about his father.

William was genuinely surprised that his father-in-law did not make an appearance or send some men back to reinforce his battalions at Oldbridge. *The old man makes it easy for me and also spares me the awkwardness of having to capture him … or worse.*

A messenger approached and told him that James and a

large convoy were already on the road to Dublin, although the narrow bridge at Duleek had slowed them up terribly. Immediately, William was asked what he wanted to do. 'We could easily catch up with him, sire?'

William surveyed the scene around him and pitied these misguided men fighting for a king who was no more. He guessed that James was returning to Dublin to board a ship to France. A mere dip of his head and his men would be off to Duleek. William, however, resisted this. *What would that solve? Yes, I could have James brought back to London in chains and imprisoned for the rest of his life, but ... what if he actually died in prison? He might become a martyr. The English are so fickle.*

William also imagined that James, if given half the chance, might repent his former behaviour and apologise for trying to force his religion upon them. *I must be careful. I cannot allow James to play the underdog to make people feel sorry for him. No, best let him go. Nobody would wish to champion a coward.*

He told his men, 'James is no longer a threat to us. Let him flee back to Louis. He is done.'

His men looked at one another in surprise, but William ignored them. Later on, he would write in his diary: *once a leader makes a decision he moves on.*

He called for his pistol and prepared to move towards the church once more. *These stubborn fellows will have to be told that James has given up on them and I am now their king, whether they like it or not.*

He wanted to get back to fighting, to prove his mettle in front of the Jacobites as well as his own men. His secretary tried to dissuade him, 'But, Your Majesty, your army is winning. There is no need to exhaust yourself further.'

William smiled. 'I will stop when it is obvious to me that I should.'

His bodyguards followed him on horseback up the hill, and William looked around for a suitable target. He could see no sign of the Irish and French commanders. *We are dealing with a headless monster that is backed into a corner. It cannot last much longer.*

The hill was crawling with his men. They had more or less surrounded the church ruins, and William could see that a trickle of them had climbed the walls to get at the enemy. He wondered about making a dramatic gesture. Surely his horse could jump that wall, with his bodyguards following, and that might rattle the last nerves of the Jacobites.

As he considered this, there was the most dreadful sound beside him. Actually, he thought the noise was somehow *on* him. His horse reared up momentarily, and William assumed the animal's ears were ringing just like his own. He experienced the odd sensation of believing that his left leg had been torn from him, though done so fast that he had no time to feel pain.

Some of his men were talking to him, shouting at him, asking if he were all right, but he could not hear a single word. He felt slightly precarious sitting on his horse, feeling that his balance was being interfered with. He wished that someone would inspect his leg and confirm to him that though it was gone, he would be all right. Losing a leg might help the English warm to him.

Then one of his men was standing to his left and holding up something small in his hand. Clearly, he wanted His Majesty's attention. William was in a daze but looked anyway. *What on earth is that, a piece of wood? Why, it looks like … a … heel.* His soldiers were pointing and laughing in relief. William looked down and found that his leg was exactly where he had left it, but the heel of his favourite boot had been blown off.

While the ringing in his ears continued he could not hear the roar of battle and it was a welcome break from the noise. William took the time to check the state of the day; the sun had begun its evening shift. He felt bone weary and was sure all the men on the hill, both Catholics and Protestants, felt the exact same way.

Eventually the break came. William saw it happen. First, it was just a handful of Jacobites who had had enough. They simply jumped over the wall and began to run in the direction of Duleek. Next, it was a few more — up over that wall and away they went. Then that tentative trickle turned into an avalanche of Jacobites dropping their weapons and taking off after their comrades.

William watched them go and did not envy them: *they have another long run ahead of them.*

In his deafness he fancied that he could hear the clanging of a bell; maybe it was the now-absent church bell ringing out from the distant past. William smiled to himself. *This place is trying to bewitch me.*

He had told his secretary that he would only stop when it was obvious. Now, encased by silence, he agreed. *It is enough.*

CHAPTER THIRTY-ONE

Malahide Castle, County Dublin

Several hours later, in Dublin, James Stuart is a very weary man. Exhausted from his long day, his nose bright red from spending so many hours sitting in the sun, all he wants to do is lie down and pull the covers over his head, but that is impossible. Protocol requires him to get dressed and ready for the evening ahead with his hosts and their guests. It may prove as treacherous as the battle, but he can see no way out of it.

At long last, his return ship is booked, and he is more than eager to step off Irish soil. If there is one thing he knows for certain, it is this: he will never ever return to Ireland and that one thought makes him happy, in spite of everything else.

He knows he has outstayed his welcome, especially after today. No doubt, because of that disastrous battle, this evening is going to be a struggle. *I don't care. I don't care about any of them!*

The gong is sounded for dinner. *Well*, he thinks, *I am rather hungry and the food is good. It is just the company that might prove tiresome.*

As he heads downstairs, he tells himself to ignore any ill feeling, *just think about getting on that ship tomorrow.*

He enters the dining room and senses that he has interrupted a conversation of which he was the starring topic. Heads are bowed momentarily, and he coolly returns the brief nods of acknowledgement. The servants are holding out the chairs, and he takes his, reaching gratefully for the glass of red wine. The cutlery twinkles in the candlelight, and his nose twitches from the heavy perfume that his neighbour has doused herself in.

James looks around but avoids catching anyone's eye. *Cowards! Why don't they just say what they are thinking?* The first course is served, oysters in wine. James concentrates on his food, too annoyed to make conversation.

There is some attempt to discuss the weather and this and that, but it is understandably difficult to ignore what has happened. His dinner companions know that he leaves in a few hours and expect never to see him again.

Finally, Lady Talbot launches herself superbly. 'Were you very hungry, My Lord?'

Irritated by the insincerity of her question, James replies unwisely, 'I am surprised I can eat at all after the day I have had.'

There, let her think upon that! They can all sit here and judge me, but what do any of them know about battle?

The longer he sits, the angrier he becomes at his hosts and their friends, and their accents and … well, *all* Irishmen. Oh, how they love to drink whiskey in copious amounts and tell sensational stories or sing dreary ballads with far too many verses. But they are fools, and he has been wrong to imagine that he could have benefitted from their help. He knows full well what has gone wrong today, and he doesn't see why he should sit there and feign politeness. He lifts his glass of wine as if to raise a toast and then says, 'Madam, your countrymen run very fast.'

She takes a sip of wine, to draw out the moment and ensure that everyone was listening, before saying, 'Maybe so, sire, but you won the race.'

CHAPTER THIRTY-TWO

Trim, County Meath

Two tired soldiers, bruised and aching, finally reached their destination. It was not Offaly, not just yet.

Paris plodded along beside them, looking unimpressed with his surroundings.

'There's Trim Castle,' said Gerald. 'It's a lot bigger than I thought.'

Jacques was studying the river as if it was an old friend he had not seen in a while. He asked, 'And this is still the River Boyne? Is it coming with us to Offaly, do you think?'

Gerald shrugged. 'There is an old saying, something about never being able to step into the same river twice.'

His companion raised his eyebrows. 'You mean that everything changes all the time. A river can only flow forward. There is no going back.'

Instinctively they glanced at the bundle lying across Paris's back.

Jacques was unsure about this, but Gerald had insisted, 'It's the right thing to do and we owe him.'

An old man pointed out the house to them. Jacques took a firm grip of Paris's reigns as he felt his courage evaporate. He glanced at Gerald who muttered, 'If it wasn't for him ...'

'Yes, yes, I know,' said Jacques. Nancy had told him the very same thing before they left Drogheda.

Gerald offered, 'Maybe they won't be in and we can just leave him with a neighbour.' He felt queasy and his mouth was dry.

As they approached the house, two red-headed children, a boy and a girl, were in the doorway slapping one another on the arm while a third red-head shrilled, 'Faster! Faster!'

They fell silent as, one by one, they felt themselves being watched. In spite of his nervousness, Jacques had to smile as he found himself faced with three miniature Josephs, complete with freckles and big teeth, who stared open-mouthed at Paris until the youngest demanded, 'What's his name?'

Jacques replied, 'He is Paris.'

The girl scrunched up her nose and stated, 'That's a strange name for a horse.'

Unable to come up with a better response, Jacques said, 'He is a strange horse!'

It was only now that she caught his accent. Giving him a cool look, she asked, 'Where do you come from?'

Glancing helplessly at Gerald, Jacques confessed, 'I am from France.'

When the children said nothing to this, Jacques felt it necessary to add, 'It is a most wonderful place many miles from here.'

The girl conferred with her brother who informed her, 'It's probably in Dublin. All the best places are!'

Jacques opened his mouth to take umbrage at this, but Gerald was anxious to press on and asked, 'Is your mother or father about?'

The youngest of the three siblings turned his head into the house and bawled, 'Mama!'

Joseph's mother appeared at the door, fixing her hair into place and finding herself transfixed at the sight that greeted her: two soldiers, one taller than the other, in rumpled uniforms, standing beside a massive, black horse. Meanwhile, Gerald and Jacques had expected to meet a red-haired woman with freckles and bucked teeth and instead found themselves rather shocked by the woman's beauty. Her hair was as black and sleek as a raven's wing, her skin clear while her teeth could not be seen until she smiled.

Horribly conscious of the children's eyes upon him, Gerald stumbled with his words. 'Mrs O'Leary. We knew ...

I mean, we were … are … friends of Joseph.'

She spied the bundle on Paris and guessed the truth from their stricken expressions. 'Yes, I see.'

The two soldiers stared at the ground, waiting on her instructions.

There was silence until the little girl asked, 'What's wrong, Mama?'

She ignored the question, only saying, 'Take your brothers and run to Mrs Murray. Ask her for some jam. Tell her I've got visitors.'

The three children tore off up the street, the little one falling behind and roaring, 'Wait for me!'

Their mother looked after them in a daze, prompting Jacques to ask, 'Are you all right, Madame? Is your husband nearby? Can I fetch him for you?'

'No. He's working above the estate and won't be back until late.'

She beckoned them to bring Joseph inside, turning away as they lifted him free of Paris. Gerald tied the horse's reins to a nearby fence while Jacques stopped in front of Joseph's mother, her son in his arms, waiting for her to lead the way.

She reached out to touch the blankets that hid her boy from sight but then changed her mind. 'There is a cot in here.'

Jacques laid Joseph on the narrow bed and followed her

to the small kitchen, where the fire was lit to heat the soup that was bubbling in the cauldron.

'I was just making the children's dinner.'

Gerald came in and looked as uncomfortable as Jacques felt.

She ushered them to the table and bade them to sit down, saying, 'You'll have something to eat and drink.'

They would have preferred to make their excuses and leave but did not know how to refuse her.

Exchanging brief looks, they sat down, careful not to scrape the legs of the stools against the stone floor.

The house was small but pleasant thanks to the flowers that decorated the room and lent it their perfume. One picture adorned the wall, a stark portrait of a dog. It was sitting up with its two front paws pressed together as if in prayer.

Mrs O'Leary saw Gerald gazing at it and said, 'Joseph drew it for me. Finn was his best friend until he died last year. Joseph was heartbroken ...'

Her voice cracked, and Gerald felt it was dawning on her that Joseph was gone forever too, just like Finn.

The silence was unbearable. Gerald waited for her to ask what had happened. Why were they sitting at her table while her precious son was at rest in the shadows?

'We're sorry!'

It was a whisper, but she heard it.

She set down two plates and sighed. 'Last night I dreamt the front door opened, and I heard him walk around this very room. I guessed he was saying goodbye.'

Gerald hoped that this was true. They had left Joseph in the forest overnight because Jacques judged that it might not be safe to collect his body until morning. But it was not an easy decision to make, to leave him there all alone. However, if Joseph's ghost had visited his home then surely that meant he wasn't scared and lonely. *Oh, please forgive us, Joseph, we were afraid. But we came back for you, didn't we?*

Jacques watched Mrs O'Leary cut the bread and paid Joseph the highest compliment he knew. 'He was a brave soldier. You can be very proud of him.'

Gerald quickly added, 'He saved our lives and another man too. He saved the three of us.'

Mrs O'Leary seemed unmoved by this incredible truth but appreciated their kindness, their good intentions. She told them, 'His father sent him off to join the army.'

Sensing that she wanted someone to blame, Gerald said quietly, 'But we all were there on the orders or wishes of someone else.'

She looked at Gerald, as if seeing him for the first time. 'And who sent you off to fight?'

Gerald was honest in his appraisal. 'My parents, I suppose,

and my tutor Father Nicholas. There have always been soldiers in our family who have fought for Ireland. It was time for me to do my part.'

Mrs O'Leary sat down, forgetting to attend to the soup. 'And how was it? Did you get to do your part?'

Gerald thought for a moment but then shook his head, unable to sum up the previous day in a few words. He had killed many men over those eight hours. Their blood was all over his clothes. He could still hear the screams and the gunfire — in particular the bullet that felled Troy and the terrifying volley that silenced Joseph forever. And he struggled to make sense of it all. Their defeat had been brutal, while the man, their chosen king, who was going to change their world, had stayed away, knowing that they would be overwhelmed. It was a wonder that there were not lots more bodies. It was a miracle.

'It could have been worse,' said Gerald to nobody in particular.

'Actually I might like to leave Ireland. At least that's what I think now.' There was something about the little kitchen that provoked him to blurt this out. He felt tired and empty. His various cuts stung, and he longed to take off the bloodied uniform. How long had it been since he sat at a table? Of course it reminded him of home, though maybe he felt freer here. Mrs O'Leary was gentle and calm and accepting

...so different from his mother who never stopped pushing him. He envied Joseph and then felt guilty for being alive but only for a second or two. Poor Joseph!

Jacques checked Joseph's mother to see if she was offended by this sudden confession. He put his hand on Gerald's arm to remind him where they were. To his surprise, however, Mrs O'Leary was immediately interested and asked the boy, 'Why now?'

Gerald spoke slowly. 'Well, I think they may be disappointed with me. I was meant to be returning in triumph.'

It was somewhat insensitive but Mrs O'Leary let it slide. She could have reminded him that, unlike her son, Gerald would not be coming home wrapped in blankets, and his mother should be grateful for that no matter what.

The boy picked at the dirt beneath his nails, oblivious to the tear that meandered down his cheek. His voice was low. 'I tried my best, I really did. I was scared and then that happened to Joseph, and Michael left. And my horse was killed. And I couldn't save him.'

Gerald had refused to think about Troy until now. How had he stood there and watched him strain in agony? He even thought of that girl swinging from the tree, though he could barely remember her features now.

'But it might not be enough for them. I might never be enough for them. I cannot make everything go back to how it was. I'm not my grandfather and I've never lived in a castle.'

Here, he looked up at them in surprise as something occurred to him. 'I don't even want to live in a castle. Is that wrong?'

Mrs O'Leary gave him a watery smile.

'I can't ... I can't ...'

Jacques tried to get his attention, but Gerald was temporarily lost to him as he sought for the right words and then found them. 'I can't hate like them. I just can't.'

Gerald pleaded with his listeners, 'But that doesn't mean that I don't love Ireland. It's just that I want to know more about the world beyond ruined graves and broken bricks.'

Mrs O'Leary stood up and fetched two bowls. She began to ladle the soup first into one bowl and then into a second one.

Placing the bowls in front of them, she spoke slowly, as if she, like Gerald, was reaching for how she truly felt. 'Lately I have wondered whether it matters to God if someone is a Catholic or a Protestant. What's in a name when all is said and done?'

Eager to join in, Jacques said, 'Yes, I know what you mean. My king likes to be called the "Sun King". When he was younger he dressed up as the sun for a party and loved his costume so much that he continues to this day to think of himself as the sun.'

Gerald and Mrs O'Leary waited politely for the French-man to make his point.

Jacques glanced from one to the other and murmured, 'I just wish I had his confidence.'

Epilogue

And so it was, twenty-three years after the 'Battle of the Boyne', that the elderly King Louis XIV lay on his death bed, shrivelled, wrinkled, tufts of long white strands of hair lifting away from his bony skull, when the arrival of his grandson was announced.

The king, who had summoned the child, nodded to have his heir brought before him. Accordingly, the five-year-old, for that was all he was, was ushered in past the relatives, family friends and his future colleagues, who stood about idly, talking in whispers, awaiting the end of an era.

The little boy showed no surprise at the sight of such a large, conspicuous audience. He nodded solemnly to his parents as he passed them. His nanny was somewhere in the background and that was a comfort to him. She had promised him the biggest slice of cake if he didn't misbehave.

Well, he would show her.

Perhaps the last person he identified was his grandfather, swaddled in clothes and blankets in the towering four-poster bed. It had been a while since he had seen him, but even he would have agreed that his grandfather was no longer the grand old man he had known.

Feeling himself being gently pushed, the boy stepped forward somewhat uncertainly, unsure of what he should say. His grandfather seemed so very far away from him, the bed being so high and vast, and he was fairly sure that he was not allowed to shout. But what if his grandfather could not hear him if he had to say something? Could he not shout then if he did it politely?

Just then, a low stool was moved to the side of the bed and a pair of strong hands easily lifted the child, guiding him to stand on it.

Ah, that's better. The boy smiled in heady relief. He and his grandfather could see each other properly, and he was almost sure that there would be no need to shout now.

Dutifully he kissed the pre-offered ancient hand as the breathless king asked, 'Do you understand that you are to take my place?'

Having been prepared for this question, the little boy proudly answered, 'Yes, Grandfather!'

A moment of silence followed, and the onlookers grew uneasy that the man had already slipped away. However, he stirred himself once more to tell France's new king: 'I have loved war too much. You must do better.'

Writer's Notes

July was a significant month for the Jacobites and Williamites. It was July 1689 when the siege of Derry ended with William's ships finally rescuing the starving city of Derry from the massive Jacobite army outside her walls.

Just a year later, in July 1690, there was the now infamous battle over the Boyne, and this time it was the Jacobites who were the underdogs, bound to fight an improbable battle with inferior weapons and numbers.

During my research I discovered the Offaly teenager Gerald O'Connor, a Jacobite, and let the story begin with him and his reasons for being in Drogheda that day, blending the scant facts about his life with fiction.

On the Williamite side, the Sherrard brothers – Robert and Daniel – made a welcome return from my novel about the siege of Derry, *Behind the Walls*. In December 1688 they had helped to close the gates of Derry against James's army, and in *Kings of the Boyne* I sent them to join Reverend George Walker to fight for King William down south.

When I heard about Jean Watson, the widowed mother

of six, I thought I might one day write an adult novel about her walk from Down to Drogheda. Then, when I got badly stuck in an early draft, I could not keep from including her in these pages.

From the moment I was asked to write this book I knew I wanted to feature the kings involved: James and William, uncle and nephew, father and son-in-law, with Louis XIV lurking in the background.

Readers should be aware that there was another shadowy figure, Pope Alexander VIII, who gave the Protestant William money. He was motivated by hatred of Louis XIV, the Catholic French monarch who appeared to see himself as a sort of god.

Of course the story of the warring Jacobites and Williamites does not end here.

Instead, it is the third July, 1691, which sees the final clash of this Glorious Revolution, at the battle of Aughrim in Galway. With over seven thousand fatalities, this is recognised as the bloodiest battle in Irish history and it marked the end of Jacobitism in Ireland.

THE THREE KINGS OF
THE GLORIOUS REVOLUTION

KING JAMES II (1633-1701)

James fled Ireland for France after the Battle of the Boyne, leaving the battle at Aughrim to his supporters. His last child, and fourth daughter, Louisa Maria Teresa, was born in 1692. Four years later there was an unsuccessful attempt, by some supporters in England, to assassinate William that only served to make James even more unpopular. Perhaps he clung onto his dream of sitting once more on the English throne because he turned down Louis XIV's offer to make him king of Poland. In his château, in Saint-Germaine-en-Laye, he surrounded himself and his family with luxurious objects, paintings and first-class musicians to attract and impress visitors who should always feel that they were in the presence of royalty.

When he died of a brain haemorrhage, on 16 September 1701, James's heart was placed in a locket and given to a convent while his brain was placed in a lead casket for the Scots College in Paris. His entrails were split between two urns, one for the local parish church and the other for an English Jesuit college. Lastly, flesh from his right arm was given to the English Augustinian nuns in Paris. Whatever was left was not buried, however; instead his coffin was placed in a side chapel where lights continually burned around it until the 1789 French Revolution.

KING WILLIAM III (1650-1702)

William became withdrawn following the death of his wife, Queen Mary, James's eldest daughter, in 1694. As king he had his enemies of course, but plenty more attest to his generous charities and concern for the tenants on his estate. A keen rider and hard worker, he was also known as a great patron of the arts. He died from pneumonia following a fall from his favourite horse, Sorrel. Legend has it that the horse stumbled into a mole burrow and that Jacobites raised a glass to toast the burrow's little owner. William was succeeded by his sister-in-law Anne, James's second eldest daughter, who was queen of England, Scotland and Ireland from 1702 until her death in 1714.

KING LOUIS XIV (1638-1715)

Louis's reign of seventy-two years and one hundred and ten days is the longest of any monarch in Europe.

A devout and pious Catholic, Louis believed in expanding France's – and, therefore, his – territory with war. Like William, his bitter enemy, Louis was a great patron of the arts and was known to have been a fine dancer in his younger days. He danced in forty major ballets and, in some of his portraits, those familiar with ballet steps might recognise certain poses that he strikes. It would appear he loved promoting his very image, commissioning vast amounts of art, including three hundred formal paintings of himself.

His health had never been strong and he kept his three physicians busy. They maintained a meticulous journal of his ailments and treatments. One operation left him with a wound that did not close for two months. He died of gangrene four days before his seventy-seventh birthday in September 1713 and was laid to rest in a basilica outside Paris.

OTHER BOOKS BY NICOLA PIERCE

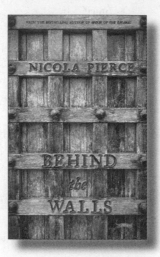

DERRY, 1689.

An anonymous letter is read out saying that every last Protestant man,
woman and child is to be murdered. Panic takes hold.

Two teenage boys, Daniel and Robert Sherrard, help close
the city gates against the approaching Catholic army.

The siege has begun.

Bombs rain down. Behind the walls, tensions grow day by day.

Trapped, the people are injured, dying, starving.

But there is no going back

Daniel and Robert are drawn into a fight to the end.'

'That calm, sunny day is one I'll always remember ... because the
twentieth of April, in the year 1910, was the day I,
Samuel Joseph Scott, died.'

Fifteen year old Sam plunges to his death whilst building his beloved
Titanic. Now as the greatest ship the world has ever seen crosses
the Atlantic Ocean, Sam finds himself on board – as a ghost.
His spirit roams the ship, from the glamour of first class to the party
atmosphere of third class. Sam shares the excitement of Jim, Isobel
and their children – on their way to a new life in America.

Disaster strikes when Titanic hits an iceberg.
As Titanic sinks to her icy grave, Jim and his family are trapped behind
locked gates ...
Can Sam's spirit reach out and save them as time runs out ...?

www.obrien.ie